Adam's Daughters

BOOK 2 IN THE WESTWARD SAGAS

David Bowles

Adam's Daughters: Book 2 in the Westward Sagas

Plum Creek Press, Inc.®
2810 Thousand Oaks #171
San Antonio, Texas 78232
210-490-9955
210-403-9072 FAX
www.westwardsagas.com
info@westwardsagas.com

ISBN 10—Print: 0-9777484-3-X
ISBN 13—Print: 978-0-9777484-3-3

ISBN 10—E-Book: 0-9777484-4-8
ISBN 13—E-Book: 978-0-9777484-4-0

Cover Art: Aundrea Hernandez
Author Photos: Lilian Foreman

Dedication

Roger M. Bowles

1936 – 2008

A long way from South First Street

Preface

Adam's Daughters: Book 2 in the Westward Sagas, is based on the actual history of the Adam Mitchell Family as well as the events of the first twenty years of our nation's founding. I have spent years researching historical and genealogical data and have written nothing that contradicts known historical facts, characters, or events.

However, I wrote the book as historical fiction rather than as nonfiction to allow me to use my imagination to create details of how events might have occurred when those details are not actually known. Everything **could** have happened as described in *Adam's Daughter's*; however, I don't know that everything did happen as I describe. See Fact or Fiction: A Note from the Author at the end of the book for more information on what is history and what is imagination.

As is common in dealing with long-ago events, there are discrepancies among different sources. In *Spring House: Book 1 in the Westward Sagas*, I spelled the names of two of Adam's daughters the way they were spelled in the sources that I had available at the time. Later, I had the opportunity to view Adam Mitchell's 1766 Bible, which is still in the family, and learned the names were spelled incorrectly. The spelling was corrected in *Book 2* to that which was written in Adam's handwriting so long ago.

When I found conflicting information, I used the sources that were the best documented and/or the information that was most supported by evidence. I also called on many experts who are listed in the Acknowledgements.

I have written The Westward Sagas to be entertaining, and I hope you enjoy them. Though they are not intended for genealogical work, all the records for births, marriages, and deaths are accurate. In Fact or Fiction, I have listed my resources to help researchers document their own genealogy work.

Acknowledgements

The Westward Sagas began years ago when I was a young boy and first heard the stories of my ancestors. So many people have helped make this book possible that I cannot list all of them here. However, I am grateful to each one.

Adam's Daughters is dedicated to my brother Roger M. Bowles, who encouraged me to write this series.

Thanks to distant cousins I have never met who contacted me to offer access to invaluable documents and resources, helping me to develop a factual story. From the beginning, my first cousins—Les Bowles, Bonnie Disney, Doris Baker, and Clara Young—have supported my efforts to research the family.

A special tip of the Stetson goes to Ann Winkler Hinrichs, descendant of John Mitchell, who willingly shared the extensive research she had done on the family of Adam Mitchell. Jerry Mitchell, descendant of Hezekiah Mitchell, has also generously given me the benefit of his research.

The special ladies in the Christian Writers Group of the Greater San Antonio Area have increased my knowledge and improved my writing through their helpful feedback at our weekly critique sessions.

Friends Mamie Carter, Dorothy J. Breezee, Paul Ruckman, Carol Cordova, Katherine Goodloe, Harry M. Fife, Jr., and Ron Kipp served as advance readers. I appreciate their valuable insights, which strengthened the book.

Betty Jane Hylton of the Washington County Historical Association assisted me with local information, such as the creeks, rivers, and streams of the region. She took me on my first trip to the area to Knob Creek and pointed out where the McMachen and Mitchell families lived.

The Jonesborough Library has an extensive section on genealogy of Washington County residents, and the

Washington County Courthouse provided valuable historical and legal documents. Thanks to both very helpful staffs.

Richard and Freda Donoho of Limestone, Tennessee, provided much information on Reverend Samuel Doak, his school, and the Washington College. I have attended services in the beautiful Salem Church where Reverend Doak preached and where Adam Mitchell worshipped.

Aundrea Hernandez did an outstanding job of the cover design capturing the time period, the Chester Inn ca. 1797, and my image of what I thought the three oldest daughters of Adam Mitchell would look like.

Donald Mace Williams, author of *Black Tuesday's Child*, provided me with literary guidance and encouragement.

Lillie Ammann edited and formatted *Adam's Daughters*. The process of producing a book is similar to what I imagine giving birth to a baby would be like. As Peggy Mitchell was a midwife delivering babies, Lillie is a midwife helping authors give birth to their books.

The contributions of all of these individuals made *Adam's Daughters* a better story—more accurate and more entertaining. If any inaccuracies or inconsistencies remain, the errors are mine.

The Adam Mitchell Family

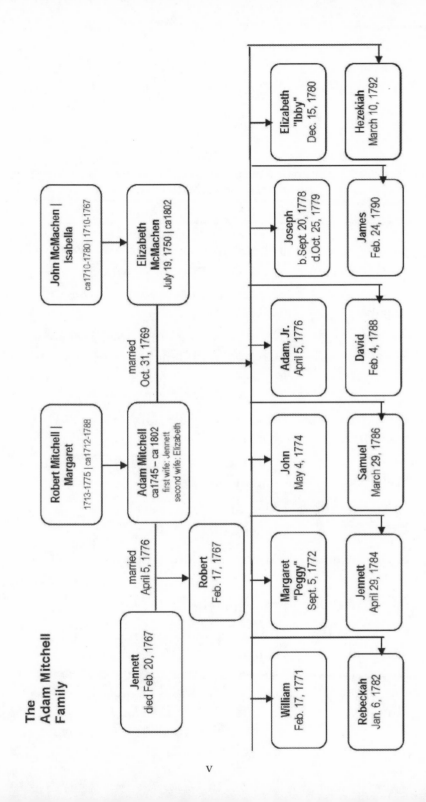

John McMachen | Isabella
ca1710-1780 | 1710-1767

Elizabeth McMachen
July 19, 1750 | ca1802

Robert Mitchell | Margaret
1713-1775 | ca1712-1788

Adam Mitchell
ca1745 – ca 1802
first wife: Jennett
second wife: Elizabeth

married
Oct. 31, 1769

married
April 5, 1776

Jennett
died Feb. 20, 1767

Robert
Feb. 17, 1767

William
Feb. 17, 1771

Margaret "Peggy"
Sept. 5, 1772

John
May 4, 1774

Adam, Jr.
April 5, 1776

Joseph
b.Sept. 20, 1778
d.Oct. 25, 1779

Elizabeth "Ibby"
Dec. 15, 1780

Rebeckah
Jan. 6, 1782

Jennett
April 29, 1784

Samuel
March 29, 1786

David
Feb. 4, 1788

James
Feb. 24, 1790

Hezekiah
March 10, 1792

Characters

Cast of Characters in *Adam's Daughters*

(See also The Children of Adam Mitchell, which includes the members of Adam and Elizabeth Mitchell's family)

Character Name	Description
Albrecht, Charles	Custom manufacturer of pianos in Philadelphia who applied for the first piano patent in America
Allison, Elizabeth	Fiancée of Robert Mitchell
Annan, Reverend and Mrs. Robert	Minister of the Pine Street Presbyterian Church in Philadelphia and his wife
Armstrong, Lieutenant John	First Regiment of the U.S. Army; Assistant to Secretary of War Henry Knox
Avery, Waightstill	Attorney respected in North Carolina and Tennessee
Balch, Reverend Hezekiah	First minister of the Hebron Presbyterian Church
Barnes, Mary Ann	Young lady John Mitchell wanted to court
Bawn, Michael	Miller on the Little Limestone Creek
Bowles, Chief also known as Duwali (which means Bold Hunter)	Cherokee Indian with white father. *Author's Note: After many years of research, I have found no connection between my Bowles family and Chief Bowles (1765-1836). Had I have found any relationship I would have been proud to claim kin.*

Cast of Characters in *Adam's Daughters*

(See also The Children of Adam Mitchell, which includes the members of Adam and Elizabeth Mitchell's family)

Character Name	Description
Caldwell, Reverend David and Rachel	Minister of the Buffalo Presbyterian Church at Guilford Courthouse and his wife
Chester, Doctor William P.	Early Jonesborough doctor who built the Chester Inn on Main Street
Coffee, Joshua	Illiterate pig herder
Cohen, Mr. and Mrs.	Stable owners and boarding house operators in Philadelphia; Mr. Cohen was brother of Rabbi Jacob Cohen
Cohen, Rabbi Jacob; Rebekah; son Abraham	Rabbi in Philadelphia and his wife and son; Rabbi Cohen was brother of Mr. Cohen
Daniel	Jonesborough blacksmith; son of slaves freed by John McMachen; friend of the Mitchell family
Deaderick, David	Owner of Deaderick's Dry Goods Store in Jonesborough
Doak, Reverend Samuel	Cousin of Adam Mitchell; pastor of Salem Presbyterian Church; husband of Esther
Doak, Sister Esther	Wife of Reverend Samuel Doak
Ezekiel (Zeke)	Negro stable boy at Mr. Cohen's stable; son of Mattie

Cast of Characters in *Adam's Daughters*

(See also The Children of Adam Mitchell, which includes the members of Adam and Elizabeth Mitchell's family)

Character Name	Description
Fain, Captain John	Indian fighter; son of Nicholas Fain; brother of Samuel and William; brother-in-law of Elizabeth; husband of Nancy McMachen
Fain, John Rueben	Son of Captain John and Nancy Fain
Fain, Nancy McMachen	Wife of Captain John Fain; daughter of Mr. Mac; sister of Elizabeth Mitchell, Rosanna Fain, and Sarah Fain; married John Hammer after the death of John Fain
Fain, Nicholas	Friend of Mr. Mac; father of John, Samuel, and William
Fain, Nicholas	Oldest son of Captain John and Nancy Fain
Fain, Rosanna McMachen	Wife of Samuel Fain; daughter of Mr. Mac; sister of Elizabeth Mitchell, Nancy Fain, and Sarah Fain
Fain, Ruth	Daughter of Captain John and Nancy Fain
Fain, Samuel	Son of Nicholas Fain; brother of John and William; brother-in-law of Elizabeth Mitchell; husband of Rosanna McMachen
Fain, Sarah McMachen	Wife of William Fain; daughter of Mr. Mac; sister of Elizabeth Mitchell, Nancy Fain, and Rosanna Fain
Fain, Thomas	Son of Captain John and Nancy Fain

Cast of Characters in *Adam's Daughters*

(See also The Children of Adam Mitchell, which includes the members of Adam and Elizabeth Mitchell's family)

Character Name	Description
Fain, William	Son of Nicholas Fain; brother of Samuel and John; brother-in-law of Elizabeth Mitchell; husband of Sarah McMachen
Hamilton, John	Registrar of Guilford County, North Carolina, who purchased 107-acre Mitchell homestead adjoining Guilford County Courthouse
Hammer, John	Second husband of Nancy McMachen Fain
Jackson, Andrew	Lawyer, State Prosecutor for North Carolina, friend of Robert Mitchell and Judge McNairy (later 7th President of the United States)
King, Jesse	Father of children who attended Hebron School; brother of Lucifer
King, Lucifer	Father of children who attended Hebron School; brother of Jesse
Love, Colonel Robert	Captain Fain's superior officer; in charge of safety from the Indians
McDonald, Molly	Youngest daughter of Mr. McDonald; barmaid at the tavern
McDonald, Mr.	Innkeeper of the tavern in Abingdon, Virginia; father of Molly; brother-in-law of Sheriff Preston
McDuffy, Captain Patrick	Captain of the Lady Ann sailing out of the Port of Amsterdam

Cast of Characters in *Adam's Daughters*

(See also The Children of Adam Mitchell, which includes the members of Adam and Elizabeth Mitchell's family)

Character Name	Description
McMachen, Isabella	Wife of John McMachen; had died before Mr. Mac moved west; mother of Elizabeth Mitchell; John Blair McMachen; and Nancy, Sarah, and Rosanna—all married to Fains
McMachen, John (Mr. Mac)	Father of Elizabeth Mitchell, John Blair McMachen, and three daughters married to Fains—Nancy, Sarah, and Rosanna; County Registrar and landowner
McMachen, John Blair	Son of Mr. Mac; brother of Elizabeth Mitchell
McNairy, Judge John	Mitchell neighbor in Guilford Courthouse who grew up with Mitchell children; friend of Andrew Jackson
Macay, Spruce	Lawyer in Salisbury under whom Judge John McNairy and Andrew Jackson apprenticed
Mathes, Elder Alexander	Elder of the Salem Presbyterian Church
Mattie	Negro housekeeper for the Cohens; mother of Ezekiel (Zeke)
Miller, Peter	Neighbor of Adam Mitchell
Mitchell, Margaret	Matriarch of the Mitchell family; Adam's mother
One Feather	Fictional renegade Indian/ highwayman

Cast of Characters in *Adam's Daughters*

(See also The Children of Adam Mitchell, which includes the members of Adam and Elizabeth Mitchell's family)

Character Name	Description
Preston, Sheriff Robert	Sheriff of Washington County, Virginia
Ross, James	Husband of Mary Mitchell; brother-in-law of Adam Mitchell
Ross, Mary Mitchell	Wife of James Ross; sister of Adam Mitchell
Sevier, Governor John	Only governor of the State of Franklin; first governor of the State of Tennessee; friend and neighbor of Adam Mitchell
Smith, Anne Witherspoon	Twice-widowed mother of Reverend James Witherspoon; stepmother of James Smith and William Smith
Smith, James	Stepbrother of Reverend James Witherspoon; brother of William Smith
Smith, William (Willie)	Stepbrother of Reverend James Witherspoon; brother of James Smith
Taylor, Major Christopher	Indian fighter ; landlord of Judge John McNairy and Andrew Jackson during their five-month stay in Jonesborough in 1788
Thompson, Jake; Sara; Robert; John	Teamster and his wife and sons from Philadelphia
Tipton, Colonel John	In charge of Indian affairs and leader of the Anti-State of Franklin movement.

Cast of Characters in *Adam's Daughters*

Character Name	Description
Trapper John	Adam Mitchell's old friend, who had disappeared during the Battle of Guilford Courthouse; rediscovered 1796
Trollinger, Henry Jacob	Owner of Trollinger's Station in the New River Valley of Virginia
Trollinger, John	Youngest son of Henry Jacob Trollinger
Witherspoon, (Reverend) James (Jimmy)	Childhood friend of Mitchell children who became a Presbyterian minister; first graduate of Washington College
Young, Jennifer	Friend of Peggy Mitchell; daughter of Joseph
Young, Joseph	Mitchell neighbor; father of Jennifer
Young, Robert	Mitchell neighbor

Chapter One

Under the Apple Tree

Six-year-old Rebeckah Mitchell sat cross-legged in the hayloft of the barn. Her older sisters, Peggy and Ibby, lay next to her, still fast asleep. From her vantage point looking out the loft door, she could see the sun rising. Its brilliant light rose ever so slowly behind the tall sycamore trees that lined the banks of the gently flowing Knob Creek, a short distance down the hill from the house and barn. The steam that rose from the spring-fed creek mesmerized the freckle-faced girl as she watched the vapors drift up into the sky and disappear into the faint rays of sunlight.

She heard the whinnies and clippity-clop of horses coming from the direction of Jonesborough. Where could they be going so early in the morning? Rebeckah hurried to the other side of the barn, trying not to wake her sisters. She found a knothole in one of the rough-hewn boards at just the right height to give her an unobstructed view of two wagons on the road from town.

Two men rode in a large freight wagon with a long wooden box in the back, and a man and woman followed in a carriage. *Today isn't Sunday,* Rebeckah thought. *Why are they dressed like they're going to church?* Both turned toward the Mitchell farm house. Lulubelle, the family's yellow-haired dog, began to bark; Elvira, the donkey, brayed; and the white leghorn chickens started their barnyard chatter as the visitors approached.

The noise woke sixteen-year-old Peggy, who said, "What's happening?"

"We've got visitors coming," Rebeckah answered.

"Who is it?"

"Don't know—two wagons coming from town."

1

Ibby, who was eight, woke, yawned, and looked out the hayloft door from high up in the gable of the barn.

"It's Uncle Samuel and Mr. Miller in the first wagon." Ibby slowly stretched her arms up over her head as far as they would go.

Samuel Fain was married to Rosanna, their mother's sister. Peter Miller was a neighbor. Both were elders of the Salem Presbyterian Church just on the other side of Jonesborough.

The girls watched through the loft door as their parents stepped out of the log house to greet the visitors. Their father, Adam, was holding two-year-old Samuel, and their mother, Elizabeth, was cradling baby David, who was just weeks old.

The sisters climbed down from the loft, brushed the hay off the clothes they had slept in, ran through Grandmother's garden, and greeted their uncle with a hug.

Uncle Samuel asked their father, "Where do you want us to unload your mother's coffin?"

"For now just put it on the sawhorses in the barn."

Reverend Samuel Doak and his wife, Sister Esther, pulled into the yard in their carriage. Reverend Doak was not only their pastor at the Salem Presbyterian Church, but he was also Adam Mitchell's maternal second cousin and long-time friend, just four years younger than Adam.

Sister Esther said, "Adam, I am so sorry that you lost your mother."

"Grandmother isn't lost. She's in the house in her bed. Isn't that right, Father?" Rebeckah stood with a hand on her hip and her head tilted, looking to her father for an answer that didn't come.

"Look, everyone," Sister Esther said. "I've been up since way before daylight cooking. I have here in the back of our carriage fresh baked biscuits, eggs, ham steak, and red eye gravy for your grits. Come on now. My Dutch ovens can't keep breakfast warm forever. It's going to be a long day."

Elizabeth asked Peggy to get the fresh boiled coffee that was warming on the fireplace hearth inside the house.

Peggy hesitated at the door for a moment, dreading to see her grandmother's corpse. When her mother had asked her to take Ibby and Rebeckah to the barn last night, she had told Peggy the end was near for Grandmother Mitchell.

As soon as she entered the house, Peggy understood why her parents had needed them out of the way. The furniture had been rearranged, and the long wooden table board where the family ate every meal had been moved outside. The mirror over the oak chest was covered with black fabric that her mother had purchased from Deaderick's, the new dry goods store in Jonesborough. Mother said it would remain up until a proper period of mourning had been observed. *I wonder how long that will be,* Peggy thought. *How can I comb my hair without a mirror?* Then she reminded herself why the mirror was covered.

Peggy heard her mother calling, "We need that coffee out here now. The men are waiting!"

Peggy rushed out and set the large pewter pot on the table board.

Elizabeth looked at the pot and brushed a tear from her eye. "Seeing this pot reminds me of being in the spring house with Mother Mitchell during the Battle of Guilford Courthouse."

"So this is the pewter she hid from the British troops." Peter Miller said.

"Your mother was a real hero, wasn't she?" Sister Esther poured Adam his coffee.

He answered, "When that British officer asked her to remove herself from the trunk she was sitting on, she refused to budge. That's just the way Mother was."

"And the British didn't get the pewter so they couldn't turn it into musket balls and use it against us!" Rebeckah, now leaning against her father, finished the familiar story about her grandmother.

"That's right," her father said. "You weren't born until the next year, but your mother, sisters, and brothers were with her in the spring house when Cornwallis' soldiers found them."

"And Robert was hidden behind Grandmother's petticoats with your dueling pistol, and he would have fired if the soldier hadn't given up and left," Rebeckah said.

"Robert was just going on fourteen then, but he would have defended his family. Thankfully he didn't have to. After my mother chastised the young officer for harassing an old woman, he just turned and walked away."

"Speaking of your firstborn, where is Robert?" Mr. Miller asked.

"He and William rode out early this morning towards Little Limestone Creek, and then on to Greene County. They went to get my sister and brother-in-law, Mary and James Ross, and their children to escort them back for the burial."

Mr. Miller said, "That's a good idea. There'll be less chance for an Indian attack with two armed horsemen escorting their wagon."

Reverend Doak came out of the house rolling up his sleeves. He, along with Elizabeth and Sister Esther, had just finished last minute preparations for the viewing of Margaret's body. "On the way here, I asked Elder Mathes to start tolling the church bell."

Peter responded, "The congregation has been praying for Mrs. Mitchell as everyone knows she's been ailing for weeks. When they hear the bell ring seventy-seven times, they'll know it's for her. There aren't any other seventy-seven-year-olds in these parts."

"Adam," Reverend Doak asked, "where is the spot in your apple orchard that your mother wished to be buried?"

"This way, Pastor."

Samuel and Peter, who already had shovels over their shoulders, followed Adam and the pastor to the gravesite.

Elizabeth came out of the house and handed Peggy a bundle of clothes. "Peggy, take the girls down to the creek and wash up. Then take them back to the hayloft to change."

Peggy nodded and called her sisters.

The men made good time digging the grave in the fine sandy loam of the Mitchells' apple orchard, but the sun was high when the last spade of red dirt was pitched out of the ground.

Back at the house, neighbors were arriving with the few fresh flowers blooming this early in the spring of 1788. These were added to dried flowers scented with pine tar, cinnamon, and vanilla to help cover the stench of death. All the doors and windows of the house were open wide, and the fireplace was snuffed to keep Grandmother Mitchell's body as cool as possible until she was laid to rest.

Elizabeth's brother, John Blair McMachen, rode up just as the elders returned from digging the grave. "I'm sorry I wasn't here to help. I just got back from delivering the news of Mother Mitchell's death to the people in Jonesborough."

Elizabeth hurried to the group of men and spoke to John Blair, who was still in his saddle. "Please bring Father to the house. I want him to have some time alone with Mother Mitchell before the reverend starts the memorial service."

John Blair nodded. "I'll bring him right away."

Rebeckah, who had been intently listening to every word the adults said, began to sob. "She isn't dead! She's just sleeping!"

Adam picked Rebeckah up and carried her to the family table. He asked Peggy to gather the children for a family talk. Peggy found twelve-year-old John and ten-year-old Adam at the swimming hole on the creek throwing flat stones, making them skip as they hit the water. She already had Ibby and Jennett, who was five, in tow as she approached the table. Samuel held one of his mother's apron strings as she stood with baby David in one arm and the other arm holding Rebeckah close to her side.

Reverend Doak stood out of hearing range under the shade of a nearby chestnut tree. He nodded to Adam and Elizabeth, reassuring them of his support. Neighbors and friends recognized that the family needed to be alone together at this time and gave them the needed distance. The group of women talked about how they would miss Margaret's fall apple-paring socials and her quilting parties. The men remembered the stories they had heard of her heroism during the Battle of Guilford Courthouse.

Adam spoke to his family. "Children, we have lost Grandmother Mitchell. I should have gathered you around me sooner for this talk. My heart was so sorrowful I just couldn't talk to you before now." He looked at the young girl clinging to her mother. "Rebeckah, I'm sorry I didn't explain to you about her passing."

Elizabeth hugged Rebeckah tighter. "I also."

Rebeckah looked at her parents, her eyes filled with sadness and questions. "I just don't understand—Sister Esther said we lost her; you just said she is passing; the last time I saw her, Peggy and Mother said she was sleeping. I want to see her now. Please?"

Adam looked at his wife. Elizabeth nodded her approval, took Rebeckah by the hand, and led the family to the back stoop of the house. She asked the rest of the family to wait until after Rebeckah had seen her grandmother.

Rebeckah looked at the body and then back to her mother. "Grandmother looks like she's comfortable now."

"She is, Rebeckah. Grandmother Mitchell is now in a better place." Elizabeth motioned for the other children to gather at the foot of the bed, which was now completely covered with flowers.

"A better place? Where?" asked Rebeckah.

"Heaven—where all good Presbyterians go," Elizabeth answered.

"How did she get there?" Ibby asked. "It looks like she's still on the bed."

"Her spirit just floated up to heaven," Elizabeth said.

"Like on a cloud?" asked Ibby.

"Yes, that's right. She just floated up on a cloud." Elizabeth motioned upward with her hand.

"I saw her leaving early this morning down by the creek," Rebeckah said. "She just floated up into the sky."

Adam and Elizabeth looked at each other but didn't question her.

Ibby said, "I didn't see her."

"You couldn't—you and Peggy was asleep. I watched her from the loft of the barn. She just floated up to Heaven, pretty as you please, just like Mother said." Rebeckah nodded, making a gesture toward the sky with her palms up.

Ibby started to rebut her story but Peggy shushed her, halting the sibling rivalry.

Adam said, "I'm sorry we didn't let you see Grandmother sooner. Your mother and I thought we were doing the right thing at the time. We should have just told you she had died and gone to Heaven."

Peggy, who had been especially close to Grandmother Mitchell, broke down in tears and reached out to touch her grandmother's hand. The family had lived with Mother Mitchell in Guilford County, and after the battle, her father had brought Peggy, her brothers William and John, and their grandmother to live with Aunt Mary and Uncle James Ross. Adam had returned to Guilford Courthouse, and more than a year passed before the rest of the family moved over the mountains to Knob Creek.

Throughout the day, the gathering of neighbors and church members continued to grow in front of the Mitchells' log cabin. They were coming up the lane on horseback, on foot, and in carriages and farm wagons. Uncle Samuel and Mr. Miller stayed busy greeting the arrivals and letting them know that Reverend Doak would start the service as soon as the family had said their goodbyes to their loved one.

John Blair and his brother-in-law William Fain carried the frail John McMachen, known by family and friends as Mr. Mac, from his home on the hill overlooking the Mitchell farm. They crossed their strong arms to make a seat out of their extended arms and hands for Mr. Mac to sit upon for the trip down the steep hill and across the road and farm field.

The octogenarian had been one of the first settlers in the area, who with his only son John Blair, and free slave Samuel, had homesteaded thousands of acres in the Washington District. He built one of the first permanent homes at the head of Knob Creek. Mr. Mac offered his daughter Elizabeth and son-in-law Adam any of his lands to farm and build a home if they would just take up residence near him. Mr. Mac promised that he and Margaret would take good care of the older children until Adam could move the rest of the family.

The McMachens were so well-known that the community dropped the Machen part of the name all together. When people tried to recall the McMachen name, they sometimes came up with McMahon, McMackin, or some other McM. It didn't matter—everyone knew Mr. Mac and his son John Blair.

The crowd cleared the way for Mr. Mac as he was carried to the deathbed of his dearest friend and confidant.

Mr. Mac and Mother Mitchell had first met more than a quarter century earlier when both their spouses were alive and their children were young. On the banks of the Opequon Creek near his home in Frederick County Virginia, he and Robert Mitchell had become instant friends and had decided that Mr. Mac's daughter Elizabeth should marry Robert's son Adam and bear them many grandchildren. The arrangement didn't work as the fathers had planned—Adam chose to marry his childhood sweetheart Jennett instead. She died three days after giving birth to their son Robert. Eventually Elizabeth and Adam did get together without their fathers' interference. They might not have ended up together if Mr. Mac hadn't moved to Guilford County to be near the Mitchell family after his wife Isabella died.

When the men carried Mr. Mac into the crowded room, Elizabeth said, "Let's leave your grandfather to be alone with Grandmother."

"No, Elizabeth," her father protested. "I think Margaret would have wanted all her family around her in this little time we have left before she is placed in her coffin."

Reverend Doak stuck his head in the door. "It's getting late, and we should proceed."

"Would you please wait for Robert and William to have a few moments with her when they get here?"

"It's all right, Mother. We've been here with you looking through the window."

Robert's voice took Elizabeth by surprise. The small cabin was so crowded she hadn't seen her oldest sons or Adam's sister Mary.

Mary said, "The pastor is right. We should start as many of her friends and neighbors have been here for a long time, waiting to see Mother and pay their respects. Even Governor Sevier and Judge McNairy are here."

The family stepped outside after Adam asked Mr. Mac to stay seated and to do the honor of accepting the condolences of the mourners as they came through the cabin.

Reverend Doak called the crowd together around the small porch for prayer and a short eulogy. After the service, he announced the cabin was open for viewing the body, then he extended an invitation to the McMachen home for the customary Scots-Irish wake that evening.

The Mitchell family stood near the entrance as their family, friends, and neighbors worked their way to the front of the house. The Governor of Franklin, John Sevier, had ridden to Knob Creek from his home on the Nolichucky River.

"Thank you for coming, Governor," Adam said. "I know that you are busy with the affairs of the state and trying to settle this Tipton matter."

"Yes, I have been, but I had to pay my respects to your mother who did so much for the wounded after the Battle for Guilford Courthouse. I look forward to saying a few words about her at this evening's wake, if I may."

"Of course you can, Governor. It would be a great honor."

"Where is Mr. Mac?"

"Inside next to Mother," Adam answered.

"I should have known. Side by side till the end!"

"He's taking it hard, Governor. He loved her very much."

Next in line was newly appointed Judge John McNairy, whose family had lived near the Mitchells in Guilford County. He attended the log cabin school for boys taught by David and Rachel Caldwell. Adam's oldest sons, Robert and William, were his classmates. The judge and twenty-one-year-old Robert had been getting reacquainted in the evenings at Murphy's Tavern.

Judge McNairy had brought Andrew Jackson, a friend and fellow lawyer. Both had served their internships practicing law under attorney Spruce Macay in Salisbury. Judge McNairy and Andrew had recently rented the loft in Christopher Taylor's cabin. With thirteen children in the family, the Taylor house was cramped. In the evenings, rather than dining with the family, the attorneys joined Robert and friends at Murphy's Tavern for a meal, washed down with several tankards of ale. Mrs. Taylor, who didn't need two more at her supper table, appreciated this arrangement.

However, when her boarders came home a little tipsy, they tripped over the children asleep on the floor and woke them, causing Mrs. Taylor anguish. She solved the problem by having Mr. Taylor build a crude ladder on the outside of the house leading up to the window of the loft.

By the time the last mourners had passed by Margaret's flower-draped body, night was approaching, and the guests were hungry and ready to celebrate her life in the Celtic way. The family decided to bury her the next morning at daylight. The pall bearers assisted Reverend Doak in placing her in the coffin, which she had purchased along with her burial gown from Deaderick's store some months before.

Adam had been perplexed that she purchased a store-bought coffin as he had always made the coffins for family members who died.

Elizabeth said, "Adam, this is just your mother's way of letting you know how much she loves you. She knew you and I would be greatly bereaved and have much to do upon her death. I'm thankful she prepared for her burial, including choosing the site in the orchard where she wished to be buried."

The pall bearers nailed the coffin securely shut and moved it back to the sawhorses in the barn. They left the large barn doors on each side wide open so the cool of the night air circulating around the coffin with the addition of fifty pounds of rock salt inside would preserve the body until morning. They would take turns staying with her coffin until burial while the others enjoyed the festivities.

Mr. Mac's log house stood on a hill overlooking Knob Creek. The house was large by backwoods standards, and it had been the first home in the county to have a stone chimney and shake shingles shipped from Philadelphia. He had built the large home with the hope that the widowed Margaret would marry him and share his worldly possessions for the short time that remained of their lives.

Although she had rejected his marriage proposal, they had been inseparable during the six years Margaret had lived in the area. Margaret had her family's blessing to marry him if she wished. He and Margaret were both grandparents to Adam and Elizabeth's children. Adam thought of him as a father and sought his advice on major decisions, and Mr. Mac loved his son-in-law and treated him just like his own son John Blair. But in spite of all the good reasons for them to marry, Margaret told Mr. Mac that she loved him as the dearest friend she ever had, but she could never marry another after the loss of her beloved husband Robert.

They had traveled about Washington County together in Mr. Mac's open carriage made of white limousine oak. Margaret had accompanied him to social events. They had become a popular couple and were the center of attention and life of any party they attended.

Confusion often ensued as Mr. Mac introduced Margaret as his friend Mrs. Mitchell and then spoke of their grandchildren. They sat with their children and grandchildren at church. The children of the Mitchell clan called the couple their grandparents, which they were, but not in the way people expected. The couple enjoyed explaining their relationship of so many years and laughing as they told their stories to the listener. Three of Mr. Mac's daughters had married sons of friend and neighbor Nicholas Fain. At family gatherings and church socials, nearly fifty grandchildren circled around Mr. Mac, intently listening to his stories.

The wake was in full swing at the Quarters, so-called by the residents of the area because during the Revolution the local militia had stored its munitions and supplies inside. The Quarters were ideal for the purpose, high on a hill hidden in the woods. Mr. Mac would be able to see the British approaching from any direction and was prepared to blow up his own home should it look like the enemy would find the Patriots' stores of war materials.

Mr. Mac had to be put into bed after the ordeal of the day's activities. He instructed his daughters and son to carry on the tradition of a Scots-Irish wake in his absence.

Governor Sevier gave a moving eulogy describing Margaret's efforts to comfort the wounded soldiers on her farm following the Battle of Guilford Courthouse.

John Blair embarrassed Adam and Elizabeth by telling of the first meeting of the two families at the McMachen home in Frederick County, Virginia, back in 1762. Both of them were so enchanted with each other they couldn't keep their eyes off one another during dinner or at the next day's church service at the Opequon Presbyterian Church. John Blair got very emotional when he elaborated on how Mother Mitchell had become a part of his family's life and that he loved her as he had his own mother, Isabella.

After the eulogies, Adam announced, "Mother would have wanted us to carry on the Celtic tradition and sing and dance and rejoice in her life. She loved each and every one of you, so for her let's sing, dance, and rejoice."

Guests helped themselves to food from the heaping table and to the plentiful libations. The neighbors began to play dulcimers, fiddles, or whatever instruments they had brought.

Andrew bowed in front of Peggy, placing his best foot forward, and asked the surprised girl to dance.

Peggy still grieved, but she was determined not to let her tears mar the celebration of her grandmother's life. She would enjoy the evening, laughing and dancing and having a good time—no matter how sad she felt inside.

Andrew was not the best-looking young man at the wake, but he was the best-dressed man she had ever seen. Most of the men of prominence wore their hair powdered; the powder made her sneeze uncontrollably. Andrew used no powder and wore his dark red hair pulled back from his face and cinched at the neck. He was taller than any man she had ever danced with. He could dance to whatever the informal ensemble was playing; it didn't matter the song, for he could lead and she could follow. She gazed into his dark blue eyes; he intently gazed into hers. She had never experienced these feelings dancing with any other man. He was so graceful in every move that he made—whether it was a waltz or a Virginia reel.

Peggy began to feel a little woozy. Maybe it was the applejack. She had to sit down.

Andrew led her to a chair and asked, "Miss Mitchell, are you all right? Can I bring you something to eat?"

She realized that she hadn't eaten since the early morning breakfast prepared by Sister Esther. "Oh, yes, please."

While he was gone to get the food, she thought back over the evening. No one had ever called her Miss before; it sounded nice. Her cousins and brothers and the boys at Martin's Academy just called her Peg. Mr. Jackson treated her like a lady, and she liked that.

Andrew returned with some pulled pork on a piece of toast. "You should eat this."

Soon after she ate, she felt much better. "Thank you for your thoughtfulness."

"It was my pleasure to be of service to such a lovely lady. Would you like to take a walk?"

"Yes, I would, Mr. Jackson."

"Please call me Andy. That's what my friends call me."

She looked at the couples dancing. "May I call you Andrew?"

"Call me anything you wish, just not Mr. Jackson."

"And you may call me Peggy."

The couple walked down the hill toward the Mitchell home and Knob Creek.

Peggy said, "I'd like to show you my favorite place."

The approach of Lulubelle, the family dog, startled Andrew. Peg knelt to pet the yellow-haired canine, whose tail was wagging rapidly after having missed the usual daily attention she demanded.

Peggy took Andrew's hand and said, "This way," as she ducked under the dangling branches of a weeping willow. She dropped his hand when they had to walk single file to follow a narrow path toward the creek—Peggy in the lead and Lulubelle at the rear, nosing Andrew in the seat of his britches every step he took until they reached the creek. At this late hour, the almost-full moon reflected on the smooth surface of the pond, and the stars glowed brightly on this clear night.

"I see why this is your favorite place." Andrew took her hand again.

Peggy looked down at their clasped hands and pulled hers back. She'd only intended to guide him to the creek. "My father and older brothers made this pond. They built a dam out of limestone boulders; it was hard work and took most of a summer to finish."

"I can tell it took a lot of work."

"Father will start building a grist mill on this very spot, just as soon as he has enough timber cut and dried. I like the pond as it is. In the summer, it's our swimming hole and where the family bathes. It's not fair that the boys get to swim more than the girls." Her frown turned to a smile. "But I sneak down alone more often than anyone knows." She frowned again. "Once the mill is built, it will never be a place I can come and be alone."

14

"Why is that?"

"My grandfather, Uncle John Blair, and the Fains and the Millers will all be using the new grist mill. It's a joint effort to provide a mill near the farmers east of Jonesborough." She sighed. "My poor father and the other farmers around here have to haul their grain all the way to Little Limestone Creek to be milled by Michael Bawn. Grain is lost on the road as well as their time."

Andrew turned to face her and stepped closer. "Peggy Mitchell, I envy you."

She looked at him in surprise. "Why, Andrew?"

"You have such a close family and so many friends." He bent down to pet the dog.

"Don't you have family?"

He looked up at her from his crouched position. "No, it's just me. My father died before I was born, and the only thing I have to remember him by is his name, which my mother gave me. I had two older brothers, but they both died at the hands of the British. My mother died of cholera after her trips by foot to Camden to secure my release."

"You were a prisoner of war?"

"Yes."

She stepped closer to him. "But you're so young."

"I was only thirteen when I was captured."

"Did they hurt you?"

"This scar on my face was from a British officer's sword."

"I noticed your scar but had no idea you received it in combat."

"It wasn't combat, Peggy. A British officer demanded that I clean his muddy boots after he had destroyed my aunt's home. I refused, and he took a swing at me with his sword. I raised my left hand to deflect the blow, but was wounded on my left hand and face." Andrew's lips tightened to a grim line. "I shall hate the British forever for what they did to me and my family."

"I'm sorry for your loss. I didn't know."

"Very few people know. John does; he's my best friend and now my boss."

"Your boss? I thought you were an attorney."

"I am, but I have been appointed the prosecuting attorney for the state of North Carolina. John, uh, Judge McNairy and I will soon head for Nashville to set up one of the state's three courts."

"When will you be leaving?"

"As soon as we've recruited enough travelers to make a caravan large enough to discourage the Indians from attacking us."

"Will you be coming back to Jonesborough?"

"Yes, I must, and so will the judge. Jonesborough is the county seat of Washington County. We'll hold court here four times a year."

"Where did you grow up?" Peg looked into his steel-blue eyes.

"On Twelve Mile Creek near Waxhaw where there are lots of pine trees. My father tried to clear 200 acres and eventually died of exhaustion."

"Is that why you've chosen to enter the legal profession rather than farming?"

"I may someday have a farm of my own, but for now I see a great need for lawyers in the expansion of the West. I've acquired several clients already in Jonesborough since being admitted to the bar in Washington County."

Lulubelle started to bark, and in one swift move, Andrew had drawn a small pistol Peg hadn't seen concealed in his waistband.

A man's voice called, "Andrew, where are you?"

"Over here by the creek." Andrew returned the pistol to its hiding place.

Judge McNairy appeared and nodded at Peggy. "I apologize for interrupting." He turned toward Andrew. "The Taylors left for home some time ago. Remember, Mrs. Taylor is still mad at us for the last time we came in so late. If we leave now, we can climb into the loft before they go to sleep and prevent our eviction." He turned to Peggy. "I offer my sincere condolences."

"I appreciate your coming and bringing Andrew." She smiled, surprised to realize that she hadn't thought of her grandmother or remembered her sorrow all the time she was with him.

Andrew asked, "Peggy, when might I have the pleasure of seeing you again?"

"You can find me this Sunday as every first Sunday of the month at Salem Church, southeast of Jonesborough. Just follow the Hominy Branch, and you'll find it." She flashed an impish smile. "They still allow attorneys to go to church in the State of Franklin, you know. They're just forbidden from seeking public office."

"I'm sure the State of Franklin won't last forever, and then attorneys will have a say."

The judge held out his arm to Peggy. "Come and let the two best attorneys in Washington County escort you home."

As they approached the Mitchell home, Lulubelle realized something was amiss in the barn. She chased out Elder Alexander Mathes, who had been watching over Margaret's coffin. Andrew and John said good night to Peggy and Elder Mathes and started toward home.

"Peggy, I know how close you and your grandmother were," Elder Mathes said. "I realize that you are in pain. Is there anything I can do or get for you?"

The smile that had been on Peggy's face all evening faded. "Yes, would you let me watch over her for the rest of the night?"

"I don't know if I should leave you out here in the barn alone."

Looking up at the star-studded sky she said, "Tonight I can't think of anywhere else on this earth I'd rather be than alone with my grandmother and my dog."

"If that is your desire, my dear Peg. Should I stay at a close distance in case some Indians come up the creek looking for trouble?"

"Don't worry. If anyone comes near, they'll have to contend with Lulubelle. She'll wake the family."

Mr. Mathes chuckled. "Yes, your Lulubelle can be heard barking for miles."

After the elder took his leave, Peggy hugged the coffin tightly and said good night to her grandmother as she had every night for as long as she could remember. Sitting on the ground, her back against one of the legs of the sawhorse, with Lulubelle's head on her lap, Peg fell into a deep sleep, dreaming of the wonderful times she'd had with her grandmother.

At daybreak the family placed Margaret Mitchell's coffin gently in her grave under her favorite apple tree.

Chapter Two

Peggy's Beau

The neighbors around the Knob Creek community gathered on the first Sunday of April at Adam Mitchell's farm to travel in a caravan of wagons for the ten-mile trek to Salem Presbyterian Church to hear Reverend Doak preach. They traveled together for safety because Indians had been on a rampage. The families looked forward to the monthly services and dinner under the shady grove of trees next to the church.

The well-armed Mitchell boys—Robert, William, and John—rode on horseback ahead of the family wagon. Adam drove and Elizabeth held baby David. In the back of the wagon, Peggy, Ibby, and Rebeckah kept the youngest children—Samuel and Jennett—occupied petting the black and white kitten Rebeckah had found in the barn. Samuel and William Fain escorted their families' wagons. Behind the Fains came Peter Miller and John Blair McMachen and their families. Along the way, other church members joined the convoy.

On every Sunday except the first week of the month, the families in the area met in private homes for Bible study. Their numbers had grown to the point that the homes were too small to accommodate the congregation. Next week they would meet in the new Washington County Courthouse, only half the distance to Salem Church.

The noise of wagons rolling down Main Street woke those residents of Jonesborough who were still asleep. Guests in the town's only inn opened the shutters and peered out, trying to determine what all the commotion was about. The worshippers, who had been laughing and singing at full volume, stopped in front of the mercantile store where the shopkeeper and his son lived in a small space above the new business. The Deadericks were invited to ride in John Blair's fringe-top carriage, a place of honor for the church visitors. It would be the first time the German Lutherans had attended a Presbyterian service.

As the Deadericks climbed into the carriage, the judge and Andrew rode up to the Mitchells' wagon.

"Quite a group of Presbyterians," Judge McNairy said. "My friend and I would like to accompany you to church this morning, if we may."

"We would appreciate your riding with us," Adam answered. "When the Indians see the arms you're bearing, they'll think twice before attacking."

Andrew turned toward the Mitchell wagon and tipped his hat to Peggy. "Good morning. I'm glad to have an occasion to see you again." His manners and tone were polite, but Adam and Elizabeth saw his wink and Peg's answering smile. They realized their daughter had another interested suitor, but this time she appeared to have an equal interest in the tall, lanky, red-headed lawyer.

Though she had been named after her Grandmother Margaret, the family always called her either Peggy or Peg. All the town's eligible young men had tried to court Peg, who was tall and slim, with auburn hair and sparkling green eyes. Adam rebuffed each of them when they asked permission to call on her because he and Reverend Doak had already selected the Witherspoon boy to become Peggy's husband once he became ordained.

James Witherspoon was a relative of Presbyterian minister John Witherspoon who had signed the Declaration of Independence and founded the College of New Jersey. Samuel and Esther Doak were fond of Jimmy, an outstanding student at their Martin Academy who, even as a young boy, was determined to serve God in the ministry of the Presbyterian Church.

Adam liked the idea of having a Presbyterian minister in the family. That couldn't happen for some time, though, because Jimmy was several years younger than Peggy. The pastor had asked Peggy to tutor the boy after school to keep her time and mind occupied.

The plan had worked until now. Peg, who had never shown an interest in any man, was flirting with Andrew as he sat on his roan stallion smiling at her. Adam hoped she was just experiencing the same kind of infatuation he had felt the first time he met Elizabeth. It had seemed intense at the time, but when he got to know Jennett, he realized how different the feelings of infatuation and love were. Later, after Jennett's death, he had fallen deeply in love with Elizabeth. But that was much later, and he and Elizabeth had both matured in the meantime. Jackson would be heading to Nashville soon; Adam hoped the infatuation wouldn't have time to develop into anything more serious.

As the wagon pulled ahead, Peggy looked back at Andrew behind them engulfed in dust from their wagon. She brushed at her skirt, smoothed it with her hand, and then sat up straighter. On previous trips, she had ridden Cherokee sidesaddle. She'd wanted to do so this Sunday, but Mother had insisted she ride in the wagon to help with her younger siblings since Grandmother was no longer here to help. Peggy had prevailed on her father to tether her saddled horse behind the wagon, suggesting Cherokee would be a back-up in the event one of the other horses in the convoy became lame. Adam knew the real reason she insisted on bringing her horse was that she hoped for an opportunity to ride with the boys after the potluck dinner.

When the group reached the church, they were greeted cordially at the door by the tall, broad-shouldered Reverend Doak. The men respectfully removed their hats, but not their weapons. The pastor's long rifle leaned against the lectern, ready for any Indian hostilities that might occur during the church service or dinner on the grounds. The pews were made of long pine logs, which had been laboriously split by the broadax of Elder Mathes. The chair legs were wooden chestnut branches turned by Adam's foot-operated lathe, which he had rigged from a discarded spinning wheel.

Even with the new pews, there wasn't enough seating for everyone on the first Sunday of each month. The children gathered in front and sat on the rough-hewn wooden floor directly below the pastor's lectern. The younger men lined the side and back of the church, leaning against the log walls, propping a leg up now and then, and shifting their weight from one leg to the other. Some preferred to stand rather than sit on the hard pews.

The soon-to-be-forty-year-old preacher was the son of Scots-Irish immigrants Samuel and Jane Mitchell Doak. Jane was Adam's aunt. Samuel Doak, Jr., born on the first day of August 1749, was their third son.

At age sixteen, Samuel Jr. knew he wanted to preach the Gospel. He spent the next ten years in ministerial studies and received his bachelor's degree from The College of New Jersey in the spring of 1775.

Samuel married Esther H. Montgomery of Virginia, a sister of his good friend and classmate John Montgomery, on November 30, 1775. He preached his first sermon in the area from horseback to a group of woodsmen felling trees on the Little Limestone Creek not far from where he later built his church.

Many in the congregation remembered his sermon at Sycamore Shoals on September 26, 1780 before "The Over the Mountain Men" left for the Revolutionary War Battle at Kings Mountain. Reverend Doak comforted not only the volunteers but the families who came to say goodbye to their loved ones—many of whom would return with injuries or would not return at all.

On this Sunday, Reverend Doak preached on reconciliation. The past four years of political upheaval in Franklin had splintered the community and his church. Some members, loyal Franklinites, wished to break away from the State of North Carolina and form the State of Franklin. Others,

so-called Antis, did not want to form a separate state government, while some vacillated according to the political
winds of the moment. The controversy over the issue of the
separate State of Franklin had escalated to the point of an
armed rebellion—neighbor against neighbor—with several
killed and many wounded.

The General Assembly of North Carolina had met at
Hillsborough on April 19, 1784, and voted to cede the state's
western land to the provisional federal government. This
action left the residents of the ceded land without representa-
tion or protection from the Indians, who had received many
promises from North Carolina that would not be fulfilled.

The pastor began his sermon. "The State of Franklin is
no more, gone forever. We have lost church members John
Smith and Sheriff Jonathan Pugh, killed by neighbors who
were once their friends over a state that never was. I have
spoken with Governor Sevier. His term of office expired last
month; he has ceased to act in the capacity of governor of
the State of Franklin.

"The purpose of forming Franklin has passed since the
mother state's repeal of the Cession Act. Governor Sevier
has sent correspondence to the state capital asking for all
hostilities against the Franklinites to halt until the next
North Carolina Assembly meets. He promised that we, the
citizens of what was the State of Franklin, will honor and
obey the deliberations and actions of that body forevermore
and pray peace and order may immediately take place in
Washington, Greene, and Sullivan Counties."

The pastor used the fifth chapter of 2 Corinthians as
the text for his sermon on reconciliation. He read, "And all
things are of God, who hath reconciled us to himself by Jesus
Christ, and hath given to us the ministry of reconciliation."

The congregation prayed that peace be restored in their
church and the community between the Tipton and Sevier
camps once and for all time.

Jimmy Witherspoon, the pastor's protégé, had done
an excellent job this morning leading the congregation in

the Lord's Prayer without a stutter. He stood beside his mentor shaking hands as the congregation exited through the only door of the church. The boy beamed with pride at the compliments he was receiving from well-wishers. Even his mother, who could be quite critical of her son, gave him a slight nod of approval.

Peggy watched Andrew out of the corner of her eye as he masterfully and patiently maneuvered into line directly behind her and her best friend, Jennifer Young. Jennifer had seen Andrew and Peggy exchange longing looks all during church, communicating only with their eyes. Seated between them, Jennifer could sense the strong attraction.

"Who is he?" she whispered.

"Don't worry. I'll introduce you properly at the appropriate time," Peggy answered, also in a whisper. As they moved forward in line to stand before the pastor and their younger classmate from Martin Academy, they felt giddy. They wanted to compliment Jimmy yet impress Peggy's new suitor at the same time.

Peggy looked Jimmy directly in the eyes. "Your enunciation and diction during the Lord's Prayer has improved so dramatically. I'm proud of you." She gave him a quick kiss on the cheek.

The lovely, blue-eyed blonde Jennifer gave him a sisterly hug.

The freckle-faced boy turned the color of a large ripe peach. He tried to speak, but managed only to bob his head up and down. His lips turned blue, and he began to wheeze.

Pastor Doak said, "Jimmy, why don't you go get a drink of water? The line is almost to the end anyhow."

Jimmy nodded, coughing as he walked toward the well in back of the log structure.

Peg looked at the pastor, her forehead wrinkled. "What did we say to embarrass him so?"

"It wasn't the message," answered Reverend Doak. "Jimmy is just shy and fragile, especially around people he looks up to. Don't worry. He'll be over this in a few moments. Go and enjoy this beautiful day God has given us."

The girls moved on so the next person in line could speak to the minister.

"Reverend Doak, my name is Andrew Jackson. I enjoyed your sermon and appreciate the way you're trying to defuse the turmoil in the Tipton and Sevier matter."

"Yes, it's difficult for the church as both John Tipton and John Sevier are long-time members, serving together on the board of trustees of our school." The minister placed his left hand on Andrew's shoulder and shook his right hand. "Enough of that, Mr. Jackson. I have heard a great deal about you. It's good to hear that you came this morning to hear the Word of God and not just admire the young maidens who have held your attention so intently." He nodded toward Peggy and Jennifer.

"Both have brought me here, sir. It's been a long time since I've been able to attend a Presbyterian service."

"You are Presbyterian?"

"My mother was very much a believer and read the Bible every day of her short life."

"Is that so?"

"She wanted so much for me to go to school and be a Presbyterian minister."

"Why didn't you?"

"It's a long story, Reverend, and before I depart for Nashville, I would like very much to tell you. Perhaps you would baptize me."

"I would like that." The pastor gave Andrew one of his bear hugs, patting him on the back.

Jennifer and Peggy had not moved far from the door of the church, staying in sight of Andrew.

"Tell me all about him," Jennifer demanded.

"His name is Andrew Jackson. He's a lawyer staying with the Taylor family in their loft, as is Judge John McNairy who grew up near our home in Guilford Courthouse."

"Seeing as you already have the affection of Mr. Jackson, what can you tell me about Judge McNairy? Is he married? How old is he?"

Peggy smiled at her friend. "He's a bachelor about five years older than my brother Robert."

"That would make him about twenty-six, wouldn't it?"

"Shh—Andrew's coming this way."

Andrew bowed at the waist. The local mountain men seeing him greet the women so respectfully looked at each other in surprise at his charm with the fairer sex. Everyone could see Jackson's impeccable manners impressed the girls.

"Peggy, I've been waiting for the opportunity to speak to you."

"I have to you also, Andrew. But first let me introduce you to my good friend, Jennifer Young."

Andrew looked deep into Jennifer's sparkling blue eyes. "Beauty attracts beauty, I see. It is an honor to make your acquaintance. Madame Young, I presume?"

"No, like Peggy, I am unmarried."

"Then you must be the **young** maiden," he emphasized the word **young**, "that I have heard so much about."

Jennifer gave him a dazzling smile. "You are so witty, Mr. Jackson. It is my pleasure to meet you." She curtsied and extended her hand for Andrew to kiss.

Peggy gave her friend a look, as if warning her to stop flirting with her beau.

"Andrew, will you be joining us for the potluck dinner?" Peggy asked.

"I didn't bring anything to share."

"That doesn't matter. You are a guest and so is Judge McNairy if he would like to join us."

"It looks like John is holding court again." Andrew looked over at his friend under the elm tree. "He's most likely trying to explain the new court system to the church elders."

"What court system?"

"The one I told you about by the pond at your grandmother's wake."

"By the pond?" Jennifer wore a teasing smile as she looked at Peggy.

Andrew ignored the interruption. "The courts that Judge McNairy and I will be setting up here and in Davidson County."

"Where is Davidson County?" Peggy asked.

"About 200 miles west of here in the bend of the Cumberland River Valley, where we will build the courthouse at a place called Nashville."

Sister Esther presided over the serving table made of wide planks stretched between two farm wagons pulled up end to end. She supervised the placement of the numerous Dutch ovens, skillets, wooden vessels, and kegs of liquid refreshments. She motioned to her husband that the women were ready to start serving the food that included rabbit stew, smoked ham, venison, and fresh garden vegetables, with johnnycakes for dessert.

The sound of the ringing church bell let the children who had wandered to the Hominy Branch know that dinner was about to be served. They ran up the hill to join the adults gathered around the minister standing in one of the wagons.

"Let us pray and bless this bountiful feast and the new friends that have come today. It's a lovely spring day, the warmest in some time. If there is anyone that has a need to be baptized or to reaffirm their faith, this would be a good time and place to do it." He looked expectantly toward Andrew, but it appeared he was not ready to heed the call.

Peggy, Jennifer, and Andrew went through the line and took their food to the quilt Peggy had spread out on the green grass of a gentle hill. Andrew motioned his friend over to join them. He introduced John to Jennifer and started to introduce Peggy.

"Remember, I've known Peggy since her birth back in Guilford Courthouse."

Peggy said, "I've been told that since we left the community has really grown."

"Yes, it has. And it was renamed Martinsville after Governor Martin shortly after Cornwallis surrendered at Yorktown."

"My memory of Guilford County is not a pleasant one." Peggy gazed off in the distance remembering how the noise and smoke of war had frightened her as a nine-year-old girl. Her mind flashed back to the night after the battle. Shuddering, she once again remembered hearing the cries of the injured and dying of both armies as they writhed in pain in the farm fields below her home. She vividly recalled seeing the bodies, smelling the stench of death, and witnessing the destruction left by the invading army. She put down her plate, no longer hungry.

"Peggy, are you all right? You look—"

She cut Andrew off with a change of subject. "Where did you find that beautiful roan stallion you ride so well?"

"I acquired Waxhaw from a farmer in Salisbury in exchange for perfecting a land title on some property." His face lit in a smile. "When I first laid eyes on the colt and studied his composition, I knew that he would grow into a stallion of quality."

"Where did you acquire your equestrian interest?" Peggy asked.

"When I was a young lad, my Uncle James Crawford had horses and taught me to ride. At thirteen, I began scouting for the rebel militia around Waxhaw and eventually started to courier dispatches and messages for the officers."

"Did you name Waxhaw in honor of your home district?" Jennifer asked, trying to get into the conversation.

"Yes, as I want to always remember where I came from." He turned back toward Peggy. "I hope someday to have a nice horse farm and to breed horses for speed."

Jennifer and John looked at each other. Andrew and Peggy seemed to have forgotten there were other people sitting on the quilt.

Peggy asked, "Do you like to race horses?"

"I can think of very few things as exhilarating as a horse race, especially when I win."

"Is that so? Would you like to go for a ride?" Peggy stood and brushed grass from her skirt.

"I would like that very much, especially if you will ride behind me."

Peggy shook her head. "No, thank you. I have my horse Cherokee tied to the wagon."

"That magnificent bay mare is yours?"

"Yes. Grandfather Mac gave me Cherokee when I was twelve years old; she was just a yearling then."

"That's quite a horse for a young lady to ride." Andrew rose from the blanket. "You ride her sidesaddle, I assume."

She motioned for him to follow her the short distance to the wagon.

Neither Andrew nor Peggy heard John and Jennifer tell them goodbye.

"Have you seen the falls in the bend of the Nolichucky yet?" Peggy asked.

"No, I haven't."

"Then I'll show you."

Andrew assisted Peggy up onto the limestone upping block. She pulled herself onto the side of Cherokee's saddle gracefully. Her older brothers Robert and William, who were standing nearby, laughed at the show their sister was putting on.

"Can you believe her?" William asked.

"Peggy doesn't need a upping block or anyone helping her," Robert said.

Elizabeth overheard her sons' comments. "You behave and don't embarrass your sister. But I think you need to follow them."

"You don't trust them alone together?" William asked.

"It's not that. But with the Indians acting up, you should keep them within sight. Take your rifles—and be careful."

Robert looked over to the judge sitting on the quilt. "You want to go?"

"No." He lay back on the patchwork quilt. "I think I'll just stay here and bask in the sun and the brilliance of Miss Young."

Robert said, "I don't blame you." He nodded toward Peggy and Andrew. "I can see Cherokee is ready to be ridden, and Peggy is ready to ride."

"There she goes," William said as the brothers found a good vantage point on a high vista overlooking the meadow below. "She's about to make her signature switch."

Peggy headed across an open field still in the side stirrups, with Andrew slightly behind her. As soon as they were out of sight of the church, Peggy put her full weight on the left stirrup and raised her right leg up and over the saddle, making the change from sidesaddle to cross saddle without slowing her mount.

Andrew and Peggy stopped at a flowing spring on the Little Limestone Creek to water the lathered horses. When Peggy dismounted with ease, Andrew realized she needed no assistance from him.

"Peggy, you ride quite well for a woman."

Her face turned red. "Why do all men think that a woman should walk or ride in a buggy?"

"I meant no harm."

"I know." She took a deep breath. "I'm sorry I let my Scots-Irish temper flare."

"That Scots-Irish temper is becoming on you. I did enjoy watching you switch riding positions in your dress with Cherokee in full gallop."

This time her face flushed with embarrassment. "Not very lady-like, I suppose." She looked deep into Andrew's blue eyes.

"I never saw my mother ride a horse—most likely as she didn't have one, yet you remind me so much of her." He seemed lost in thought for a few seconds. "She could do anything a man could do, but she also knew when to act as a lady."

"Does that mean you think I don't know how to act like a lady?"

"No, I said you're like my mother, who could do anything a man could do but still knew how to act like a lady. I love to watch you ride with your hair blowing in the wind. You look so natural and at ease in the saddle."

His smile made Peggy want to melt in his arms. He pulled her gently toward him as he lightly stroked her auburn hair. They gazed into each other's eyes as they drew closer together until their lips met for the first time. Peggy drew back, unsure of her feelings. She'd been kissed before—but not like this. Andrew leaned further toward her and continued to kiss her as she pulled away.

She didn't understand what was happening, but it reminded her of the woozy feeling she got after a cup of Grandmother's applejack. She savored that feeling, and she liked Andrew. She tentatively started to return the kiss.

The sound of approaching horses interrupted the romantic moment. Andrew instinctively took Peggy's hand and grabbed the reins of both horses. He led them across the creek, wading in the shallow water and toward a thicket on the opposite bank. Andrew put his finger to his lips, reminding Peggy to be quiet. She put an arm around Cherokee's neck and her other hand on the animal's nose in an effort to keep the horse from making any sound. Her effort failed as Cherokee picked up the scent of her stablemates carrying Robert and William.

Seeing her brothers, Peggy stepped out of the thicket into the shallow creek. "Were you following us?" She stood in the running water of the creek with her hands on her hips.

"No, it's just that it's getting late and will soon be dark. Mother asked us to round everyone up for the long ride home."

Peggy put both hands on the saddle horn and pulled herself up on Cherokee. "Let's not keep the family waiting."

She gave Andrew a nod and headed back toward the church. They met up with the caravan already headed toward home. Elizabeth had made a pallet of quilts for her youngest children in the back of the wagon. Since the tired youngsters would sleep on the way home, Peggy could ride Cherokee alongside Andrew. They dropped back some distance from the noise and dust of the wagons where they could talk.

Andrew said, "I really enjoyed this day with you and dread to see it come to an end. When will I see you again?"

"If you wish to continue seeing me, you should ask permission from Father."

"Do you think he'll approve?"

She turned slightly in the saddle to look at him. "I think so. He didn't stop me from riding with you this afternoon."

"You do know that your brothers were following us the entire time, don't you?"

"They were?"

"Yes, they were in my eyesight most of the time."

"Watching?"

He nodded. "Yes, the whole time."

"Damn them!"

Andrew looked at her.

"Don't look so shocked. I hear the men use 'damn' all the time. It's probably about as ladylike as the way I ride." She snorted. "Did they see us kiss?"

"Most likely."

"Why didn't you tell me?" She slowed Cherokee's pace.

Andrew slowed his horse to stay even with her. "Would you have so graciously returned my kiss had you known your brothers were watching?"

"Certainly not!"

"Then there is your answer."

"You are a scoundrel, Mr. Jackson." She shook her head but smiled as she spurred Cherokee toward a clump of trees. Andrew chased after her, both laughing loud enough to be heard by the rest of the travelers.

"Where do you think they're going?" Adam asked Elizabeth, who was attempting to nurse baby David as the wagon bounced along the rough road to Jonesborough.

"For a little privacy, I suppose." She raised her voice to be heard over the sounds of the wagon, straining to direct the crying baby's mouth to her breast.

"What do you think of this fellow Andrew Jackson?"

"I like him. There's something about him I've seen in only one man before."

"And just who is that one man?"

"When I was about Peggy's age, we were living in Frederick County, Virginia. Father's friend Patrick Henry came to visit for a few days. Father had invited him to speak to some of the leaders of the county. I've never heard anyone speak with such persuasion—he convinced many a Tory in Virginia to become a Whig. Mr. Jackson and Mr. Henry both have the same aura of grandeur and speak as if they're royalty." She shifted on the hard seat as the baby's mouth found its target and the crying quieted.

"Lawyer hogwash if you ask me," Adam replied.

"Well, Mr. Henry became the Governor of Virginia and signed the Declaration of Independence. That's not hogwash."

"Andrew Jackson will never be a man of the stature of Patrick Henry."

"Time will tell." Elizabeth watched the young couple racing through the woods back toward the wagons, reminding her of when she and Adam first met back in Virginia so long ago.

Peggy had led Andrew into the woods where she had given him a teasing kiss while still on horseback. Then she galloped off toward the group of travelers just as they entered Jonesborough to drop off Mr. Deaderick and his son.

"Robert, make sure everyone stays together till we get to Knob Creek." Adam nodded toward Peggy and Andrew.

"I understand and will pass the word to everyone."

Robert whirled around and rode over to the young couple. "Will you help me keep the wagon train tight?" he asked Andrew. "The next few miles are thick with timber, and a raiding party of Indians could be lurking at any bend in the road. William and I will go ahead, and the Fains will protect our rear."

After looking around to make sure the wagons were close together, Andrew rode up to Adam's side of his wagon. "Mr. Mitchell, can we talk?"

"What about?"

Peggy stayed well back so she wouldn't be drawn into the conversation.

"I would like your permission to call on your daughter Peggy."

"I think it would be best if we had this discussion in private."

"Very well, Mr. Mitchell." Andrew looked straight at Peggy's father. "When can we meet for a discourse on the matter of my courtship of your daughter?"

"The evening is young, and there's still some daylight left. Why don't you follow us home? We can talk in the barn away from everyone."

"Then I shall follow you to your farm."

Though she was too far away to be included in the conversation, Peggy was close enough to hear what was said. She was impressed with the manner in which Andrew approached her father. He wasn't shy or afraid of Adam like so many of her suitors had been. She even thought her father seemed impressed with Andrew's forthright request. But she could never really gauge what Father was thinking—he was so stoic and said so little.

I wonder if he has terrible memories of the battle as I have. On the front line with the Guilford County Militia, he saw many of his friends killed and injured, and Trapper John just disappeared standing next to him.

"Damn, I hate war," she muttered.

Andrew, who had ridden back to her side, asked, "What did you say?"

"Nothing. I was just thinking out loud."

Andrew gave her a teasing smile. "Thinking out loud in that unladylike language again." His voice became more serious. "I need to drop back to tell John, I mean Judge McNairy, that I'll be riding on to Knob Creek with you."

After Andrew had told his friend of the change of plans, he and Peggy rode side by side until the Mitchell wagon turned into the lane toward their home. The McMachen and Fain families called out their goodbyes and continued on toward the Quarters.

"Stop, Father! Stop the wagon," Peggy yelled.

"What's the matter?"

"Something's wrong. Lulubelle always meets us at the road."

"Peg, you're right." Adam looked around. "And where is Elvira?" He motioned Robert closer and whispered, "Go quickly, and bring the men back quietly. Tell them something is amiss here at my cabin."

Adam climbed down from the buckboard and said softly, "Everyone stay quiet. Elizabeth, take the children to the Quarters for safety. Peggy, you go with them."

"I will not." She didn't raise her voice, but her determination came through. "I must find Lulubelle."

"It's not safe, Peggy," her father insisted.

"I'm staying."

Adam looked at Andrew. "Are you sure you want to court my strong-willed daughter?"

Andrew and William worked their way around to the back of the house while Adam approached the front door. He listened for any noise coming from the house, but the only sound was the croak of a nearby tree frog. He kicked open the front door, gun in hand. The house was empty.

He went back to the door and said, "No one is here." Then he lit a candle as the sun was setting behind the tall trees, casting long shadows that made the cabin dark inside.

The candlelight revealed the severed head of a duck and a fish strung on a piece of leather from the mirror over the oak chest. Next to the chest was a uniquely carved walking stick. It had etched designs of beaver, deer, and fish that appeared to be carved by Indians. A white rag was tied to its handle.

Peggy and Andrew began to look for Lulubelle and Elvira. The other farm animals seemed to be unmolested.

William pointed to the tannery door, which was open. He entered carefully, then called "Bring me a light."

Adam appeared with a rag lamp. About one-fourth of their tanned beaver pelts were missing.

Elizabeth and the children returned with the neighbors. The children looked for Lulubelle, calling out the name of the yellow-haired dog. Elizabeth discovered a bag of corn meal had been opened; half of its contents were gone.

Captain John Fain, a trained government Indian fighter on leave, had arrived with the group from the Quarters.

Adam asked, "What do you think of this, John?"

"Most unusual, very unlike any Indian raid I've seen."

"What do you mean?"

"For one thing, there's very little damage. You know the Quarters were attacked twice by the Cherokees before you came west. John Blair and Mr. Mac were warned by a friendly tribe of half-breeds hunting on the creek; the McMachens fled to Wolf Hills and stayed with us for a while. The Cherokees did a great deal of damage to Mr. Mac's property. Fortunately we had a lot of rain, and their attempts to burn the Quarters failed."

Adam nodded. "I remember Mr. Mac describing how they destroyed his garden, pillaged the spring house, and killed his farm animals."

"It wasn't like this raid at all. They don't seem to be trying to scare you off, and there's no rage that I can see."

"What about Lulubelle and Elvira?"

"I don't know." He looked around and signaled his brothers to join them. "Tonight we will post a watch, rotating every two hours. I'm sorry I didn't hear or see anything from the Quarters. I do remember hearing Lulubelle taking on, but when she stopped yelping after a short time, I just assumed she'd run off a varmint."

As the Fain brothers were organizing their watch, Adam heard Peggy calling from the creek below the house.

"Father, come quickly."

"I'm coming," he answered. *I hope she didn't find Lulubelle or Elvira slaughtered*, he thought as he ran to the creek.

"The pond—it's gone!" Peggy said, looking at her father as if he could explain where it went.

Adam saw that most of the water had disappeared from the pond. "How did that happen?"

Andrew answered, "Whoever started this mischief pulled the huge boulders from your dam. It could have only been done with brute force, a strong farm animal like your jenny." He put his arms around Peggy's shoulders. "Adam, if you find these heathens, I'll see that they're hung."

Joseph Young, Jennifer's father, and Peter Miller showed up with their boys after hearing of the Indian raid.

Someone in the crowd hollered, "Let's go kill some damn Indians."

"Not tonight," Captain Fain said. "I'll lead you tomorrow at daybreak. It's not wise to go hunting for Indians at night. Go home and get some sleep now. Come back in the morning with supplies for at least a week and as much ammunition as you can carry."

Judge McNairy arrived with Mr. Taylor, who said, "Andrew, we should all go home. My wife and children are there alone. We'll need to set up a watch of the premises tonight as the Fain and Mitchell families have."

It was late by the time the neighbors departed, grumbling about the mischief perpetrated on the Mitchells by the Indians. Elizabeth started to remove the dead fish and the duck head from the mirror.

"Would you please just leave everything as you found it until morning?"

"That fish already smells pretty strong," she protested.

"Just till daylight," Adam said. "I need to think this through and try to make sense out of what the intruders did, but more important what they didn't do."

Adam lay awake in bed thinking. *A dead fish, a duck's head, a walking stick with a white rag tied to it. It just doesn't make sense.*

He rolled over to face his wife. "Elizabeth, why would they go to the trouble of draining the pond?"

"Maybe they needed the water downstream."

"They could have taken all the beaver pelts, but they only took about a fourth. Lulubelle and Elvira are both missing. They're trying to tell me something."

Elizabeth turned away from him. "I am telling you something. Go to sleep now! We're safe, and that's what matters."

Peggy and Rebeckah cried themselves to sleep worrying about the fate of their beloved Lulubelle. They hoped that when morning came they would find her on the back stoop, as always guarding the Mitchell household from the varmints and spooks of the night.

Chapter Three

Crisis on Knob Creek

Adam walked the banks of Knob Creek before sunrise, looking for the trail of the culprits who had destroyed the mill pond. He was determined to find the tracks before the local militia arrived and trampled them. He found where Elvira had dug into the ground as she strained to pull the boulders loose from the dam. She'd worked so hard helping Adam and his boys place the boulders where they were, Adam thought it a shame that she was forced to undo their hard work.

Captain Fain and his brothers Samuel and William found Adam on the trail about 150 yards downstream from where the dam had been.

"Are you planning to go after the Indians by yourself?" Captain Fain asked Adam.

"No, I was waiting for you and your brothers. Did you see the tracks they left?"

"Yep. It looks like four on foot and one mounted leading your jenny. Did you notice how they've snapped a twig from a bush every so often?"

"Yes, they've a left a trail that's too easy to follow. Even where an Indian would normally cross a creek to hide their tracks, they didn't. It sure looks like that whoever did this wants me to find them."

"No doubt about it," Captain Fain agreed.

Adam turned his eyes from the creek to his brother-in-law. "Do you think they're trying to lure me into an ambush?"

"It's possible, but the flag of peace left inside your cabin leads me to believe they don't intend to harm you. It wasn't just dropped there—the flag was tied neatly."

"And what a magnificently carved walking stick it was tied to," Samuel said.

Adam appeared deep in thought but nodded his head in agreement.

The Indian fighter added, "Had they intended you harm, they would have raided the cabin while you were there, scalped the entire family, and burned your buildings as a warning to other settlers."

Adam winced at the thought. "I think I'll just follow the tracks they left for me and find out who they are and what they want." He looked down the clearly marked trail.

"I agree. But you should have a force of militiamen behind you just in case. I've already sent my oldest son, Nicholas, to Greasy Cove to apprise Colonel Love of the situation and to request as many men as he can muster to protect the residents of Knob Creek from these Indians."

By the time Adam and the Fain men walked back to the Mitchell home, nearly every able-bodied neighbor had arrived, armed and prepared for a long ride. Elizabeth had packed a haversack for Adam and her sons.

Adam wolfed down the cold breakfast his wife had made earlier. The captain joined him at the family table to discuss their options.

As Elizabeth sat in silence beside Adam, her mind drifted into the past. She remembered so well that cold March morning seven years ago when Adam had gone to war. She fed him a good breakfast, then they said their goodbyes and Adam rode off with Nathanael Greene's troops to fight the British. Today her boys would be leaving, too, possibly to fight alongside their father.

Adam said, "John, I know you've fought many Indian battles and you know what you're doing. But I want to find out what this is about before you bring the troops down on them."

"Do you have a plan?"

"I want to follow the trail they've marked so well. I'll carry the flag of peace and won't carry any arms. I don't want any militia in sight, but would like you, your brothers, and my sons to follow at a distance in case I get in trouble."

Outside someone hollered, "Let's go kill some Injuns."

Another yelled, "What the hell are we waiting for?"

Adam shook his head. "See what I mean?"

"I sure do," the Captain answered.

"Please tell the neighbor men nothing is going to happen today—we're going to wait for Colonel Love and his troops before going after the raiders. Thank them for coming and tell them to go home and wait for word from us." Adam looked John in the eyes. "Then just the six of us will follow the trail to where it takes us."

"I know the colonel wouldn't approve of your plan, so remember, I didn't agree to it."

Adam nodded. "I understand you have a sworn duty as an Indian fighter to protect the settlers from attack. I wouldn't ask you to do this if I didn't have a strong feeling that no one is in any danger."

John went outside and told the volunteers to go home until he heard from Colonel Love.

Elizabeth slowly rose from the table, removed her apron, and hung it on a kitchen peg. She stood there for a moment, holding on to the peg with both hands, staring at the bare wall. She took a deep breath then whirled around to face Adam. Her green eyes flashed as she leaned into his face. "What in the world are you thinking? You have fifty good men outside, ready and able to go after these renegades. Instead, you are sending them away so you can go after these red warriors with only our sons and their uncles."

Adam stepped back and held up his hands in front of her. "Elizabeth!" He placed his finger over his lips, then motioned with his hands for her to keep her voice down. "The neighbors will hear you. What's got into you, anyway? You're screaming like a banshee!"

"I cannot stay quiet, knowing you plan to go after the Indians with only my sisters' husbands and my sons. It's bad enough that you put your own life in jeopardy, but the lives of our boys? I will **not** allow it."

Captain Fain poked his head in the door, then stepped in cautiously as he had learned to do when one of the McMachen women was riled. "Elizabeth, may I say something? Please?"

"Say what you want, John. It won't change my mind about my husband's foolish plan." She crossed her arms and glared at him.

"Elizabeth." His voice was gentle. "Adam and I have good reason to believe these Indians just want to talk to us. Look." He pointed to the corner where the walking stick with the white flag attached leaned against the chest. "They left a flag of peace for Adam to carry, and it looks like they marked every step of the way to their camp. Adam is correct—it would be wrong to bring the wrath of the militia down on them."

Robert, familiar with his mother's temper, entered the cabin slowly. "Mother, take a look at me. What do you see?"

"My son that I love."

"Have you noticed I'm now twenty-one years old and a grown man? I'm taller than Father or Uncle John."

William stuck his head in the door. "Mother, I'm seventeen and will soon be joining the militia with Uncle John. Your boys have grown up." He looked behind him. "The horses are getting restless, and we're wasting time."

Captain Fain said, "William is right. We'd best be going."

"Would you all please leave Elizabeth and me alone for a moment?" Adam asked. "I'll be right out."

After the others left, Elizabeth took several quick breaths and nodded her head. "You and the boys always know how to convince me you're right." Her voice took on a determined edge. "Adam, you'd better not let those Indians touch a hair on my boys' heads." She took another deep breath, then patted Adam's cheek. "Peggy and I will take the children to the Quarters. I'll try to comfort Nancy. She worries so when the captain is away chasing the Indians."

"Tell your father I'll give him a full report on my return." Adam swatted her behind as he started out the door.

Elizabeth grabbed his arm and turned him back to face her, causing him to stumble a little. She kissed him. "Please be careful, my love."

Adam tightened his embrace. "We'll come home safely. Assure your father and Nancy—and yourself—of that."

The Mitchell and Fain men gathered at the creek and started down the trail left by the Indians. The sun beat down, and the air was still. They rode slowly, their eyes straining to search the long shadows of the woods for movement.

After a couple of hours, the men heard Elvira's hee-haw coming from the other side of the creek. Her braying grew louder when she caught Adam's scent.

He handed his long gun and the reins of his horse to Robert, then he placed his handgun, knife, and tomahawk into the haversack tied to his saddle horn. Adam motioned the others back into the woods and placed his finger over his lips. He moved from tree to tree as he climbed to the top of the next hill. Dropping to the ground to lie on his belly, he looked down from the cliff above the creek.

He saw a small Indian village below and Elvira with her nose in the air, savoring her master's scent. Two Indian boys were pointing in the direction the donkey was curling her nose. The camp contained only four lean-tos made of poles and covered with branches for the roof. One malnourished horse was tied to a stake. An Indian woman, most likely the boy's mother, stepped out of one of the lean-tos.

Thanks to Elvira, the Indians knew Adam was there, so he decided to show his face. He raised the white flag high, waving it not only for the Indians to see but also to make sure his kin knew he was going into the camp.

As Adam approached, the Indian woman summoned the boys. They stood beside her in front of the largest of the lean-tos, and a man stepped out of the dwelling. He wore no headdress other than a simple Indian band around his head.

From the deference shown him by the others, Adam figured he was the chief of the small tribe.

The chief, who looked to be younger than Adam, motioned for his guest to enter the lean-to. Inside Adam saw Lulubelle lying on a pile of beaver pelts, limp and covered with scratches and torn hair as if she had been in a fight with a bear. The yellow-haired dog tried to wag her tail and managed a low whine. She could barely raise her head.

The sadness in her big brown eyes tormented Adam, and he fought back the impulse to demand to know what the Indians had done to her. He walked over to Lulubelle and patted her head. The Indian invited Adam to sit on the pelts beside the dog, then took a seat facing Adam.

The chief pointed to his arm, which was covered with blue and purple bruises. "Your dog is great warrior." He spoke in understandable English. "You should be proud to have such noble animal watch your camp."

"What happened?"

"She made noise trying to chase us from your farm. My horse was afraid of her and threw me to the ground — hard." He leaned over to demonstrate how he landed on his bruised arm. "Your dog thinks she big as horse and gives chase. Horse kicks her, and yellow dog fly like a bird. We think she dead. I bring her home to my squaw who has magic healing for all living things. In two days from now, dog will be chasing rabbits."

Adam gently caressed Lulubelle. He stared at the chief, who looked nothing like any Indian Adam had ever seen. The man had auburn hair, blue eyes, and a patchy complexion with freckles on his cheeks. Adam looked around at the Indian children and saw they all had similar features.

He looked back at the chief. "You speak the white man's words well."

"My father was a white man named Bowles, and my mother a Cherokee." He pointed to an older Indian woman who had just entered the lean-to. "My Indian name is Duwali, in Cherokee means Bold Hunter."

The chief introduced his two sisters and his two sons, who all had blue eyes, and his wife, who had dark hair and eyes and looked like the Indians Adam was familiar with.

The chief went on, "My father was murdered on way home from Charleston by two men with red hair. I was only twelve."

Adam started to express his sympathy, but the chief continued.

"I found them and killed them. It took two winters, but I got revenge for his death. Their scalps hang in place of honor in my home." He pointed to them, his chest puffed out with pride.

Adam had thought the red scalps were squirrels' tails. He realized that the chief wanted him to know that he had already killed at least two white men.

In an effort to change the subject, Adam asked, "What should I call you, Chief Duwali or Chief Bowles?"

"Either is correct. I am as much like you as I am Indian. Indian is my better half."

He laughed, and Adam and the rest of the Bowles family laughed with him.

"Why did you come to my farm and destroy my mill pond?" Adam blurted out without thinking.

Chief Bowles glared wild-eyed into Adam's face. "Your pond!"

The women and children jumped back at the sound of their leader's angry voice.

Chief Bowles' reaction alarmed Adam. He regretted his impulsive question and feared that his scalp would soon be hanging in a place of honor in this lean-to.

The Indian's softer voice didn't disguise his continued irritation. "You may own ground and trees that grow on your land. You do **not** own fish and beaver that swim in water, no more than you own wind or stars in sky."

Adam just sat in silence.

"Since you build dam, my people have no fish to eat and no beaver pelt to trade. So we freed fish and beaver to swim downstream. Now ducks and geese come. Deer drink from creek near our camp." He leaned a little closer to Adam. "You have taken our hunting grounds, but Duwali will never let you take water."

That explains the dead fish and the duck head, Adam thought. "Why did you not take all of the valuable beaver pelts?"

"We not thieves like white men that killed my father for his wagonload of goods." He pointed toward their scalps. "We only took what your wall in water prevented us from trapping. Each year we take only fifty pelts." He raised his right hand and spread his five fingers. "This many for each member of my family—no more."

Adam did the quick math in his head. *That means ten Indians are living in the camp. Seven are present, so three are not here. They could be in the woods. What if they encounter my sons and their uncles?* He tried to eliminate that dreadful thought from his mind.

The chief continued, "When you stopped flow of water, we only get eighteen beaver. I take difference from your barn full of pelts so I can trade with white man called Deaderick for supplies. Like white woman, Indian woman likes things at new store." He pointed to a small mirror hanging from a pole inside the lean-to.

The Indian women burst into approving smiles when Chief Bowles pointed to what must be their proudest possession. Adam remembered the time he brought a mirror home from Salisbury to his first wife, Jennett. They lived in a little log cabin he had built for them. The cabin had a dirt floor, but Jennett had been as proud of that mirror as these Indian women of the mirror hanging in their home.

For the first time, Adam realized how similar the lives of the red man and the white man were. *We both have the same wants and needs,* he thought. *We love our families and want to protect them and make them happy and proud of us.*

Chief Bowles pointed to a long pipe and a leather pouch. His eldest son picked them up and carried them to the chief, bowing his head just as Adam's sons did when they brought him the family Bible for the nightly Scripture reading.

Whatever is fixing to happen, Adam thought, *everyone here recognizes that it's a sacred moment.*

Chief Bowles took several pinches of rough cut tobacco out of the pouch. He held them up and sprinkled some on the ground. "We must always give back portion of what we take from earth."

Adam just nodded but he thought, *What have I done to these Indians?*

The chief filled the pipe with tobacco, holding the bowl in his palm with the stem pointed toward him. Then the other son brought forward a twig burning red hot from the fire to light the peace pipe.

Each son has his special place in the ritual, Adam thought.

The chief inhaled the acrid smoke, holding it deep within his lungs for what seemed to Adam an eternity. Chief Bowles raised the pipe toward the heavens and began to chant.

Adam assumed this must be a prayer to the god of the Cherokees.

The Indian then handed the pipe to Adam, who nodded and accepted it. He inhaled deeply like Chief Bowles had done. He felt a burning sensation in his throat and lungs and tried to hold back a cough. He wrapped one hand around his throat and pointed to the lean-to entrance with the other. The young braves, one on each side, helped him, coughing and wheezing, out of the lean-to into the fresh air outside.

Adam's inability to handle the Indian tobacco embarrassed him, and he regretted that his coughing episode had interrupted the Indians' sacred ritual of peace.

However, Adam's appearance outside the lean-to averted something worse than interrupting a ritual. He had been inside for so long his kin had become worried. Captain Fain had ordered the family members into position to force their way into the camp to rescue Adam.

When the young braves brought Adam out into the fresh air, the captain signaled the group to relax and stay out of sight. They were on the same hill Adam had descended earlier, with a good view of the camp. They could see the Indian women beating on Adam's back, but they were all laughing and appeared to be enjoying each other's company. Adam didn't look like he was in trouble; in fact, he seemed to be enjoying his powwow with the Indians.

Robert and William looked at each other quizzically. Captain Fain shrugged.

They saw the young braves spread corn shuck mats out on the ground in front of the lean-to. The apparent leader of the group motioned for Adam to sit. They wished they could hear what was being said.

Chief Bowles smiled at Adam. "First time I smoked pipe of peace, my mind and spirit was not in harmony, and my lungs would not accept smoke of peace pipe. In time I teach you to smoke pipe of the Indian and the customs of my people. You can teach me white man's ways."

Adam nodded, still finding it difficult to speak.

The chief told his wife to bring something from the lean-to. She returned with a small package and unwrapped it.

The chief asked, "What is this?"

"It's ground corn meal," Adam answered. "Where did you get it?" He was sure he knew where it came from.

"From your barn." Chief Bowles poured some of the meal from one hand to the other. "Why does your meal look so different from meal my woman makes?"

"This maize was milled by Michael Bawn at his mill on the Little Limestone Creek."

"Your squaw doesn't grind your grain?" The Indian creased his forehead in a puzzled look.

The Indian women stuck their fingers into the powdery meal, then licked their fingers. Their smiles and approving sounds convinced Adam they liked the white man's corn meal.

"I'm sure my ancestors once ground their grain by hand as the Indian does today. But all my life, my family has always lived near a grist mill where we would take our grain to be milled."

"The sack in barn would take ten Indian women working many days to fill."

The chief stuck his finger into the small package of meal. He grinned at his wife and said something in Cherokee. She smiled and touched his bruised arm, speaking in Cherokee words that Adam didn't understand.

He did understand the look of love he saw in the couple's eyes. And he could tell the chief's mother was happy about what was being said as she attempted a smile, even with most of her teeth missing.

Chief Bowles said, "I asked my squaw why white man need wife if grain is ground in grist mill. She told me that why you have so many children." He laughed so hard he could barely finish his story. "White man's woman is not on knees all day using pestle to grind corn for her family. Has more time to keep husband happy."

Adam smiled and nodded but suspected his face had flushed. To cover his embarrassment, he changed the subject. "The reason I made the dam was to trap water for a mill pond on Knob Creek. The water running through a water race would power a grist mill. We could mill our own grain so we wouldn't have to haul it over to Little Limestone."

The smile disappeared from Chief Bowles' face.

Adam continued, "The mill is to be used by my neighbors and family members. We'd be glad to mill your grain if you wished. The miller keeps one bag out of each ten that is milled."

The Indian abruptly stood and motioned for Adam to rise. "We have smoked pipe of peace and understand each other better. This is good. I have many thoughts in head and must have time to think about what was said. You come back in two days and we talk more. Your dog will be ready to go home with you."

"That I will do." Adam held his hand out, and the chief took it and shook it firmly. Adam handed the flag of truce attached to the walking stick back to the Indian. "I won't be needing this. From this day on, when you see me coming, it will always be as a friend."

The chief nodded, took the walking stick from Adam's hand, and then turned to his eldest son and said something in Cherokee. The young man ran to Elvira and brought the donkey to Adam, handing the leather reins to him with a proud smile.

Adam led Elvira up the hill he had come down earlier. When he reached his sons and brothers-in-law, they recognized that something was different. Whatever had happened down in the Indian village had changed Adam. They weren't sure what had changed or why. Adam said very little all the way home.

Robert remembered his father being like this for days after he was released from the British stockade where he had been held in a pigsty as a prisoner of war. Robert knew his father would tell him what happened during his meeting with the Indians when he was ready.

As the men approached the Mitchell home, they could see a great deal of activity around the Quarters. At least a hundred horses grazed on the lush grass growing on the hillside, and as many men lounged about under the trees.

Captain Fain exclaimed, "I'm in big trouble now!"

"Why?" asked his brother Samuel.

"It looks like the colonel has brought his entire militia over from Greasy Cove, and our local militiamen have joined in to go after renegade Indians that don't exist. Damn, I wish I hadn't been in such a hurry to summon the colonel's help."

"Just let me do the talking," Adam said. "Your only involvement in this was as my brother-in-law, not as a captain of the militia. I'll take full responsibility for creating the alarm."

The militiamen were in high spirits as John Blair had provided them with ample supplies from his father's distillery. The McMachen, Fain, and Mitchell women were making bread and carving up hams and turkeys from the smokehouse for the hungry volunteers.

The McMachen sisters ran down the hill to greet their men. Elizabeth looked for Adam. Nancy, Rosanna, and Sarah hurried towards their husbands, the Fain brothers John, Samuel, and William.

Robert and William Mitchell dismounted first. Elizabeth hugged them tightly and said to the older men, "Thank you for bringing my sons safely home to me."

"You're welcome, my dear sister," Captain Fain replied. "Thanks to Adam, we were never in any danger from the Indians."

Neighbors Robert and Joseph Young, who had both consumed considerable distillate of corn, approached, and Robert spoke loud enough for all to hear. "If you went Indian hunting, where are the scalps?"

Major Christopher Taylor, who had earned his title in the Battle of Kings Mountain, had also obviously been enjoying the McMachen corn whisky. "Hey, Indian Fighter," he called to Captain Fain. "Did you kill any Indians?"

Adam noticed young children listening to every word the adults spoke. "Let's not talk of such things in front of the children."

Nancy whispered to her husband, "Colonel Love is here with his troops, and he sure has his drawers in a wad, John."

"I can imagine."

Overhearing the couple's conversation, Adam said, "Let me talk to the colonel."

"It doesn't work that way in the military, Adam. Only I can report to my commander." He put his arm across Adam's shoulder. "But thanks for the offer."

A young militiaman who looked about seventeen rode up. "Which one of you is Captain Fain?"

"That would be me."

"Captain Fain, sir, Colonel Robert Love requests your presence alone at the Quarters, the house on the hill, sir." He saluted the captain.

"I know where the Quarters is, soldier." Captain Fain returned the salute even though he was out of uniform, and the young soldier rode away. He looked at Adam. "See what I mean?"

"Yes, I do." Adam nodded, then turned to his sons. "Boys, take care of the horses while Uncle John and I go to the Quarters."

As Robert and William approached the barn, Peggy appeared. "Give them to me." She reached for the reins of all the horses.

They handed her the reins and spoke to Andrew, who stood beside Peggy.

"Did you ride over with Major Taylor?" Robert asked.

"Yes, I couldn't let my landlord go off to capture renegade Indians without me."

William said, "I see you're not over there drinking with him."

"I'd rather keep Peg company here in the barn. You go take care of yourselves. Peg and I will see that the horses are fed and watered."

When Adam and John reached the Quarters, Adam went to Mr. Mac's room while the captain met with Colonel Love in the adjoining office.

The captain entered the room, which contained a small desk, rope beds, and several small chairs. Captain Fain saluted. The colonel gestured for him to sit.

"What the hell were you doing taking civilians on an Indian raid?"

"It was not a raid, sir."

"Then why did your son come to my home with such an urgent request, a request for military assistance, a request that he said that was from you, his father, who is one of my officers?"

John squirmed in his seat. "Sir, at the time I sent my son to seek your assistance, I thought we were dealing with an Indian uprising. It was dark and, unfortunately, I didn't have all the details."

"Your son told me farm animals and beaver pelts had been stolen, the Mitchell house ransacked, and their mill pond destroyed. Is that what happened, Captain Fain?"

"Yes, sir, it is."

"That certainly sounds like the makings of some serious Indian mischief. And that I will not tolerate in my district."

Adam knocked lightly, then opened the door without waiting for an answer. "Colonel Love, may I say something, sir?"

The colonel scowled and gave a huge sigh. "Who the hell are you?"

"Please let me explain, sir," Adam said, once he had been invited in and introduced. "Captain Fain went with me and my sons as my brother-in-law. He never represented himself to anyone as an officer of the state's militia, and he was never seen by the Indians."

The colonel shifted in his chair but didn't say anything.

Adam continued, "Chief Bowles did what he did to make me realize the problems I had created for his people when I built the dam for the mill pond. We smoked the pipe of peace together and are working out our problems peaceably."

The door opened again, and Mr. Mac shuffled in. "Adam, did I hear you say you met Chief Bowles?"

"Yes, Mr. Mac. I was with him and his family this afternoon."

Though he looked weak and fragile, Mr. Mac's face lit with a huge smile. "So my good friend Duwali is back on Knob Creek where he belongs. That's wonderful news."

"You know Chief Bowles?" Adam took Mr. Mac's arm and helped him into a chair.

"Yes, it was your friend Trapper John who introduced us shortly after I homesteaded this place in 1776. Duwali was just a young buck—maybe twenty—back then. The Quarters wouldn't be here today if it weren't for Chief Bowles."

"What do you mean?" Adam asked.

"Twice he warned us that the Cherokees planned to raid the Quarters and burn us out. Both times we were able to retreat to Wolf Hills for protection."

Colonel Love turned to Mr. Mac. "Is this Chief Bowles a half-breed, with red hair and freckles?"

"Yes," Adam said.

Mr. Mac nodded.

"I am well aware of this Indian and his family. They have been on the outs with Chief Dragging Canoe, head of the Chickamauga tribe of the Cherokee Nation, for some time. Chief Bowles and his family pretty well stay to themselves. I think he is shunned by his people because he is half white." He shrugged his shoulders. "Others say it has to do with Indian politics."

"I'll be meeting with Chief Bowles day after tomorrow," Adam said.

Three pairs of eyes turned to focus on Adam.

"For what purpose?" asked Colonel Love.

"It's kind of personal, sir." Adam wasn't ready to share his experience and dilemma with them.

The colonel looked into Adam's eyes. "I am in charge of keeping the Indians in line. The safety of the settlers in Washington County is my responsibility. I report directly to Colonel Tipton on Indian affairs. If you know something, you are obliged to report it to Captain Fain or me."

"It's just that I must go back to get my dog Lulubelle. The Indians have been caring for her. She was injured by Chief Bowles' horse when Lulubelle chased after the chief's runaway mount."

Colonel Love rose, indicating the meeting was over. He extended his hand toward Adam for a handshake. "Mr. Mitchell, I encourage you to make a friend of the chief and keep Captain Fain posted of what you find out from this Indian." He ushered Adam toward the door.

"Yes, sir."

"If no one wishes to file a formal complaint, I will just note in my government journal that unknown vandals perpetrated a prank against your household making it appear that Indians were involved, and the offenders are unknown."

"I would appreciate that," Adam said.

"Mr. Mitchell, will you please send my aide in so I can have him explain to the militia and volunteers waiting that there is no Indian crisis on Knob Creek at the present time. The men will be dismissed." He placed a gentle hand on his host's feeble shoulder. "My men from Greasy Cove and I will partake of Mr. Mac's generous hospitality tonight and ride out in the morning."

Adam nodded, assisted Mr. Mac out the door, and sent the aide inside.

Colonel Love gave his instructions to his subordinate, then motioned for him to shut the door on his way out. "I will need a few more minutes alone with Captain Fain."

The colonel spoke to Captain Fain in a low voice so the family wouldn't hear his verbal reprimand. "Don't you ever make a damn fool mistake like that again!"

Captain Fain stood at attention in front of his commanding officer. "I will not make that mistake again, sir."

"At ease, Captain. Now that this crisis on Knob Creek is settled, the military can better concentrate on the Cherokee Indians to the west. They are so rightfully angered at the white man that I don't know if peace can ever be made." The colonel sat down and picked up a stack of papers on the table.

Captain Fain relaxed his stance but remained standing.

Colonel Love said, "You will need to get your affairs in order quickly and enlist as many men as you can. Then head west toward James White's fort on the Holston River where the settlers have already forted up in fear of the Indians. Your father and Mr. Mac have discussed your service to the militia with me already. I am keenly aware you lost your brother David in an Indian battle. Your wife and family do not want you to go on this campaign against the Indians and rightfully so."

"You've discussed this with Nancy?" John didn't try to hide the disbelief and shock that his commander would commit such an unmilitary act as discussing his orders with his wife before informing him of the mission.

Colonel Love raised his head from the papers in his hand. "She overheard your father and me talking about it. I am sorry that she heard about your orders from me. If there was anyone else that had your youth and understanding of the Indian problem, I would send them in your stead."

"Sir, after my brother David was killed by the Indians, I volunteered to become an Indian fighter. That is what I do. I'll be ready to leave with my men on your orders, sir."

"This will be a dangerous mission, John." Colonel Love rose from his seat and motioned the captain toward the door. "I will have more details in the morning. You are dismissed for now."

Captain Fain saluted and did an about face toward the door.

The assembling of the militia had turned into a great party at the Quarters. Many of the men stayed for the festivities that lasted until morning.

With all the activity going on around them, Andrew looked for a chance to speak to Adam alone. The young lawyer saw him walk off into a clearing where he appeared to be gazing at the stars in the heavens.

"A beautiful sight, isn't it, Mr. Mitchell?"

"Yes, it is, Andrew. And a wise Indian chief informed me today that I don't own the wind or the stars in the sky over my land—or the water for that matter."

"Perhaps he is correct, but as long as we have eyes to see, we can enjoy looking at the stars and the water, and as long as we can feel the wind in our face, it is ours for the moment."

Adam looked at Andrew. "Well said, Mr. Jackson. You are very articulate and should make a great attorney."

"Coming from you, I consider that a great compliment." He cleared his throat. "You might recall we had plans last night to discuss my calling on Peggy. However, the Indian raid on your property spoiled that opportunity. May I discuss this with you now, sir?"

"All right, but let's walk over to my place where we have a little privacy and can partake of some special nectar of the grain I keep for honored guests." He turned toward his home. "Many think that Mr. Mac's whisky is the best in the county, but personally I like mine better. Please don't ever tell him I said that."

When they arrived at the barn, Adam poured whisky into a silver quaich that Mr. Mac had recently given him. The drinking vessel was a prized heirloom that according to legend had been brought from Ireland to America by Mr. Mac's father. Mr. Mac claimed it had been given to an ancestor by Bonnie Prince Charles while the McMachen family was in Scotland.

Adam said, "When Mr. Mac gave me this some months ago, I knew that his time on this earth was coming to an end. He's been giving all the members of his family pieces of his treasures since Mother died. He seems to have lost his will to live." Adam's emotions welled up inside him as he thought of the long relationship he had enjoyed with his father-in-law. "Damn, I'm going to miss him." He handed the quaich to Andrew and turned aside to wipe the tear he didn't want his guest to see.

"I'm sure you will, Mr. Mitchell. I spent a good deal of time with him today, and you are correct that he is aware the end is near for him."

"Why do you say that?"

"He wishes to get his affairs in order." Andrew took a swig of the corn whisky and returned the quaich to Adam. "One issue he is greatly concerned about and he asked me to discuss with you is the filing of your mother's will."

Adam poured more whisky into the quaich. "That is something I intend to have attorney Waightstill Avery handle at the summer session of the court."

Adam noticed that Andrew frowned and clenched his fists at the mention of the well-respected lawyer's name.

"That is Mr. Mac's concern, sir. There won't be a session of the court in Jonesborough again until late fall."

"Why would Mr. Mac be so concerned over my mother's will?"

"As the Washington County Registrar, he is aware many legal documents are missing from the courthouse in Jonesborough. After numerous raids between the Franklinites and supporters of the mother state, records of Washington County are in shambles. It will take years to get them in order."

"Andrew, you heard Reverend Doak say during yesterday's sermon that the State of Franklin is no more." Adam sipped on the whisky.

"Yes, that is what the good Reverend Doak said, and that is what he believes because that is what his friend John Sevier told him."

"The governor should know whether it is or isn't."

"It's not that simple. As the appointed prosecutor for North Carolina, I have information that some of the promoters of the State of Franklin are still in rebellion. Land speculators, I've been told, have spoken to representatives of Spain and offered to lead a movement that would align the Westerners with the Spanish empire."

Adam set the cup on a sawhorse and leaned back with his arms crossed. "Then nothing is settled about the State of Franklin?"

"Not yet," Andrew said. "That's why Mr. Mac wanted me to advise you not to file your mother's will in Washington County, at least not until after the North Carolina Assembly meets in November."

Adam shook his head. "I don't think it's fair to my mother to wait until next fall to file her will."

"Mr. Mitchell, I'll be glad to file it for you in the new Davidson County Courthouse as soon as we get set up in Nashville. Judge McNairy and I plan to ensure that all records are safe there. The judge told me how your father's land grant mysteriously disappeared from the Rowan County Courthouse before Guilford County was established. You have had experience before with missing records."

"Yes, I have, and I suppose your proposal would please Mother. If Mr. Mac likes the idea, let's do it." He smiled at

Andrew and raised the two-handled drinking vessel. "Now before we get interrupted or I fall asleep as it's past my bedtime, let's discuss the original purpose of our meeting."

Andrew, who had sat on the sawhorse, slapped his knees. "Mr. Mitchell, as you and everyone in the county are aware, I am very interested in Peggy. I have had the fortuitous opportunity of seeing her on three different occasions, all at times that have been quite stressful for her and your family. I have been very impressed with how she has handled herself in each situation. I would like your permission, sir, to court your daughter."

Adam looked deeply into Andrew's eyes for a few seconds before he responded. "I've heard many good things said about you since you arrived in Jonesborough. My wife has even compared you to Patrick Henry, whom her father introduced her to many years ago in Virginia. However, I have some concerns about rumors I've heard from your past that occurred while you lived in Salisbury."

The young lawyer flinched. "I am honored to be compared to the likes of Patrick Henry. Those rumors are most likely about a few indiscretions of a young man who had not yet learned how to handle his liquor. I did some damage to furniture in the Inn at Salisbury one evening with friends of mine. The charges were dropped, and my friends and I made full restitution to the innkeeper."

"What about the story of your association with harlots?" Adam glared at him.

Andrew looked straight at Adam. "I did while in Salisbury invite a couple of prostitutes, a mother and daughter, to an elegant ball as a practical joke. The prank backfired on me, as the well-known prostitutes were shunned by the guests, some of whom were their clients." He cleared his throat. "The host and hostess were terribly embarrassed. I have made amends to all that were involved and will never do anything like that again."

Adam nodded. "I also understand that you are a gambler."

"I have been known to bet on a cockfight or a horserace from time to time. A friendly wager makes for a more interesting sporting event, don't you think?"

"I appreciate your straight answers to my questions, Andrew." He paused to clear his throat. "Now, just what are your intentions with my Peg?"

"Sir, I have never been married, but I desire a good wife. I feel that Peggy can fulfill my requirements."

Adam rose from his position on the sawhorse and looked down at the young man. "Have you discussed this with Peg?"

"It would not be proper without your permission, Mr. Mitchell." Andrew started to rise, then sat back down when he realized how close Adam stood to him.

"If you were to marry Peg, how would you support her? You have no home—you're sleeping in a rented loft."

"Sir, I lost my father before I was born, and my mother died when I was only thirteen. I have pretty well raised myself and spent the last two years learning the law." His voice was filled with pride. "I was admitted to the bar in Jonesborough recently and expect to be admitted in Greeneville before I leave for Nashville. In addition to the small salary as the state's prosecutor, I have my growing law practice."

"Andrew, my Peg is much like her mother. She has a great attachment to her family and friends. I seriously doubt that she would wish to accompany you to Nashville." He shook his head, then smiled. "You are a very good solicitor, and if anyone can convince Peg to leave home, it would be you. You have my permission to court Peg, and you are welcome in my home anytime. I wouldn't mind having a lawyer in the family."

"Thank you, sir."

Adam stepped back, motioning toward his cabin. "The hour is late. My wife and my bed await me."

"I look forward to hearing about your visit with the Indians." Andrew rose and held out his hand.

Adam shook Andrew's hand and said, "If you can break away from Murphy's Tavern on Wednesday evening, you may come for supper. I will give you an update on our powwow."

"Thank you, Mr. Mitchell. I bid your leave and look forward to seeing you Wednesday evening."

Chapter Four

The Planting Stick War

Peggy heard her father up before daybreak starting the fire for her mother to cook breakfast. Adam enjoyed the quiet time of the morning while everyone else was sleeping. He could meditate and read the Bible.

From her bed in the loft, Peg saw his weathered face in the faint light of the flickering fireplace and sensed he was deeply troubled. She slowly pulled back the covers so she wouldn't wake Rebeckah. Peggy climbed down to join her father. After she poured coffee into her own mug, she refilled his without saying a word. Adam nodded his thanks but didn't look up from the family Bible.

As Peg sat at the family table directly across from her father, she thought, *Each one of us has a special place at this table, and we go to it automatically when the family gathers, whether for a meal or conversation.*

There had been little time for family conversation lately, though. Life had been hectic with the death of Grandmother, then the Indian raid on the farm, and now spring planting.

Looking deep into her pewter mug, Peggy said, "I miss her." She started to cry when she looked at the empty seat that had always been her grandmother's.

"So do I." Adam reached across the table for his daughter's hand. Your grandmother had a good life."

"I know." Peg wiped a tear from her eye.

Trying to cheer her, Adam said, "I'll be bringing Lulubelle home today."

"I want to go with you, Father. Please — please?"

"I thought you might." He looked at her with the grin that had been absent from his face for some time.

Peggy answered with a huge smile of her own.

Elizabeth slipped into the kitchen. She'd overheard the conversation and recognized the emotions at the table. She was careful not to intrude or say anything that would take away from this special moment.

She began to stir the red hot coals on the limestone hearth with an iron poker, creating more flames that gave needed light to the room.

Elizabeth cleared her throat and waved away the smoke. It irritated her nostrils and made her feel like she was choking. She turned to Peggy. "Would you gather some more eggs—I know those chickens have laid more eggs than we've found. Your brothers will be here soon from the bunkhouse, and they'll expect breakfast to be ready. I hope one of those boys will remember that I asked them to bring a side of bacon from the smokehouse."

Adam grinned at his wife. "I invited your favorite attorney to dinner tonight."

"Waightstill Avery is coming to our home for dinner?" Peg asked in an excited voice.

"Not Mr. Avery, your new admirer—Andrew, the lawyer who reminds your mother of Patrick Henry." Adam winked at Elizabeth, who was warming the Dutch oven over the embers.

"I assume he asked permission to court me."

"Yes, and I was very impressed by his decorum." Adam nodded to his wife in approval, as if she had been correct in her observations of Andrew.

"Hurry, Peg, and gather us some eggs as I start cooking what's in the basket."

"Yes, Mother." Peg threw a shawl over her shoulders and took the empty egg basket from Elizabeth's hand.

"I overheard you tell Peggy you were taking her with you. Are you planning to take Robert and William?"

"No, I need all four of the boys to start the planting as we're getting a late start. You know I always have my seed in the ground by now. Tomorrow I'll harness Elvira and join the boys in the fields. Today I need the donkey to pack the provisions your father wants me to take to Chief Bowles."

"It seems strange. The Indians raid our home and steal our corn meal and pelts, then set about destroying all the work you did on the mill pond. And now you're taking them gifts."

"I created a grave injustice to Chief Bowles and his tribe when I stopped the flow of water to their camp. I have prayed for God's forgiveness, and I hope the Indians will forgive me as well."

After breakfast Robert and William harnessed Elvira and tied the peace offerings to the packsaddle. Peggy and Adam saddled their horses, said their goodbyes, and headed out for the camp of the Indians.

Peggy spoke loudly to be heard over the noise of a dozen hooves hitting the hard limestone rock along the creek bed. "What did he say?"

"What did who say?"

"Andrew."

"He asked permission to court you."

"Father, I know that. You told me already. What did Andrew say about me?"

"That he desires a good wife and he thinks you could fulfill his requirements."

Peggy said nothing after that. She rode now in silence thinking, listening to the water's gentle flow and the noise of horseshoes plodding out a steady beat. *Mr. Jackson thinks I could fulfill his requirements! What does he think I am? Some breeding mare for his stable? A wife to bear him a passel of children like my poor mother, who's had an infant on her hip since the day she married? I think not!*

Adam said, "It's just over the next ridge."

The Indian children spotted their guests and waded across the creek to greet them. The tribe's women, shielding their eyes from the morning sun, looked surprised when they saw Peggy. They began excitedly chanting, "The paleface woman that rides like the wind."

"Peg, I think they know you." Adam watched the children running around in circles as he dismounted.

Before he had his feet on the ground, Peggy was off Cherokee and holding the reins of both horses.

Chief Bowles, his mother, and his wife had joined the welcoming party.

"The woman that rides like the wind is from your tribe?"

"Yes, this is my oldest daughter Peggy who wanted to come and thank your wife for mending our Lulubelle."

The chief's wife entered the lean-to and brought out the very excited dog on a short rawhide leash. Peggy fell to her knees, hugging her pet as its tail wagged rapidly back and forth. Elvira began to bray, and Lulubelle barked back at the donkey.

"Your dog is ready to chase rabbit now."

"I never doubted that your wife would make her well. We have brought you gifts from our farm and the McMachen Quarters to show our appreciation," Adam said.

"You mean Mr. Mac, who lives," he pointed up, "high on the hill in big house?"

"Yes, my wife's father, John McMachen."

"Mr. Mac is your wife's father?"

"Yes, and the grandfather of all my children," Adam answered.

"How is he?" the Indian asked with a look of concern.

"His mind is strong—his body is weak."

"Tell him for me that his friend Duwali wishes his strength to return soon."

Adam and Peggy removed the packages from the donkey. They handed the sacks of corn meal, a smoked ham, and a side of bacon to the teenage braves, who nodded in excited appreciation.

Adam and the chief entered the lean-to and the others followed. The chief and his family were polite but not as friendly as they had been on the first visit.

After he and Adam were seated, their host motioned to Peggy and the others to sit.

"My people appreciate gifts from your family."

The women nodded in agreement.

"Chief Bowles, I was not aware when we met that you knew Mr. Mac. He told me how your warnings about Indian raids on his home saved his property and his life."

Speaking sternly, the Indian said, "Adam, I must have your word not to speak of my warnings to Mr. Mac. I have enough trouble with my people."

"You have my word."

"Will you ask Mr. Mac and family to never speak again of this?"

"Yes, I will." Adam sensed something different in the chief from the meeting of two days earlier. *Where is the laughter? The family appears to be uncomfortable with us here, and the chief is so stoic.*

He asked, "Chief Bowles, what is wrong?"

"You brought the Indian fighter and four other men to my camp. They waited in woods watching us smoke peace pipe. This man is paid to kill my people by your governor. Is that not so?"

"Captain Fain is paid to keep the peace. He is married to my wife's sister and is Mr. Mac's son-in-law. I did not bring him as an Indian fighter but as a family member whose only concern was my safety. The other men you mention were also family members."

"If they are in woods waiting today, they have likely already been scalped. I must warn you that all your people should pack belongings and move back over mountains. It is not safe for white man on this side of mountain."

"My daughter and I are alone today, and I am unarmed. We came only for our dog and to bring you gifts."

"You must go back over mountains before next full moon."

"I can't do that."

"Then you and your family will perish at hands of Cherokee."

Peggy's eyes widened, and she tightened her hold on Lulubelle. The dog picked up on her anxiety and growled at the chief. Peggy stroked Lulubelle's fur until the raised hair on the back of the dog's neck lay down again.

"The Chickamauga Cherokee have many large tribes. Like white man, they now have long guns and many horses. Tribes have banded together to drive white man from lands of Cherokee."

"Are you going to join in this effort?"

"For safety of my tribe, I must."

"If you go to war against the settlers, the soldiers will come after you, and your family will never be safe."

"If I refuse to join the Cherokee cause, the other chiefs will kill my family."

"I don't understand. You have lived peaceably near the settlers for many years. Mr. Mac owns this land that you are camped on and will let you stay on it as long as you wish. We will not let anyone hurt you."

"You or your soldiers cannot protect us from ourselves any more than Indian can keep your brothers from across water from killing you." He shook his head. "No more talk of this. We will be leaving soon to join our Indian brothers at Running Waters."

"Chief, is there any way this Indian uprising can be stopped?"

"If your Governor Sevier had kept his word to Cherokee Nation at Dumplin Creek, there would be no war with Indians today."

Adam just shook his head, knowing the Indian was right. The State of Franklin not only ignored the treaty but had established its capital at Greenville in the heart of the Cherokee Nation, a boundary established three years earlier by representatives of the provisional federal government.

Peggy, trying not to listen to the frightening talk, scooped up a handful of dirt from the floor of the lean-to. She held it up and watched it trickle through her fingers, just as she had done with the dirt from the floor of the spring house as a child during the Battle of Guilford Courthouse.

For a short moment she was back in the spring house, putting the fears of war out of her mind—distracted by a handful of dirt. However, the distraction was only momentary; soon she again heard the sounds of battle and men crying out in agony.

The chief stood and placed his hands on Adam's shoulders. "Duwali has warned you. Go now and prepare your family for what is to come. Do not come back." He reached for the hand-carved walking stick Adam had returned on the first visit. "This is for you to remember a friendship that can never be."

No one said a word as Adam and Peggy rode slowly out of camp with Lulubelle and Elvira following close behind. The spring flora was in full bloom making it difficult to see into the thick underbrush. Adam saw signs of movement in the woods and heard the bird calls used by Indians to alert one another of the enemy's movements.

Both horses and Elvira were making the nervous sounds they often made when a predator was near. Lulubelle was having a hard time keeping up. Adam, without a gun or a knife and with his daughter's life now in his hands, regretted his decision to bring her.

I must stay calm. What should I do? God, please help me. Something told him to get on higher ground rather than to go up the creek. He was not far from the field his sons were planting. He motioned for Peggy to follow him, and as he headed up the hill, he saw an ominous sight.

"Peggy," he said. "We have company."

"I see the Indian on top of the ridge."

"Yes, and he's well armed. When I give the word, head for the open field at the top of the ridge." *Damn, I hope the boys are armed today.* "I'll be behind you with Elvira and Lulubelle. Now, go and don't look back!"

Peg leaned forward and clicked her heels into Cherokee's sides. The mare, as always, responded instantly to her command. Adam followed close behind. Both horses ran like this was another one of those family races with a friendly wager involved.

When Adam topped the ridge, the Indians realized their prey had outwitted their ambush and gave a blood-curdling whoop. The warriors on horseback turned and chased after Adam while others scrambled out of their hiding places back onto their mounts.

As Peggy outdistanced him, Adam felt thankful that she had a fast horse and natural equestrian abilities. He thought, *The Indians are right. She does ride like the wind.* He watched her disappear from sight in a brown cloud of dust as the sound of the Indians grew louder, telling him they were gaining ground.

Elvira was holding him back, and he considered turning her loose. However, his fear of what the Indians might do to her and his need of her for spring planting gave him the strength to hold on to her rein. He wondered where Lulubelle was.

From the direction of his field, he could see several trails of dust coming toward him at great speed. It looked like at least five riders, and he would make six. Thinking the riders were from the local militia, he said out loud, "Thank you, God."

As the riders got close enough for the Indians to see them, Adam stopped and turned toward the advancing warriors. Sitting up high in his saddle, he pulled out the walking cane Chief Bowles had given him and raised it over his head defiantly. He hoped it would look like a gun to the Indians. There appeared to be no more than six braves pursuing them. *One on one,* Adam thought.

As the riders got closer, he saw it wasn't the militia. It was Peggy, Robert, William, John, and Adam riding towards him waving something over their heads.

The planting sticks they were waving must have looked like guns to the Indians. They turned and ran back into the woods when they saw the hard-riding horsemen coming to confront them.

As his unarmed rescuers approached, Adam asked, "Where's your guns?"

"Don't have any," Robert answered.

"You and William were running head-on into an Indian raid with your sister; John, who isn't shaving yet; and Adam, who just turned twelve. And you had no weapons except your planting sticks?"

"Yep."

"What the hell were you thinking, Robert?

Robert spat out a chaw of tobacco. "You were in trouble and needed our help. That's what family does. Mitchells don't think about it. We just do what needs doing. That's what you and Grandfather taught us."

He turned his horse and headed back toward where he had left off planting.

Adam, finding words to express his feeling difficult, said, "Well—I, uh, thank you, Robert." He sat on his horse shaking his head as Robert rode off as if nothing out of the ordinary had happened.

"You're welcome," he called back. "Now I need everyone back planting except Peg. Mother needs her at home. She says we got a special guest for dinner tonight."

William grinned and shook his head. John and Adam Jr. looked in awe at their father and sister who had just survived an Indian attack. They sat waiting in their saddles for some response or direction from their father.

Adam shifted in his saddle, putting his full weight into the stirrups, trying to give his aching buttocks some relief. "You heard Robert. Let's get back to work." Silently he gave thanks to God for what had just happened. "Peg, head for home. William, you go with her and then come right back. Stay in the open as much as you can."

Peg said, "Thank you."

"For what?"

"Taking me with you. Our time together today was special."

"I nearly got you killed."

"But you didn't." Peg saw Lulubelle coming out of hiding in some tall grass at the edge of the corn field. "Come, girl, it's time to go home."

Adam said, "If you ever want to go with me again anywhere, it's best not to tell your Mother about the Indians chasing us."

"I won't say a word."

When they reached the barn, William wheeled around on his horse and headed back to the field. It took Peggy a while to unsaddle her very tired horse. A mixture of lather and dust matted Cherokee's usually shiny coat from head to tail. Peg hurried to curry the mare and put her into the horse pen before her mother could ask any questions.

No one was in the house, and her mother didn't answer her call. *Where are Mother and the children?* They weren't in the smokehouse or the chicken coop so Peg headed for the creek. The sight of her mother's dress covered with blood and floating in the shallow water alarmed her.

"No," she said. "Oh, no, please God. Not my mother and baby brother and sisters!" She reached into the water and picked up the wet and bloody dress. She held it tight against her bosom, sobbing and crying out in anguish.

She jumped when she heard, "Peggy what is wrong with you?"

She turned to see her mother standing behind her, looking so pretty in her best dress with her hair freshly done. *Am I dreaming?* she thought.

"Where are the children?"

"The babies are asleep on a pallet underneath the willow tree. Ibby and Rebeckah are downstream. What's wrong with you?"

"With me? There's blood all over your dress floating in the creek. That's what's wrong with me. Then I couldn't find the children."

Her mother took the bloody dress and tossed it back into the creek. She pulled her daughter toward her for a hug, and then pushed her back. "I've spent the last two hours washing clothes, bathing babies, and primping for your gentleman caller. I am not going to let you soil my clean clothes. How in the world did you get so dirty?"

"Father and I had a friendly horse race on the way home."

"Here is a bar of last winter's soap with the leaves of lavender you like so much. Take off that dirty dress and get in the creek and make yourself pretty for Andrew."

Sinking into the refreshingly cool creek, Peggy asked, "Where did all that blood on your dress come from?"

Elizabeth sat on a large boulder watching the children begin to stir on the pallet. "I culled six of those big old white leghorn hens this afternoon that hadn't been laying enough eggs to earn their keep. That hatchet was so dull those old birds just bled all over me."

"Is chicken what we're having?"

Elizabeth ignored the question as she admired her beautiful daughter. Peg's hair was full and curly; she had beautiful long legs and a radiant smile. No wonder Andrew was so infatuated by her.

"Chicken? Is that what we're having, Mother?" Peggy spoke louder.

"No, I just spent the afternoon chopping their heads off and Ibby and Rebeckah are downstream plucking them just for the fun of it."

They both started laughing so hard they woke the children.

Elizabeth said, "I'm heading to the house now so as to slow cook those tough old birds."

"Please, Mother, will you wait so I won't be alone?"

"Lulubelle is here for you. And since when are you afraid to be alone?"

"I'm not really afraid, but I'd like your company."

"All right, but you must hurry."

When they were back at the house, Rebeckah and Ibby peeled potatoes while Elizabeth and Peggy prepared the chickens.

Near suppertime, Peggy checked on the chickens that were slowly roasting in two large Dutch ovens hanging just over the embers on the hearth. "Set the table for twelve tonight."

"Who's the extra place for?" asked Rebeckah.

"Peg's new beau, Andrew. that she is so cow-eyed over." Ibby made a childish face at her sister.

Elizabeth put her hands on her hips. "Girls, I do not want you making fun of Peg. Tonight is a special occasion."

Rebeckah asked, "What's a special o-quasion?" trying hard to sound out the new word.

"Like when it's your birthday," her mother said, giving Rebeckah a pat on the head. "I hear horses coming. Why don't you go see who it is, girls?" After the girls left, she said, "Peg, the men will be in shortly so I just want you to know that I like Andrew and I can tell he likes you. He is a very determined young man that will never be content with the life of a farmer. He is different from the men we know from here."

"What are you trying to say?"

"It's just that he would never choose to live the life that your family has always known."

"That's what I like about him—that he is so different."

Baby David began to cry. Elizabeth picked him up and carried him to the rocker by the window to nurse. She looked out the small windowpane and saw Andrew and Adam in what looked like a serious discussion. Adam and the boys must have met Andrew on the road. She thought, *I hope Adam is not already discussing the dowry with Andrew. Not on the first visit, like my father and father-in-law back in Virginia. Not much I can do about it, if he is.* Rocking vigorously, she patted baby David on the back, hoping for a small burp of gas, just as she had done with one baby after another for what would soon be nineteen years.

"Peg, go tell the men dinner will be ready in a few minutes."

When Peg got to the barn, she saw Father and Andrew talking. Not wanting to intrude on their conversation, she turned to go back into the house. Adam motioned for Peg to come join them.

Watching through the window, Elizabeth thought, *That's strange for Adam to invite Peg to join the men's conversation. And I wonder why Robert and William are nodding their heads.*

Rebeckah and Ibby entered the house and flounced down at the table with sullen looks on their face.

"What's the matter with you girls?"

"They were talking about being chased by Indians, and they made us come in the house."

Hmm—wonder what that's all about, Elizabeth thought. "Remember, we have an honored guest so mind your manners at the supper table."

"Yes, Mother," the girls said in unison.

A few minutes later Andrew was seated at the place of honor directly across from Adam. He appeared to really enjoy the chicken and gave Elizabeth glowing compliments on her cooking skills. She enjoyed the praise and said that her daughters, especially Peggy, had all helped in the preparation, assuring Andrew of her oldest daughter's culinary ability.

"Well, then, my compliments also to Peggy."

Peggy blushed.

The Mitchell family was not as chatty as they usually were at the evening meal. John and Adam were especially quiet. Having been warned not to say anything of today's events, they didn't have much to talk about.

Andrew, reaching for another piece of chicken, broke the silence. "We had a visitor from Philadelphia at the courthouse today."

"Did they have any news on the ratification of the Constitution?" Adam asked. "It's been seven months since the Constitutional Convention."

"He told us that last month Rhode Island rejected the Constitution—the first state to do so. South Carolina should reach a decision any day. Word from the Capital is North Carolina plans to reject it also."

Adam furrowed his brow. "Does that mean it might not get ratified?"

"No, the delegates are saying that Maryland, New Hampshire, and Virginia will vote in favor. Rhode Island's and North Carolina's rejections won't matter—only nine states are needed to ratify."

Elizabeth, who usually ignored discussions of politics and the labor pains of founding a new federal government, asked, "Andrew, would this gentleman be headed back to Philadelphia in the near future?"

Adam looked at his wife. *Why would she ask such a question?*

Andrew answered, "I assume he will as soon as his work is done."

"Work? What kind of work is he doing in Jonesborough?" Elizabeth asked.

"I am not at liberty to say, except that he is here on official business of the provisional government."

Adam reached for another piece of chicken. "Who sent him?" He looked at Andrew for his answer.

"He plans to call on you tomorrow. He can answer that question for you."

"The boys and I are working hard to get our seed in the ground. We've already lost several weeks of the growing season. We don't have time to be entertaining some Philadelphia lawyer."

"He's not a lawyer. He's Lieutenant John Armstrong of the First Regiment, U.S. Army."

Elizabeth said, "Adam, you must make time to see him. It isn't often someone from the nation's capital comes to Jonesborough and wishes to see you."

"If Lieutenant Armstrong wants to talk to me, he can find the boys and me in the corn field by the road where we met you this afternoon. We'll be there every day from daylight to dark till the planting is done. "

"I will give the lieutenant directions to your field when I see him in the morning. Mr. and Mrs. Mitchell, this has been a most wonderful meal, and I have enjoyed the conversation. The evening is getting late and I would very much like to take a stroll with Peggy before I take leave."

"Certainly," Adam said. "But please just stay near to the house and look out for Indians."

"After today's events, I will be cautious of any movement in the dark, and, as always, I am armed."

Elizabeth thought, *Is anyone going to tell me about today's events? What's so bad they don't want me to know about it?*

Andrew helped Peggy pull a cape over her shoulders and held the door for her. The couple stepped outside into the cool air of the April evening. Lulubelle waited by the stoop, wagging her tail, ready for some attention that never came from the couple engrossed in each other. Peggy suggested they go in the barn. With the farm animals penned up for the night, she felt safe, knowing that the animals would create a ruckus should the Indians approach.

After Andrew and Peg left the house, Elizabeth passed a small cypress bucket around the table, into which the family members scraped their food scraps to feed to Lulubelle in the morning.

Elizabeth said, "Rebeckah, I need you to wash down the table board."

"That's Peg's job."

"Tonight you get the honors, and Ibby can help you."

Adam sensed Elizabeth's growing irritation. He motioned for his son John to bring the Bible to the table. If he could get the Bible reading started, he could delay the questioning that was sure to come.

He read verses from the Bible and asked the children what the passage meant. Their answers often made their parents proud that their children were so knowledgeable of the Scriptures.

Elizabeth and Rebeckah finished cleaning the kitchen and joined the family. Elizabeth seemed to be listening to the children, but she shrugged her shoulders up and down and breathed deeply. Her hands lay on top of the table, one over the other, her right hand twisting the wedding band on her finger. Adam and the children recognized these to be signs that Mother wasn't happy.

The conversation stopped when she looked sternly down the long table at each child, then directly at Robert. "It is obvious that your father has no intentions of telling me what happened today with the Indians. Someone please tell me."

Rebeckah and Ibby sat wide-eyed, eager to hear about the Indians. John and William looked down at the table. Robert fidgeted and looked at his father with raised eyebrows, and Elizabeth turned her gaze to her husband.

Adam—who had fought in the Revolutionary War, survived being a prisoner of war, and recovered stolen goods from a band of robbers without fear—feared the wrath of the Scots-Irish woman he had married almost nineteen years ago.

He stammered, "Well— Elizabeth, uh, well, I was just waiting for Peg—to come in—so we could discuss it—as a family."

"Adam, Peggy was with you. She knows what happened! I am waiting to hear about the Indians from you."

She pointed with both hands toward her ears, and Adam knew that she meant for him to start talking.

He told the story of Chief Bowles warning them to move back over the mountains and a brief version of the Indian chase. He neglected to tell Elizabeth that the chief said the boys might have been scalped if they had been there.

"You were attacked after taking gifts?" She shook her head in disbelief.

"I don't believe Chief Bowles' family had anything to do with the Indians that tried to attack us. Apparently they have intimidated him and his family, threatening them for befriending us."

"Well, we intimidated them with our planting sticks today," Robert said.

The boys started laughing at the thought of what they had done. Elizabeth was not amused.

"Should we take the warning serious?" Elizabeth asked.

"Yes, we should, and get prepared to fight should it become necessary."

Peggy and Andrew came in the back door, and Andrew said it was time for him to take his leave.

"When you get home, please apprise the Taylors of the warning about the Indian uprising," Adam said. "Tomorrow remind everyone you see to attend the church services at the courthouse this Sunday. I will see that Captain Fain is there, and we can make plans to protect ourselves from the Indians."

"I will post a notice on the courthouse door and at Deaderick's in the morning." Andrew headed for the door, hurrying to make it home before the Taylors retired for the evening.

Adam said, "Be careful on the way home. Watch for those renegades."

After Andrew left, the boys went outside to their sleeping quarters. Elizabeth put the babies to bed while Peggy tucked the younger girls in.

Shortly, curled up on the feather bed next to Adam, Elizabeth heard the familiar sound of coyotes howling. Or was it the Indians she heard? She stared at the crescent moon coming through the small glass window pane high on the wall, reflecting in the mirror over the dresser.

Tonight, Elizabeth, who had endured the horrors of battle, trembled in fear.

"Will it ever end?"

"What?"

"The fighting. As long as I can remember it's been this way. When I was just a young girl, Tory raiders came to our home on the Opequon Creek and threatened to hang my father for his political views. We moved to Guilford County to get away from the Tories and ended up hiding in the spring house while the British destroyed our home. I cannot bear to lose another home." She started to cry on Adam's shoulder.

He let her cry, holding her tightly. "God will not give us more than we can handle."

Peggy heard her parents' conversation and recited over and over what she had just heard her father say. She now realized what a close call they had today. What if the Indians had kept coming and had seen that they had no weapons to defend themselves? She fell asleep praying that her father was right—that God would never give their family more than they could handle.

The next morning, Elizabeth was her usual self. She said "Adam, please ask the lieutenant from Philadelphia if he would be so kind as to deliver your mother's deathbed letter to David and Rachel Caldwell when he passes through Martinsville on his way to Philadelphia."

Adam, with a grin, put the letter in his pocket. "Now I understand your interest in when the soldier was going back to Philadelphia. I should have known you had a reason."

"I couldn't trust a letter of such importance to just anyone. Being an officer in the Army should make him trustworthy and dependable. Don't you think?"

"Once I meet him, I will know his mettle and will decide then if he should be the one to deliver Mother's letter."

Peg had asked to go to the field to help with the planting, and Adam had agreed. He could always use an extra hand at planting time, and he suspected Peg wanted a break from her responsibilities for the children. Elizabeth didn't like her daughters doing man's work. Adam, on the other hand, had no objection. He remembered his first wife, Jennett, working beside him in the fields when she was about Peg's age.

Adam, Peg, and the boys loaded the farm wagon with seed, drinking water, and lunch—corn bread and a Dutch oven filled with slow-cooked deer meat. The guns and ammunition were wrapped in a deer skin for protection from the elements. From this day forward, the Mitchells would always have their weapons loaded and at the ready.

After planting several rows, they noticed a lone rider on a magnificent bright bay mare with black legs, mane, and tail.

As he approached, Peg thought it was the most beautiful horse she had ever seen. The rider was a very attractive man of about thirty years.

"Mr. Adam Mitchell?" the stranger asked, extending his hand to Adam. "I am Lieutenant John Armstrong."

"I have been expecting you," Adam said.

"It is an honor to meet you. I have heard many good things from Judge McNairy and Andrew Jackson about you and your family. I also offer my sincere condolences on the loss of your mother."

"Thank you, Lieutenant Armstrong. Now how may I be of assistance to you and the Army?"

"I have been sent by Henry Knox, Secretary of War, to confirm or disprove a rumor that the State of Franklin is planning an armed invasion of Spanish Louisiana."

"You're not serious?" Adam tried not to laugh.

"The Secretary of War is taking the allegation seriously enough to send me as a special agent of the government to investigate."

"The Franklin Militia can't keep the Indians out of our gardens and chicken coops. How could the Secretary of War think they could take on the Spanish Empire?"

"It could be done with the help of the British."

"Are you implying that the citizens of the State of Franklin might join forces with the British?"

"Yes. If the Westerners secured Spain's holdings, they would have control of the Mississippi River and the Port of New Orleans for navigational purposes."

Robert, William, Peggy, John, and Adam Jr. were amazed as the stranger and their father continued to talk about the great river and the vast lands to the west of Knob Creek—a world the Mitchell children knew little about.

"Lieutenant, you need to understand that the only reason the State of Franklin ever petitioned to break away from North Carolina was because the settlers west of the mountains could not depend on the North Carolina Militia for protection from the Indians after the Cession Act."

"I am surprised that you sound as if you are in support of the Franklinites."

"Why are you surprised?"

"Neither you nor any of your family members signed the petition delivered to the North Carolina General Assembly last December."

"I am curious as to how you would know that," Adam said. "But you are correct. Not one member of the Mitchell, McMachen, or Fain families signed the petition to separate from the mother state."

"Why not?"

"The families met at the Quarters, and we prayed over the matter under the guidance of Reverend Doak. After we prayed and discussed it, we chose not to sign."

"Your father-in-law is a close friend of John Sevier, the Governor of Franklin, I have been told."

"Everyone in Washington County is John's friend, except for John Tipton. Remember that it was John Sevier that led the volunteers to King's Mountain, where his own brother Robert lost his life. Three of my brothers-in-law, all named Fain, fought at King's Mountain, along with their father Nicholas. His only daughter Elizabeth's husband Andrew Evans was there, too. For anyone to think that John Sevier — or anyone who fought or had family who fought at King's Mountain — would now plot with the British to acquire land from Spain is ludicrous."

"I have heard of the bitter rivalry of the two Johns and the killing of Sheriff Pugh."

"In answer to your question about John McMachen not supporting the Franklin petition, you must realize that as the state's Registrar of Washington County, it would have been improper for him to sign."

"And your reason for not signing the petition?"

Adam put a hand on Robert's shoulder, the other on William's, and nodded towards Peg, John, and Adam. "You are looking at the reasons, Lieutenant. They, their mother, and grandmother were on the battlefield hidden in the spring house on our farm that adjoined the Courthouse of Guilford County. They endured hours of artillery and small arms fire. After the battle, they witnessed the carnage of war and smelled the stench of death."

Peggy rolled her shoulders forward and shuddered. Hearing her father speak, she remembered the smells of death and the bloody bodies lying in the fields outside their home.

Robert looked out to the field, trying not to remember anything that had happened after the battle. He had just turned fourteen and was forced by the British to help bury the dead as the rest of the family watched from what was left of their home.

"My family needs peace, Lieutenant. That's why I didn't sign the Franklin Petition."

"What do you think will come of this government of Franklin?"

"North Carolina has reconsidered the cession of the western lands. If, come July, the state's General Assembly endorses the federal Constitution and agrees to provide the settlers protection from the Indians, there is no reason for the State of Franklin to exist."

"I agree. That is what I will report to the Secretary. It appears the rumor was nothing more than a ploy to create distrust of John Sevier and the Franklinites. I will be forever indebted to you for your forthright answers to my questions of this matter and would appreciate your not discussing my being here with anyone."

"I will hold this meeting in confidence. Now, I have a question for you. Will you be going by way of Guilford Courthouse on your way back to Philadelphia?"

"If you mean Martinsville, as it is now called, I am."

"Would you be kind enough to deliver my mother's deathbed letter to Reverend David Caldwell at the Buffalo Presbyterian Church?

Looking Adam directly in the eyes, Lieutenant Armstrong asked, "Did your mother really negotiate with General Cornwallis for the release of all the captured soldiers and militiamen after the battle on your farm?"

"She did."

"Then, sir, it would be an honor for me to deliver her letter as an officer of the Army." He reached for the letter and placed it in his saddlebag.

"I wish you Godspeed, Lieutenant Armstrong."

The soldier saluted, turned his bay mare toward Jonesborough, and then cantered out of the Mitchells' corn field and down the road until he was out of sight.

Chapter Five
The Proposal

Daniel, the town blacksmith, saw the Mitchells' wagon coming down Main Street toward his stable and blacksmith shop. He dropped his hammer and ran out to greet his friends. Offering a hand first to Peggy and then to John, he helped them off their horses as William pulled the wagon into the livery stable.

"I sure am glad to see you." He gave each a warm hug and shook his head. "Look at all of you—you all grown up."

John beamed with pride at being considered an adult by someone he so admired. William removed the tackle from the team as Daniel smiled his trademark grin and opened the gate to an empty pen for the horses.

"Peggy, you're still the prettiest girl in Washington County."

"Why thank you."

Daniel, the son of freed slaves, had moved to Washington County with the McMachen family before the Revolution. He looked much older than his thirty-three years. His short hair and beard had patches of gray. A hulk of a man, he walked with a severe limp from being thrown from a wild horse he'd tried to tame for Nicholas Fain.

"It seems like only yesterday I seen you coming down this street in that wagon with your Grandmother Mitchell and all her possessions. I'm sure going to miss her."

Peggy touched his arm. "I know. We all miss her. You should know that in her last days when she couldn't come to town with us, Grandmother Mitchell always wanted a full report on how you were doing when we got home."

He sniffed back a tear, and John patted him awkwardly on the shoulder.

William cleared his throat. "We need you to check all the horses' feet for loose shoes—we can't afford to have a horse throw one running from Indians."

"I heard about your scrape with the Cherokees." Daniel shook his head. "You all go on and take care of your business in town, and I'll take good care of your horses."

John looked at Daniel and asked, "Can I stay here with you."

Daniel and John turned to Peggy and William for approval.

"That's fine," Peggy said.

Peggy headed for Deaderick's Store with the list of needed provisions while William delivered two large crocks of his father's special whisky to Murphy's Tavern. Since Andrew and Judge McNairy came to town, the sales of Mitchell-made whisky had picked up considerably.

While the storekeeper filled the Mitchells' order, Peggy busied herself looking at the notices tacked to the bulletin board. The one announcing Jonesborough's First Annual Beaver Run caught her eye.

"What is a beaver run?" she asked.

"It's a horse race, Peggy, for beaver pelts."

"I don't understand."

"It's simple—every entrant pays six pelts or forty shillings. The winner will receive five pelts or thirty shillings per contestant."

"How many horses are entered?" she asked.

"Only five have paid the entrance fee so far, but once it is announced at church this Sunday I expect there will be more—maybe ten or twelve horses. Your new beau Andrew Jackson is entered."

"Really?" Peggy did the math in her head. *That's 50 to 60 pelts or 20 pounds sterling. That's a lot of money. I could further my education and maybe one day do something besides take care of babies.*

"Fact is the beaver race is Mr. Jackson's idea—quite a thinker he is."

"If I were to enter, will you not tell a soul until we are lined up for the race?"

"Well, er, are you sure you want to run against men, especially with Mr. Jackson being your beau?"

"Yes, I do. That's why I don't want you saying a word to anyone. Promise me." She put a finger to her lip when she noticed Andrew entering the store. She hadn't seen him dressed for court before, and she thought he looked almost as handsome as he did on horseback.

Mr. Deaderick nodded his head that he would keep the secret and went back to filling the order.

"Good day, Peg," Andrew said. "I was eating at Murphy's when William came in, and he said you were here."

"We're about done. Aren't we, Mr. Deaderick?"

"Yes. I will load everything for you once William gets here with your wagon."

"Your apple brandy, eggs, and corn meal are on the wagon. Be sure to get them off. Father says they should take care of today's supplies."

"More than enough. Please tell Adam I need as many small brown jugs of his special whisky as he has the next time one of you comes to town. For some reason, it sure is getting popular around here."

"I know." Peg smiled at Andrew, knowing he and his friends were introducing her father's special recipe to the townspeople.

"I would like to show you something, Peg. Let's walk over to the courthouse." Andrew opened the door and slipped his arm under hers once outside the store.

The new one-room log courthouse smelled of the fresh-cut pine timbers used to build it. Peggy couldn't figure out what Andrew wanted to show her as she attended church there three Sundays of the month. He asked her to sit on a wooden bench next to his work table, which he stood behind.

"I have something to ask you, and I needed a private place in which we could talk. I have asked Judge McNairy and Attorney Avery to extend the court's recess for another hour."

"What could be so important as to hold up the business of the court?"

"You are."

She twisted nervously on the hard pine bench. "Thank you for the compliment, but what makes me so important?" She looked into Andrew's steel-blue eyes.

"I have been properly courting you for several weeks now with the blessings of your father and Reverend Doak."

She frowned and stiffened, holding on to the bench with both hands. "Reverend Doak is aware of your courting me? When did you last speak to him?"

"Last Sunday after church services."

"That was the business you told me you had to tend to?" She looked down and traced the dust on the rough wooden floor with the toe of her shoe.

"Yes, it was, and the minister baptized me. He said he would not condone our marriage otherwise."

Andrew looked down at her, as if watching for her reaction. He scowled when he saw her clenched fists and her frown.

Peggy sat rigidly, staring first at the floor and then up at the ceiling. She said nothing, but she shook her head.

"Did you hear what I said?"

"Yes."

"Please, say something."

"I don't know what to say. You have already talked to everyone that is near and dear to me about our marriage but have not discussed it with me."

"I knew that the pastor's blessing had to be secure before you or your family would consent to my marriage proposal."

"Mother, Father, and the reverend told me that they had chosen James Witherspoon for my husband." Her brow furrowed into a puzzled expression.

"The pastor mentioned young Jimmy and his plans for the two of you."

She jumped up and put her hands on her hips. "That was discussed? You talked about that—about Jimmy?"

"What's wrong?" Andrew reached out to put a hand on her shoulder.

Peggy backed away from him. He tried to put a hand on each shoulder, but she went for the door before he could touch her.

"Don't go," he pleaded as she stormed out the door.

She passed Judge McNairy and Mr. Avery in a huff.

Attorney Avery turned toward the judge. "It appears the marriage proposal was not taken well by the bride-to-be."

"It certainly appears that way," the judge responded as he watched Peggy hurrying toward the livery stable.

Attorney Avery pulled out his pocket watch. "Well, there's no need for us to tarry any further. Shall we get back to work?"

William and John were coming down Main Street towards Deaderick's in the wagon with the saddled horses tethered to the tailgate.

Peggy crossed over to the store and waited for her brothers under the canopy next to the keg of rock salt and other supplies that needed to be loaded on the wagon.

"What's taking you so long?" Peggy asked, tapping an impatient foot.

"We've been waiting on you," William answered. "Andrew told me you would be another hour at the courthouse."

"Mr. Jackson seems to provide everyone my schedule except me."

Her brothers looked at Peg, then at each other, but didn't say another word. They sensed Peg's displeasure and went about unloading the brandy and eggs and loading the family provisions.

The shopkeeper came out to give each of the siblings a piece of candy. "Tell your mother and father I appreciate their business and I look forward to seeing you all this Sunday at church services in the courthouse."

Peg led Cherokee to the limestone upping block in front of the store and threw her right leg over the saddle, not bothering to sit sidesaddle. Her mother wouldn't like it, but she didn't care.

When Peg entered the house, she found her mother in a dither. David was colicky and running a high fever. Rebeckah and Ibby were arguing. Samuel was wandering around the room sucking his thumb. The smell of burning food hovered in the air. Peggy removed the Dutch oven from the fireplace. She put her young sisters to tending to Samuel so Elizabeth could give her full attention to the ailing baby.

Elizabeth looked at Peg. "Look how quickly you brought everything under control. I don't know what I will do if you marry Andrew and go off to Nashville." She spoke through trembling lips, still trying to nurse the sick baby.

Peggy knelt by the rocking chair, placing a reassuring arm on her mother's shoulder while patting the feverish cheek of her baby brother with the other hand. "Don't worry, Mother. I won't be going to Nashville any time soon. Where are Father and Robert?"

"Cutting some large timbers in the woods by the creek," Elizabeth answered.

"Why do they keep cutting timber? Father no longer plans to build the mill house."

"They need to clear another field for planting next year. The logs can be used for the church and school your father is always talking about building."

***

The next Sunday, Elizabeth and Robert were disappointed they couldn't hear Hezekiah Balch preach. The two baby boys were both sick, and Elizabeth stayed home to care for them. Robert stayed with them to guard against an Indian attack.

This would be the first opportunity for the congregation to hear Reverend Balch preach. A graduate of Princeton

College, he had preached in York, Pennsylvania before moving to the State of Franklin in 1784. His friend and fellow Presbyterian minister Samuel Doak had referred him to Adam to help organize a church for the Knob Creek Community.

John Blair McMachen, a church elder, introduced the visiting preacher to the congregation. Reverend Balch proudly delivered the good news he had just received from family that his home state of Maryland had voted to ratify the U.S. Constitution, making it the seventh state to vote for forming the United States government.

After the sermon, Mr. Deaderick announced the beaver race that would be held immediately after church on the second Sunday in June. Thirteen horses were entered already, and he expected at least twenty entrants in the four-mile race. The women of the church would prepare food to sell to raise funds for the soon-to-be-built Hebron Presbyterian Church.

Andrew had skipped Sunday services to work with Waxhaw. As the potential purse had doubled the additional entries, he hired a jockey and trainer. He took the race seriously and planned to win.

Peggy had her own plan to win the beaver run. The plan included getting Cherokee in condition for the grueling race and learning everything she could about the course and the competition. The thought of winning this race consumed her, and she felt exhilarated, having never felt such passion in her young life.

The next morning after breakfast had been served and the table cleared, Peg said, "Father, I have business in town that I need to take care of today, and Mr. Deaderick needs as many small brown jugs of whisky as you have. He said he needs them right away."

"I can't spare any of your brothers to go with you, and it's too dangerous for you to go alone—especially with a delivery."

"Why can't one of the boys go with me?"

"I have a huge pine tree to bring down today. I need the help of all the boys."

"I need to do this today. It's important."

"I understand about the unfinished business, and it is wise of you to wish to address it in a timely fashion."

He thinks I'll be talking to Andrew. I have no intention of doing that. But I'll let Father think that's my important business so he won't ask any questions.

Adam suggested, "Why don't you go to the Quarters? One of your uncles might be going to town."

Peg climbed the hill to Grandfather's home and saw Captain Fain's horse saddled and tied to the hitching post. *It looks as if Uncle John is going somewhere this morning.*

"How is Grandfather this morning?" Peg asked Aunt Nancy.

"He hasn't been alert the last few weeks, but he's alert today. I know he'd love to see you. Go on in."

Peggy stepped into the room and greeted her grandfather.

"Margaret, is that you?" the old man mumbled.

"It's Peg, your oldest granddaughter." She thought he was delirious and speaking of her namesake, Grandmother Mitchell, as he sometimes did.

"Yes, and your given name is *Margaret*. You were named for one of the loves of my life, your Grandmother Mitchell."

"That's correct, and I miss her." She hurried to his bedside, giving him a hug and a kiss on the forehead. She was happy that he appeared to have all his faculties with him this day.

"What brings you today, my child?"

"I try to see you every day, but the last few times I came you were asleep."

He whispered in Peg's ear as if telling her a secret. "Last night Nancy made me a hot toddy that gave me a good night's rest. I feel quite well this morning. Now, tell me about the Indians. I overheard your father telling John the story. I want to hear it from you."

Peggy looked at her Uncle John standing by the door with his coffee cup in hand. She waited for approval to repeat the story. The family had become careful of what they told Mr. Mac for fear of exciting him. Her uncle's approving nod and wink told her that the Indian fighter also wanted to hear her version of the much-told story.

As she repeated the details of the Indian encounter, Mr. Mac's eyes closed and he seemed to doze off. "I wish I could have seen my grandchildren run off a pack of marauding Indians with planting sticks," he murmured before falling into a deep sleep with a smile on his face.

"Father will sleep the rest of the day." Nancy covered his shoulders with his favorite quilt. Mother Mitchell had made it for him, and it had the design of the Quarters in its center and the name of every grandchild embroidered around it.

"Uncle John, I saw your horse saddled out front. Are you going somewhere?"

"I am riding over to Isaac Anderson's place to try and convince him to enlist in the campaign against the Chickamauga Indians."

"Will you be going through town?" Peg asked.

"I could. Why do you ask?"

"I have business in town, and Father will not let me go alone."

"That's wise of Adam. I'll be glad to escort you to Jonesborough; you'll have to wait for me, though, on my return from the Andersons' farm."

"I can wait at Daniel's for you."

"Get your team harnessed. I'll meet you at the road as soon as I say my goodbyes to the family." He was always careful to speak to every family member before he left because of his dangerous job.

Peggy, excited that her plan was working so well, ran down the hill toward the barn, making it before the men left for the woods. Adam and the boys helped her load the whisky and harness the team—not that she couldn't do it herself, but with their help Peg would be able to get to the road sooner to meet Uncle John.

She tied Cherokee to the wagon and threw her combination saddle in the back. She hoped Daniel could make it into a saddle suitable for racing.

They arrived at Deaderick's just as the store opened for business.

"I see you have a military escort this morning—quite impressive," Mr. Deaderick said to Peggy as he waved to Captain Fain riding out of town. "Sure appreciate your bringing the little brown jugs to me. I am completely out of stock."

"These are all Father had. He has plenty of whisky in barrels but no more crocks."

"I have two boxes of dead soldiers I've been hoarding for just this instant. I'll get them."

"What do you mean dead soldiers?" She shuddered.

Seeing her anguished look and knowing she had survived a major battle, the storekeeper said, "I'm sorry. I should have said empty jugs. Just empty crock jugs—dead soldiers was what the patriots during the Revolution called them when they finished their daily ration of spirits. They just cast them off as they couldn't carry empty jugs marching off to battle."

"They just left the jugs?" *Like they left the dead soldiers,* she thought.

"Yep. Then the camp followers picked them up and sold them back to distillers and merchants after the armies broke camp. That's how the camp followers survived."

"Just how much does Father pay you per jug?"

"He gives me a schilling credit for a pint and two schillings for the gallon size."

Hmm—all I need is about forty brown jugs for the entry fee.

"Where can one find these dead soldiers?"

"Wherever men drink."

Thinking of where men drank, she decided Murphy's would be her next stop.

"Are you still intending to run in the beaver run?" Mr. Deaderick asked.

"Yes. I'll have the entry fee by the end of the week. Have you told anyone that I'll race?"

"Not a soul, not even my wife."

"Oh, I should have said earlier. Congratulations on your marriage. I'm looking forward to meeting your new wife," Peggy said. "Please don't tell anyone about my entering the race."

He nodded though it was obvious he was not excited about her being in the race.

At Murphy's, Peg found three pint jugs and one gallon jug. Behind the courthouse, she found two more. She felt confident she could raise the entry fee on her own.

Arriving at the livery stable, she called, "Daniel where are you?" She looked around the dusty stable for the blacksmith, getting no answer. She removed the tack from the team and led the horses into the only empty pen. Fortunately the pen couldn't be seen from the street, and the wagon was pulled far into the barn.

I hope Andrew doesn't learn I'm in town. I'm just not ready to talk to him, and if I were, I don't know what I would say. Where could Daniel be?

His dapple gray mare was in its stall. Peg knocked on the tack room door where Daniel slept, but he didn't answer.

Peggy scooped a handful of cracked corn out of a bin in the corn crib as a treat for Cherokee, petting her with one hand and feeding her with the other.

She heard the sounds of chickens and pigs. *He must be feeding the hogs out back. How can he stand the smell of this place?* Peg leaned forward, looking through a crack for a glimpse out back.

"How long have you been here?" Daniel startled her by coming in the front of the large barn-like structure.

"Just long enough to pen the horses and give Cherokee some cracked corn."

Daniel reached for the thick leather blacksmith chaps hanging next to the furnace. "What brings you back to town so soon?"

"A delivery to Deaderick's and to call on you for help."

"My help—how can I help you?" He strapped the chaps on his legs to protect them from the hot embers of the fire and the red hot tools of his trade.

"I want to race Cherokee in the beaver run."

"Who'll be the jockey?" Daniel bent down to light the kindling to ignite the furnace.

"I will."

"That's what I was afraid you were gonna say."

"Why would I want to hire a jockey? I usually win."

"That's true, but you've only raced family and friends. With a purse this big, this race will have some serious competition. You could get hurt."

"Will you please help me?"

"You know that your beau Mr. Jackson is running Waxhaw and the idea for the race is his?"

"Yes—yes. But please don't call him my beau."

Daniel said, "I thought—"

"He is not my beau. Not—back to the beaver run. No one except Mr. Deaderick and now you know I intend to race."

"Why such a big secret?" Daniel pumped the bellows with his foot to fire up the raised brick hearth for the day's work.

"Because Father and especially Mother would not approve."

"If you was my daughter, I know I wouldn't." He pumped the bellows harder.

"Why?"

The blacksmith turned his attention away from the furnace and sat on a discarded buckboard across from the three-legged milk stool where Peggy sat. He looked her in the face and said, "Listen to me. It's a long race, with over twenty horses. Money-hungry men from who knows where, nothing but winning on their mind or having their way with some pretty girl. If you were to be thrown, they'd run right over you."

"That's why I came to you." She gave him her most charming smile. "No one knows more about horses and racing than you do. Will you please help me?"

"You know if I do everyone in your family and your Mr. Jackson will be mad at me."

"No one will know, unless you tell them as I certainly won't. Andrew is **not my** Mr. Jackson. If I win, I'll give you a fair share of the purse for being my trainer—say one-tenth."

"That's more than fair," the blacksmith said with an approving nod. "If I agree, you must do as I say. Is that understood?" Looking into Peggy's face for a sincere answer that didn't come, he said louder, "**Is that understood, Peggy Mitchell?**"

Reluctantly nodding her head, she said, "**Yes.** Now, please tell me where the race will be run?"

Daniel traced the route of the race in the dirt with the pointed poker he used to stoke his fire. "The race will start directly in front of Deaderick's and pass Murphy's, the court-house, and my stable. Then down the hill toward the springs of Little Limestone Creek, going across the creek, then along the creek bottom to the other end of town. Then back across the creek, up the hill, back to Deaderick's for the finish."

"How do you know this is the route?

"'Cause Mr. Deaderick asked me what would be the best course for the race and that's what I suggested." Daniel returned to tending the fire.

"Isn't it dangerous to cross the creek twice? Why do you say that is the best course for the horses? "

"It's what's best for the spectators that matters. The race is for them." He spoke loudly over the sound of the bellows he was pumping again.

"Why so?" Peggy hollered.

"This race will be the biggest happening here since Jonesborough hosted the first State of Franklin convention some four years ago come August. Mr. Deaderick says he expects at least three hundred people in town for the race."

"Where will they come from?"

"From all over the state." He moved closer to the open doors of the livery stable. "Look, Peggy. After those twenty-some-odd horses come galloping down the street and head for the creek bottom, the crowd can run to the back of the courthouse and from that knoll over there see the race continue along the other side of the creek."

Peggy looked intently at the creek bottom as Daniel pointed.

He continued, "Once the horses cross back over the creek and start up that steep incline over yonder, the horses and their riders will be completely out of view of the crowd. That's not good for you or Cherokee but convenient for the spectators."

"Why do you say it's convenient for the spectators?"

"The people who are paying for the best seats under Deaderick's' canopy can rush back to their place and see the winner cross the finish line." Daniel's animated gestures and voice indicated his excitement and anticipation of being involved in the race.

Peggy also felt the excitement of the moment, visualizing herself on Cherokee racing down Main Street with a large crowd cheering her on past the finish line. Peggy and Daniel sat quietly for a moment enjoying the visual image that Daniel had described.

She shook herself back into reality. With a grave look upon her face, she asked "Why did you say getting out of the spectators' view was bad for me and Cherokee?"

"My mother always said the devil does his work when the angels ain't watching."

"Meaning?"

He paused a long time. "I know many of the men that will be in the race. Most are good hardworking farmers and trappers who would do anything for their neighbors. But with a purse of 40 to 50 pounds, a good man might do things that he normally wouldn't."

"Like what?"

"Grab you and pull you off your horse, for one thing." He picked up the poker. "Remember, you promised to do what I say do. So listen to me and listen good. Cherokee is as great a horse as I have ever rode. I halter broke her as a young filly for your grandfather right here in this corral. I know her disposition as well as anyone."

"I know you do. That's one of the reasons I want your help."

He pointed to the dusty road in front of the stable. "When the starter fires his shot in the air, Cherokee is going to bolt as she always does, wanting to be immediately in the lead. You must hold her back until you have crossed the shallows of the first creek crossing. Once off that slippery limestone rock and on the dry grass of the creek bottom, spur her on with all you got."

Peggy jumped up from the stool and gazed off in the direction Daniel pointed. "And then what?"

"You need to jockey Cherokee to the outside, away from the creek as you don't want to be forced into the water by a herd of wild riders. It's important that you be one of the first to forge the second crossing of the creek. If you aren't, the other horses ahead of you will have created a muddy mess at the base of the steep incline leading back up to the street. This is where the horses will slip and be spooked and riders thrown. You must avoid that mess, and remember the first horse and rider safely to the top of the incline will most likely win the purse."

For the first time, Peggy thought of the many hazards in the race and the unfortunate consequences, including injury to her beloved horse, that could occur during such a long run. She shook off the thought and concentrated instead on the vision of crossing the finish line in front of the best horses and riders in the state.

During the next few weeks, she and Daniel met every day to prepare. Determined to keep her participation in the race a secret, she told her parents she was taking Cherokee for early morning rides. The family was accustomed to her riding her horse every chance she got, but were worried about her being out alone with the ever-present risk of Indian attack. However, she convinced them that she would stay close enough that the family could hear Lulubelle barking if she encountered any unfriendly strangers. *After all,* she thought, *where Daniel and I are working is that close to the house so I'm not telling a lie. I'm just not telling them everything.*

Daniel bartered for a British-made racing saddle that was much lighter in weight than her combination saddle, and he worked Peggy and Cherokee hard. A week before the big day, Daniel pronounced horse and rider ready to race.

Chapter Six

The Hebron School

Peggy wrote *October 18, 1795* on the blackboard, then, satisfied her schoolroom was ready for the day, sat at her desk. She stared out the small window of the one-room log building that served as both the schoolhouse and the Hebron Presbyterian Church. From her desk, she could see the morning sun casting a brilliant orange glow on the wooden crosses under her grandmother's favorite apple tree. She realized it had been more than seven years since Grandfather McMachen had been buried next to Grandmother Mitchell.

She wondered if her father had intentionally placed the window where he had or was it just happenstance? Either way, seeing the graves of her grandparents provided her daily inspiration to teach.

Her father and brothers, with the help of the men of the Knob Creek Community, had labored all summer to get the building ready for the fall semester of school. John Blair McMachen donated the land; Samuel Fain and Peter Miller bore a good share of the cost.

She watched Aunt Nancy's children—Ruth, Thomas, and John Rueben—cross the shallow creek on their horses. Peggy was happy that her Aunt Nancy had married a fine young man like John Hammer after Uncle John had been killed by Cherokee Indians at Cittico eight summers ago.

John had originally attempted to court Peggy when he started his search for a wife. He was a handsome young man and a devout Christian from good German stock. Peggy was impressed that he had built a fine home for his bride-to-be before knowing who she was. He called it "Walnut Grove" as the first settlers had named the area for the large cluster of walnut trees on his farm. But in spite of all his good qualities, Peggy wasn't interested. She explained that she had all the children she could care for at the moment with her aging mother recently giving birth to James and Hezekiah. She introduced the young bachelor to her aunt, who had already proven to be a prolific bearer of children and in need of a husband. Peggy smiled, knowing that she had been the matchmaker, but she sometimes wondered if she had made a mistake by not accepting his marriage proposal.

Jennett, Peggy's thirteen-year-old sister, had the honor this morning of ringing the bell that signaled the start of the school day. Jennett couldn't hold back her enthusiasm any longer. She opened the door slightly and asked, "Isn't it time to ring the school bell, Miss Mitchell?"

Their parents had told Peggy's siblings they should always refer to her as either Miss Mitchell or Teacher during school out of respect for her position.

More students arrived as Jennett rang the bell with such vigor that the new blue gingham bonnet her mother had made tumbled from her head, revealing long, auburn hair.

The students, who ranged in age from eight to sixteen years of age, began to enter and find seats on the simple log benches lined up in front of the teacher's desk. The children of Uncle Samuel, Uncle William, and Uncle John Blair, as well as Peggy's six younger brothers and sisters, attended. In addition to the relatives, children of the Miller, King, and Young families were students of the school.

After the Morning Prayer and Bible study, sixteen-year-old Ibby took the younger students outside to the large cypress tree in front of the school where she worked with them on reciting the alphabet over and over until they had memorized it.

For the older students, Peggy taught a civics lesson, not an easy task as the ongoing organization of the nation was in a constant state of turmoil. Peggy's students were to be the first generation of native Tennesseans following the sixteenth state's approval come June. Her first job was to teach them to spell Tennessee, which was named for a meandering river that flowed through it.

Peggy had heard that Andrew Jackson had recommended the state's new name. She'd also heard that he had taken a wife, a divorced woman named Rachel that he'd met in Nashville. In spite of his high-handedness, she had felt bad at his disappointment when she turned down his proposal. She hoped that he was happy and that his wife could give him the family that he desired.

What is it with men—why do they think of women as just brood stock to bear their children? Even my own father—God knows I love him—has impregnated Mother with twelve children. Two are just babies, and I'm twenty-three years old.

She saw her father carrying a large Dutch oven with steam coming from under the lid, He had several loaves of her mother's fresh-baked bread under his arm. *I don't know how I could run this school without Mother and Father, but I do hope they're finished making babies.*

"Students, bring your slate boards to me, please. Mr. Mitchell is bringing our noon meal. Rebeckah, would you please tell Ibby and the children to come in to eat?"

Each student was required to bring a wooden or pewter porringer from home on the first day of school. It was their personal drinking vessel, used to dip water from the water bucket and to eat their noon meal that was served hot every day.

The headmistress of the school where she had interned stressed the importance of a warm meal for the students. Reverend Balch had arranged the internship through a friend at a dame's school in York, Pennsylvania. A quick study, Peggy had been certified as a teacher in two years.

The stipend for schooling could be paid to Peggy in coin, pelts, or farm products. Coin was in short supply but there was always an abundance of pelts and farm products, not only for educating the children but also for Peggy's work as a midwife. After helping her mother and aunts in birthing dozens of children over the years, Peg had become well known as a midwife. With no doctor available, she was called out on many a cold night to assist in the birth of a child or handle a medical emergency.

She gladly accepted silver belly beaver pelts after she learned their value after winning the beaver run. She had taken the cumbersome load of pelts with her to York to trade for books and supplies for her new school. The headmistress introduced Peggy to a young furrier from New York, John Jacob Astor. Mr. Astor was impressed with the mountain girl and took her to dine while he was in York on business. Their time together was strictly business as the furrier was a happily married man. Wishing to establish trade with the trappers of Knob Creek, he paid 200 pounds sterling for her pelts and made her an agent to procure tanned hides for his company.

On this warm September day, the students took recess outside, giving her time to grade their slate boards from this morning's exercises. She had opened the window for fresh air.

Suddenly loud voices distracted her attention from the slate boards. She heard her eight-year-old brother David arguing with Peter Miller's son of about the same age.

"She did too!" David insisted.

"Did not!" the Miller boy replied.

"Did too!" David hollered louder.

Peggy reached the boys just as they were about to go after one another with fists flying. Being the oldest girl in a family with nine brothers, she had a great deal of expe-rience breaking up adolescent fisticuffs before they turned into outright brawls. She grabbed each boy by an ear and led them back into the one-room school. She seated them on the bench directly in front of her desk.

"Boys, will you please tell me what this bickering is about?"

They looked at her, then at one another.

"One of you had better speak up." She looked from David to the other boy and back to David. "Say something."

"What does bick-ering mean?"

"It means fighting."

"We weren't fighting. We was just arguing," David said.

"Then what were you arguing about?"

"You and Cherokee,' David said.

"You were arguing about me and my horse?" Peggy shook her head.

"He says you couldn't have whipped all the men that raced in the beaver run. I told him you did and I seen you do it."

"David, you were there but you were just a baby. I doubt that you saw much of the race." She asked the Miller boy, "Why do you find it so hard to believe that I won that race?"

"Cause you're a girl!"

"I see." She walked to the window and called, "Ibby, ring the bell. Recess is over."

As the students came in, Peggy had the girls sit on one side and the boys on the other. They looked around, wondering about the sudden change in seating arrangements.

The teacher looked at the students for a few seconds. "I told you this morning that we would practice cursive writing using quill and ink. Events during recess lead me to believe we need to have a lesson in equality. Who knows what the word equality means?" She wrote the word on the slate board behind her desk.

Rebeckah raised her hand slowly.

"Please tell us, Rebeckah."

"It means we are all equal."

"Who says that we are all created equal?"

"The Bible," Jennett answered.

"It says we're all equal in the Declaration of Independence," Rebeckah added.

"Some people think that because I'm a woman I couldn't have won a race against a bunch of men. What do you girls think of that?" She pointed towards the girls' side of the room. She heard a mixture of comments from both the girls and the boys.

"Why couldn't a girl win a race against men jockeys if she had a good horse to ride?" She waited for an answer that didn't come.

"Students, the horse is the one running—not the jockey. The jockey simply has to ride the horse and let the horse know what to do. A woman can do that, don't you think?"

The girls nodded in agreement, but the boys seemed to be having some difficulty digesting this.

"Will you please tell us how you did it, Miss Mitchell?" Ruth asked.

"I used my brain." Peggy pointed her index finger at her temple.

"You outsmarted the men, didn't you?" Rebeckah said more as a statement than a question.

One of the boys said, "Sounds like you tricked them."

"It wasn't a trick. Our friend Daniel helped me train. His knowledge of the course and his expertise with horses allowed us to develop a well-thought-out plan to win, something the men failed to do."

There was a scratch at the door followed by one low-pitched bark. The children laughed, knowing it was Lulubelle who always joined the class after recess. Peggy motioned to Thomas, who was nearest the door, to let her in. The dog made her customary grand entrance as the students giggled. The children looked forward to her daily visit, but the lesson stopped as she slowly made her way to a pallet in the corner near the schoolmistress's desk. Everyone watched as the aging dog plopped herself down then let out a deep sigh. Here she would sleep until school was dismissed.

"Now, where was I?"

"You were telling us how you won the race," Ibby said.

"I held Cherokee back, staying away from the other horses until I got to the last crossing of the creek. Just as Daniel my trainer had said, several horses balked at crossing the unfamiliar water. Two riders were thrown from their horses into the water. They pushed and shoved one another, trying to keep the other from getting back on their horse. While the ruckus was going on, Cherokee and I quietly crossed the creek far to the left of the melee and started up the hill, crossing the finish line way ahead of the rest."

"See, I told you," David said to the Miller boy.

"That's enough from you, David." She gave him her most severe teacher look, then turned to the rest of the class. "So now you all know how I won the race. Let's discuss other things that a woman can do as well as a man."

Usually quiet and shy, John Rueben raised his hand. "What about farm work?"

"Women do farm work all the time. Your mother took care of the pigs and cows while your father was off fighting the Indians." Peggy bit her lip, wishing she hadn't mentioned John Rueben's deceased father.

"I remember Mother taking us with her to do the farm work," John Rueben said.

His sister Ruth and brother Thomas nodded in agreement. Peggy felt better seeing that the Fain children weren't saddened by her mention of their father.

"What else can women do?"

"Teach school like you," said Ibby.

"Yes, but some people think only men should do the teaching. Have any of you heard of Mary Wollstonecraft?"

No one raised a hand.

Peggy lifted the lid of the drop-leaf teacher's desk, reached in, and pulled out a leather-bound book. She held it up for the class to see. "This book was written by Mary Wollstonecraft the year Grandmother Mitchell died. Miss Wollstonecraft is a teacher who lived in London and wrote a novel titled *Mary*. She later wrote *A Vindication of the Rights of Woman* and *Original Stories from Real Life*. Her writing says that women must be thinking and acting beings in the course of their lives. I have read all her works and agree with her that women are not put on earth just to procreate and be obedient servants to men."

A student raised his hand. When Peggy recognized him, he asked, "What does procreate mean?"

"Having babies," Rebeckah answered then put her hand over her mouth, realizing she should have let the teacher answer.

Peggy gave her sister a stern look. "That is correct, Rebeckah, but in the future, please raise your hand, and I will acknowledge you to give the answer."

"Yes, Teacher," Rebeckah said, her face turning red.

"If there are no more questions on equality, we should get back to this afternoon's lesson in penmanship using quill and ink. Mr. Mitchell prepared these quills from the plumage of pheasants he killed last spring." She handed each student a feather. "You can tell from the bright colors that these birds were cocks. The tail feather of peacocks makes the best quills, but pheasant is the next best."

"Be very gentle," Peggy cautioned as she demonstrated the proper technique of holding a feather quill between the thumb and index finger. "Students, this is the most powerful tool you will ever hold in your hand." She raised her quill up high for the class to see. "Like our founding fathers you can pen a Declaration of Independence, write a book like Mary Wollstonecraft, or send correspondence to a friend in a faraway place."

"Where's the ink?" Ruth asked.

"In good time. Today we will practice with a dry quill to get familiar with the light touch and feel. Remember this is much different than writing with a pencil or on a slate with a piece of chalk. "

Peggy spent the rest of the afternoon working with the students as they made imaginary circles and lines with the pheasant quills.

"Tomorrow we will work with indigo ink, which I will prepare tonight. Wear old clothes as ink spills are sure to happen. Class is dismissed."

It didn't take long for the school house to empty. Ibby, however, lingered after class as always to help her sister straighten up the room for tomorrow.

"Peg, tell me more about Mary Wollstonecraft," Ibby said as she erased the slate board.

"Why don't you read her book?" Peg handed the volume to her sister.

"Thank you." Ibby caressed the leather cover.

When Peg was satisfied the schoolroom was ready for the next day, she and Ibby went home to the one-room log cabin they shared with Rebeckah. Their father had built the girls' room next to the original cabin. He had added a span of roof and floored the space between the cabins to keep his daughters dry and out of the mud when they came into main house. Lulubelle considered this open space between the cabins, which the family called the dog trot, her domain.

After dinner, Peggy carefully filled a small apothecary jar with the indigo ink that Adam had meticulously made from a recipe given to him many years ago by Reverend David Caldwell. Her father had spent days perfecting the ink to the correct viscosity and color for the students' use. Rebeckah watched her sister strain the precious liquid through an old rag to remove any excess sediment.

Rebeckah's job was to carefully open six walnut shells with a jackknife. The shells could not be crushed in a nut cracker as each half of the nut's turtle-like shell was needed to hold a small dab of ink for the students to work with. The delicious meat from the walnuts was Rebeckah's reward for making the crude ink wells.

Ibby curled up in bed, totally engrossed in the book Peg had given her to read. "Where did you get this book? I like what she has to say."

"It was given to me by someone that asked I never reveal where it came from, and I will honor that request."

"Why would it matter, Peggy? It's just a book." Rebeckah crinkled her freckled nose.

"Mary Wollstonecraft's work is much more than a book. Her thoughts on paper should be an inspiration to any woman who reads them. Many men feel threatened by her views, and my benefactor could lose her job for giving me this book. Unfortunately, far too many of our sex cannot read or write and will never know of Wollstonecraft's dreams for womankind."

"I've never heard you speak with such passion," Ibby said.

"I do feel passionate about her work and hope to someday meet her."

"Would you go to London to see her?" a wide-eyed Rebeckah asked.

"I would like that," Peggy answered.

"I wish to go to Europe before I marry and have children." Ibby pulled the covers up to her chin.

"I hope you both have the opportunity to travel and learn more of the world before you marry. With a proper education, there is no limit to what you may achieve. Now, no more talking. Your teacher needs her sleep. "

The next morning, the students were excited about writing with ink. The day went well, but Peggy was concerned about the King children, who hadn't shown up for school. She thought it strange that all the children of both brothers, Lucifer and Jesse, were absent. Peggy decided to ride over to Jesse's home, which was closest, after school to make sure all was well.

Chapter Seven

Tragedy

As she approached the log cabin, Peg saw Jesse and his oldest boy Jonathan with axes in hand trying to remove a large tree stump next to the house. The younger boys were running about playing. They looked well but were dirty and still in the clothes they wore to school the day before.

"How are you today, Mr. King?"

"Fine, I reckon." He held the ax defiantly across his chest with both hands.

"Is Mrs. King ailing?" Peggy tried to act as if she wasn't intimidated by him or his ax.

"She just fine."

"That's good. Can you tell me why the children did not come to school today?"

"They will not be going to your school no more."

"Why?" Peggy tried to block the afternoon sun from her eyes with her hand.

"Don't like what you teaching my young uns."

"You don't like me teaching them to write with a quill?"

"They too young to be learning about making babies."

"What are you talking about, Mr. King?"

"Last night while doing my husbandly duty, my youngest asks if the missus and I were procreating. I asked what that word meant and he said you told him it means making babies."

"That word did come up in class yesterday, and it is a very proper name for describing the method that God has given us to populate this vast new frontier. Which, I might add, that you are doing a very good job of, and I am sure God will reward you for your efforts."

"Thank you, Miss Mitchell. I always try to please God." Jesse stood a little taller with his chest puffed up with pride.

"Is this the reason your brother Lucifer's children stayed home from school today?"

"We discussed it and thought it best for our children to keep them away from your school."

"Because your son learned a new word, a word that you think is vulgar, you are keeping them from going to school? Your children, with the exception of the baby, know how babies are made. They were in your one-room cabin watching that cold night last February when I delivered her. You might recall that your wife was in labor most of the day and would have died had I not been here to assist her, Mr. King."

"That's why we named the baby Margaret—after you, Miss Mitchell—and I will always be thankful to you."

"Keeping your children from school is a fine way of showing it." Peggy's face reddened.

"Nothing personal, you understand. Lucifer and I just don't want our children being told wives shouldn't be obedient to their husbands. Like some writer you were telling the students about."

"Does Mrs. King feel the same way?"

"Don't rightly know as I didn't ask her."

"Then I think I will ask her." Peggy dismounted from Cherokee and led the horse to the hitching post.

"Mrs. King, I need to speak to you." Though she spoke loudly, she didn't get an answer.

"No need to bother her about this," Jesse said.

Peggy pulled the latch string to the door of the cabin and opened it. Inside the cabin was a mess as if there had been a big fight. She heard someone crying and saw a woman on the bed.

"Please just go away, Miss Mitchell. I don't need any more trouble."

Peggy pulled back the bedding to reveal a badly beaten woman she could barely recognize as Mrs. King.

"Who did this to you?" Peggy demanded.

"I fell bringing in the firewood."

"Looks like a herd of buffalo trampled you."

She called to the oldest boy, "Jonathan, bring some fresh well water and be quick about it."

"Do you see what he did to your mother?" she asked as she took the wooden bucket from the terrified boy a couple of minutes later. The child looked at his mother's bruised and bloody body in horror and began to cry.

"Jonathan, fetch my medicine bag, please. It's tied to my horse."

"Jesse didn't mean to hurt me, Miss Mitchell. I know he didn't. He just lost his temper, that's all."

After cleaning the woman's wounds, Peggy directed her attention to the baby beside its mother. Lifting the precious seven-month-old child, Peggy turned her gently from side to side to make sure she wasn't harmed.

She had Jonathan start a fire. "When did you eat last?" she asked him.

"Last night."

"I bet you're hungry?"

"Yes, ma'am."

"Go fetch as many eggs as you can find before it gets any darker."

Peg found a bag of corn meal and started preparing corn bread.

She fed the children, but Mrs. King was hurt so badly she couldn't swallow.

How could a man do this to anyone, much less the mother of his children?

She heard the sound of horses being ridden hard and fast. *Most likely Father and my brothers worried about me.*

"Peg, is everything all right?" The question came from her brother John, who was just two years younger than Peggy.

Seeing Mr. King standing behind John, she said, "Mrs. King had an accident, says she fell carrying in the firewood. Isn't that right, Mr. King?" She glared at him in a way that revealed her anger towards him and let her father and brothers know that everything was not all right.

"That's what happened." Mr. King nodded nervously as Adam and Robert looked at his wife.

They could tell even from the doorway that her injuries were not the result of a fall.

"What can we do to help, Jesse?" Adam asked.

"Nothing I can think of. Miss Mitchell fixed supper and done cleaned up my missus. She'll be just—."

Peggy interrupted Jesse before he could finish. "Father, I will stay tonight with Mrs. King and will try to stop the internal hemorrhaging with hot packs and bellis. I need John to stay—I might need his help. If you and Robert would take Jonathan and his younger brothers home with you and get them ready for school in the morning, that would be a great help. Ibby knows my school plan and can carry on in my absence."

"What do you mean internal hemorrhaging?" Jesse looked at Peggy for an answer.

"She's bleeding from the inside, and I can't see the injury."

"If you can't see, how do you know she's bleeding inside?"

"Anyone that has taken such a severe beating, er, I mean fall—with so much bruising about the stomach would have internal bleeding. I have no idea how bad it is."

"Is she going to die?" Jesse asked.

"I don't know." Peggy shook her head.

"I am so sorry. Please tell me she'll be all right." Jesse started to cry.

Adam placed a hand on Jesse's shoulder. No one said a word as Peggy soaked a rag in the water bucket, wrung out the excess water, and placed it on the woman's forehead.

The man stared at his unconscious wife, who occasionally whimpered a moan. "She can't die. I need her."

Silence fell over the room. Then Adam said, "Jesse, help me harness your team to your wagon. We best get your children on to my place as it's getting late."

The men left Peg tending to her patient.

"You don't need to take the boys, Adam. I can take care of them, I reckon," Jesse said.

"It's all right. Ibby and Rebeckah can look out for them until your wife gets on her feet. We'll bed the boys down in the school house."

"You won't mention this to Reverend Balch, will you?"

"As an elder of the church I must advise him that a member is badly injured and in need of prayer and round-the-clock nursing."

"Please, Adam."

"You and Mrs. King both said she fell carrying wood. Is that what happened?"

"Well, yes."

"Then, what is your concern?"

"Nothing, I guess."

"If she lives through this, Jesse, I would either bring in the firewood myself or have Jonathan fetch it. That's the way we Mitchells do it as gathering wood is a man's job."

Both Robert and John nodded in agreement.

Adam lifted the terrified children up into the wagon as Robert tied Adam's horse to the tail gate.

"Keep an eye on Jesse. I never have trusted him. There's something about him—he won't look you straight in the eye when you talk to him," Robert whispered to John.

Adam called out to John as they pulled away from the barn. "I will send someone to relieve you come daylight."

John and Jesse stood waving at the children, who didn't wave back.

"I'll just sleep in the barn." Jesse sauntered off shaking his head and mumbling to himself.

"How is she?" John asked his sister as he entered the cabin.

"She's not doing well; I'm afraid she's getting a fever."

"Anything I can do?"

"Yes, pray and keep Mr. King away from me."

"Are you afraid of him?"

"No, but I'm afraid of what I might do to him."

"Watch that temper, Sis! Anyway, Jesse says it was an accident."

Peg yanked the cover back. "Does that look like an accident to you?"

John turned away in horror at seeing black and blue marks about the size of a boot across her midsection.

"He stomped her while she was on the ground." Peg held the covers back so her brother could see.

"What should we do?" he asked.

"Not much we can do. They both say it was an accident," Peggy said. "She loves the dumb ox."

"I think he loves her also," John said.

"Why do you say that?"

"He said if she died he would miss her."

"The selfish bastard said 'I need her.' He didn't say anything about missing her." Peggy's voice started to rise.

John shook his head to warn Peggy to calm down, then changed the subject to their brother Robert's courtship and upcoming marriage.

"What do you think of Elizabeth Allison?"

"I think she'll make Robert a good wife, and I enjoy her company."

"I've met a girl I want to court."

"Are you going to tell me who it is?" Peggy carried the baby to the rocker and sat down.

"Mary Ann Barnes."

"Really? How did you meet her?"

"At a party honoring Governor Sevier. James, the governor's son, introduced us. I asked her to dance, and she said yes."

"I thought you didn't like to dance?" Peggy patted the baby as she rocked.

"I don't, but I would have done anything to get to know her better."

Peggy laughed, and for a moment John's story served its purpose of taking her mind away from the savage beating of this frail little woman.

Peg leaned back in the high back rocker and closed her eyes. John sat on the bench of the supper table, laid his head on his arms, and soon fell asleep. They were both awakened by the crying of the baby and a new and ominous tone to Mrs. King's moaning.

"John, you'd better get Mr. King."

John entered the barn quietly. The distraught man sat on a pile of straw in the corner with a crock of corn whisky between his legs, obviously drunk. He cast his teary eyes up at John— the first time Jesse had looked him in the eye. The light of a lamp revealed that one eye appeared to look away from the other. John thought, *No wonder he doesn't look at people when they speak to him.*

"She dead?"

"Not yet, but her time has come. You want to be with her?"

"No, I just want to remember her as she was."

"All right. I'll be in the house if you need me."

When John entered the cabin, Peg was pacing the floor with the crying baby, trying to comfort her by caressing and talking gently. She tilted her head toward the child's mother, then looked at her brother and shook her head.

"Well, she won't have to suffer any more beatings now." Peg spoke through tears.

John nodded.

"Is he coming in?"

"I don't think so."

Peggy shook her head. "That's what I figured. He doesn't want to see what he did."

The sound of a gunshot cracked in the quiet night.

"Sounds like it came from the barn." John hurried out the door.

He saw Jesse on the ground, his betsy rifle lying beside him, with a large hole in his forehead and blood spattered all over the barn.

"Damn him!" John stomped around in circles. "Damn him," he screamed as loud as he could as he walked out of the barn.

Peggy was headed toward the barn with the baby. "What happened?"

"Sis, no need for you to go in there. Nothing you can do."

"Are you sure?"

"Yes, I'm sure."

"You mean these children have no parents? Please, God, tell me this is a bad dream."

A light morning mist was beginning to fall. John said, "Take the baby back in the house. She doesn't need to be wet and cold on top of everything else."

Hoofbeats sounded on the road. A lone rider was approaching.

"It's Father. He and I will take care of everything in the barn. You go inside with the baby."

Adam rode up. "I heard a gunshot."

John took Adam into the barn to show him what Jesse had done.

"Father, what do we do now?"

"I'll ride over to tell his brother Lucifer." He shook his head. "I sure don't like delivering this kind of a message."

"I can keep busy digging graves while you're gone."

"Let's wait. We don't know of the family's wishes. Stay with Peg—she'll need you more. I think it's best we leave the bodies just as they are so Lucifer can see for himself what actually happened. I don't want him to think we had anything to do with it."

While Adam was gone to deliver the news of the couple's deaths, John and Peggy had a chance to talk alone, something that was difficult to do in such a large family.

"Peg, as the oldest of the girls, you're like a mother to the rest of us—all eleven of us. I know you take your responsibility seriously and have little time for frivolity." John leaned forward and put his arms on the table. "I often remember how you comforted me in the spring house during the battle."

Peg started to respond, but John cut her off. "Sis, will you ever marry?"

"If I find the right man, I might."

"What was wrong with Andrew Jackson or John Hammer?"

"Nothing was wrong with either, I suppose. It was not the right time for me to give myself totally to another person. I had to be there for Mother. She couldn't take care of all you by herself after Grandmother Mitchell died. I also abhor violence like we have seen here."

"Was Andrew violent?" John asked.

"Not towards me. He had pent-up anger inside him, though. He would never do harm to me like this. He was gentle with women and children and he loved horses, but if a man crossed him, they had hell to pay." Peggy laughed. "He had quite the temper."

"Like the time he challenged Waightstill Avery to a duel or the bare-knuckled fight he had down in the hollow."

"He would have killed poor Mr. Avery had Reverend Doak and I not intervened."

"I know Robert was Andrew's second as Judge McNairy refused to get involved. Robert and William were there and witnessed everything. What do you mean you intervened? "

"When William came home and told us that Andrew had challenged Mr. Avery to a duel on the hill south of town, I rode into Jonesborough to persuade him to drop the matter."

"Was this after you spurned his marriage proposal?"

"Yes. You see, according to Judge McNairy, Mr. Avery kept ridiculing Andrew about my storming out of the court-house the day he proposed. Mr. Avery passed me on Main Street and saw how upset I was. Apparently he chided Andrew constantly about it. Then when Avery questioned Andrew's legal acumen, Andrew was so rankled that he challenged him to a duel."

"I never knew that."

"It's the first time I ever told anyone. Had I not tried to stop him, I would have felt responsible for whatever happened."

"What did you do?"

"I saddled Cherokee, and William got on his horse. We rode hard and caught up with Andrew and Robert on their way to the hill. I informed Andrew that if Mr. Avery or Robert were hurt in his silly altercation, he would have hell to pay. I also reminded him that Mr. Avery was the most respected lawyer on both sides of the mountains and should he be harmed Andrew's career in the legal profession would come to an end."

"Well, it worked apparently. Mother wouldn't let me go—said I was too young. She tried to stop you and William as I remember."

"I don't know that Andrew took heed to my warning as much as Reverend Doak's chastising and threat to out him from church."

"William and Robert both said Andrew and Waightstill fired their shots in the air, then shook hands and the feud was over," John said. "Wasn't that silly?"

"Not if you understand a man like Andrew. He was a young man with nothing but a fine horse, no family. What people thought of him mattered more than anything. Everyone knew and respected the honorable Mr. Avery, and Andrew was quite jealous of that. Once he challenged Avery to the duel, he wouldn't call it off for fear of being called a coward. He earned more respect by not hurting Mr. Avery."

John pondered what she said for some time, watching her tender way with the King baby, and then asked her a question that had been lingering in his mind for a good while. "Sis, do you wish to have children?"

"When I'm not teaching a classroom full of children, I have James and Hezekiah who are like my own. I have the tannery, the still, and the horses to take care of. There's no time left for childbearing." She took a deep breath. "Tell me how you plan to win the Barnes girl over with all the men who are courting her."

"With the Mitchell charm, of course!" John's face lit with the big grin Peggy so admired.

"Just don't be too confident. I hear a matrimonial bond for her has already been issued to a suitor by your friend the county registrar."

"James didn't tell me about that." John looked perplexed.

"Would you go milk the cow that's in the corral next to the barn? She appears to be fresh." Peg laid the baby down beside its mother for what would be the last time. "Without her mother's milk, we'd best get her accustomed to cow's milk as soon as we can."

"Will she grow up the same without her mother to nurse?" John asked.

"Look at your brother Robert. He lost his mother just three days after birth. I doubt that he ever tasted his mother's milk, and he did just fine."

"I often forget that Robert had a different mother from the rest of us," John said on his way out to milk the cow.

As he was returning to the house, Lucifer King and Adam rode up the trail.

Seeing John with the milk pail, Lucifer sneered and asked, "You be taking a dead man's milk?"

"Yes, seeing that Mrs. King is dead, Peggy will be trying to get the baby to accept cow's milk."

"Peggy here too?" Lucifer looked agitated.

Adam thought agitation was to be expected of a man who had just lost a brother and sister-in-law.

"She found Mrs. King in a bad way. When she didn't come home, the boys and I came looking for Peg. She and John did everything they could to save Mrs. King. They stayed up all night tending to her and the baby."

"Tell her how much my family appreciates her efforts. Let's see my brother first."

"This way." Adam pointed toward the barn. "John, better get that milk to Peg before it clabbers."

Once Lucifer saw the undisturbed ground around his brother, he realized what happened.

"He did this because his woman died?"

"I think you will better understand when you see her body."

Adam put an arm on his shoulder as they entered the house.

Upon seeing the disarray inside the cabin, Lucifer said, "What kind of woman leaves her home looking like this?"

"One that is beaten to death by her husband." Peggy jerked back the covers to expose the body.

"Jesse did that?" Lucifer asked.

"Sure looks that way," Adam answered.

"I knew there was trouble brewing. Jesse just couldn't leave that whisky alone. Never dreamed it would come to this." Lucifer stood gazing down at his dead sister-in-law, shaking his head.

"We're here to help. Just tell us what you would like us to do first," Adam said.

"I don't want anyone else to see their bodies. Would you help me to dig one grave and put them both in it?"

The next day, Reverend Balch held a graveside service. It was a sad occasion around the Knob Creek Community. Three boys and their baby sister were now orphans.

Lucifer approached the Mitchells as the family was about to leave the King farm.

"I appreciate all you did for my brother and his wife." He looked up at Adam and his boys on horseback.

Turning his attention to Peggy, he removed his dusty hat and turned it nervously in his hand. "Miss Mitchell, my brother has accumulated a good many beaver pelts in the barn, and with the additional mouths to feed, I could sure use some extra money."

"Certainly, just bring them with you when you bring the children to school next week."

"I wasn't planning on our children going to your school no more."

"Is that so?" Peggy held the reins of the team tightly in her hand. She looked at the orphaned children of the Kings and bit her lower lip to keep from crying.

"Nothing personal, you understand—just not schooling the children no more."

"Then I suggest you find another fur broker to market your pelts. Nothing personal, you understand, Mr. King. But if you don't trust me to teach your children, we shouldn't be conducting business. And please don't bother to come for me when your missus is ready to give birth to her next baby." Peggy popped the whip, and the horses pulling the wagon moved forward. Her father and older brothers followed on horseback.

"What was all that about?" her mother asked.

"Just business, Mother."

The next week, Lucifer King's children and his three nephews were waiting at the schoolhouse with a load of fine quality beaver and otter pelts when she arrived.

Chapter Eight

Statehood

The storefronts on Main Street displayed decorations of red, white, and blue. Flag bunting of the same colors adorned the entrances of many homes. Long banners of stars and stripes announcing statehood were stretched across Main Street on both the east and west ends of Jonesborough. The oldest town in the newest state was in the midst of celebrating its statehood as well as the twentieth anniversary of the nation's independence.

The young Mitchell boys—Samuel, James, and David—sat wide-eyed in the back of the bouncing wagon. Peggy drove and Rebeckah held on tight to the seat of the buckboard with both hands as they crossed the deep ruts cut in the street by the heavy freight wagons on their way west to Knoxville and Nashville.

The only inn had a sign out that read No beds to let. Visitors were paying to sleep in barns and chicken coops or camping on the banks of Little Limestone Creek.

Proud Tennesseans came from all corners of the mountain region to partake in the Fourth of July festivities that included horse races, special church services, parties, and the opportunity to hear their hometown hero, Governor John Sevier, speak.

Peggy and Rebeckah brought their little brothers with them to pick up provisions. Ibby and Jennett stayed at home with their ailing mother and baby brother Hezekiah.

"Good morning, Peg, Becka." Mr. Deaderick nodded a welcome at the girls and then waved to the Mitchell boys, who sat down on the inside bench at the front of his general store.

David Bowles

"Can I give the boys a piece of rock candy?" The merchant already had his hand inside the pocket of his shop apron where he kept the sweet treats.

"That's why they're here, Mr. Deaderick. You've spoiled them and every child in the county with your candy."

He gave each a choice of a candy from his hand, called each boy by name, and then offered a piece of candy to Rebeckah, who eagerly accepted while Peggy graciously declined.

"I want you ladies to take a look at the large selection of fine fabrics just arrived from Philadelphia. Look at this imported black satin. It would make you a fine dress to wear when you go to York to trade your pelts." The merchant proudly rolled out a yard of the shiny fabric and invited them to feel it.

"I will be going to Philadelphia, and I'm sure I can buy ready-made gowns there of the same cloth." Peggy stroked the elegant fabric with the palm of her hand. "I do need a large bolt of linsey-woolsey for work clothes."

Mr. Deaderick had frowned when Peggy mentioned ready-made gowns, but he replaced the frown with a forced smile as he showed her the serviceable material. "It is available in blue or grey. Which do you prefer?"

"Blue is good." Peggy nodded approval.

"I have the supplies ready that your brother Adam ordered yesterday when he delivered the apple brandy. My son David will load your order while I get your linsey-woolsey."

Peggy looked around to make sure no one else was listening. "Is Dr. Chester in?"

"Yes, he's upstairs in his office that used to be my living quarters. Just go on up. I know he looks forward to finally meeting you."

Peggy said, "Rebeckah, stay here and keep your brothers in line."

She knocked lightly on the office door of the new physician who had set up shop above Deaderick's Dry Goods Store.

124

"Come in," Dr. Chester called out as he came toward the door of the cramped quarters of his temporary office.

Peggy opened the door carefully to a cluttered room full of boxes.

"May I help you?" Dr. Chester asked.

"I'm Peggy Mitchell. I wanted to meet you and welcome you to Jonesborough." Extending her gloved right hand to the doctor, she tried to keep her hoop dress from brushing against the dusty boxes stacked in the small room.

"I'm so glad to finally meet you, Miss Mitchell. Please excuse this mess. I have heard many good things about you."

Dr. Chester shook Peg's hand with enough vigor to convince her that he was sincerely glad to make her acquaintance.

"Is that so?" Peggy looked approvingly at the large array of surgical tools on the table next to his desk—tools that she had read about but had never had the opportunity to see. *Now we finally have a real doctor, and I like him.*

"You have quite a reputation for nursing the sick and injured back to health."

"I try but sometimes I fail, as with Mrs. King."

"I heard of the unfortunate incident at their farm. You did all you could for the poor woman. Medicine is a difficult profession, and there is so much we do not know about the human anatomy. Tell me, Miss Mitchell, where did you learn about medicine?"

"From *Beecham's Family Physician*."

"So you taught yourself using *Beecham's*." Dr. Chester nodded. "I'm impressed."

"Thank you for the compliment, Doctor Chester, but I need your medical advice."

"Are you ill?"

"Not I, but my Mother," Peggy answered.

"What are her symptoms?"

"She hasn't been herself for some time. Sleeps most of the day and falls asleep at the table board nearly every night."

"Sounds like a case of melancholia to me, but I would need to examine her to make a diagnosis." Dr. Chester sat down at his small walnut desk, turning his chair to face Peggy and pointing to a three-legged stool for her to sit.

Peggy shook her head." I don't know if she would allow that. Since we moved to Washington County, only Grandmother Mitchell or I have ministered to her health. The last physician to examine her was Dr. Caldwell when we still lived in Guilford Courthouse. He helped Mother in the birth of Jennett some thirteen years ago."

"Can you bring your mother in?" Dr. Chester asked.

"She won't leave the house except to go to church, which is just a stone's throw from our home." Peggy sighed. "She hasn't been to town in a long time. "

"What if I came to visit, which I had already planned to do to seek your father's advice on the construction of the inn? You could suggest to her that as I was already there and she hasn't had a medical examination in thirteen years that she allow me to examine her in your presence."

"That may work."

"Good. I'll be at your farm before dark."

"Thank you. Please come hungry and join us for supper."

"I'd like that." Dr. Chester rose and opened the door.

Mr. Deaderick met her at the bottom of the stairs. "Miss Mitchell, may I speak to you for a minute? You're paying the trappers a higher price for pelts than I can offer so you must be getting better prices than I am. May I ask what price you are getting for beaver pelts in Philadelphia? "

"You may ask, but I cannot tell you." Though she intended her response to be matter-of-fact, she saw Mr. Deaderick bristle and realized she had offended this man who was a dear friend of the family and the largest buyer of their farm products. "It's just that I've never sold any pelts in Philadelphia, therefore I have no idea what price I'll get until the transaction is complete. I sell by the lot and not the piece. If you would like me to make an offer for your furs, I am prepared to pay you in new federal coinage."

"Please make me an offer."

Peggy looked over at her brothers, who were weary of waiting on their sister and were antagonizing Rebeckah with their boyish antics. "I must attend to other matters at the moment, but I'll come back tomorrow without these hooligans to grade your inventory and make you an offer." She glared at the boys.

"That will be good of you." Mr. Deaderick chuckled at the sight of Peggy pulling David and Samuel toward the wagon by their ear, followed by James. *One tough school-teacher, that Miss Mitchell.*

The trip would not be complete until the boys and Rebeckah combed the town for dead soldiers. While they gathered crocks, Peggy went to the courthouse to pick up the mail and the Knoxville Gazette. The Gazette's owner, George Raulston, delivered mail to the courthouse free for anyone who subscribed to his newspaper.

Peggy thought, *I'll be glad when the Post Office takes over the mail delivery at the end of the month.* John Waddell, the son-in-law of Governor John Sevier, had been selected the first Postmaster of Jonesborough, and mail would be available at his home until a post office was built.

She shuffled through the stack of newspapers and letters and saw a small, official-looking envelope addressed to her father. The yellowed envelope was stained and wrinkled and sealed with a bright red wax on the flap with the initials J.H. embossed boldly in the center of the seal. The outer circle of the seal could not be read. It appeared that when the writer pressed his official seal to the wax it slipped, blurring the small letters. It had a Martinsville, North Carolina postmark dated March 15, 1796. Peggy wondered what the letter could be about as she headed toward Knob Creek.

As the wagon turned down the lane toward the family's log house, Rebeckah pointed out a strange-looking horse tied to the hitching post. "Looks like we have company for dinner."

"That strange-looking horse is the mule of soon-to-be Reverend Witherspoon." Peggy gave the reins a shake, and the horses picked up their pace.

"How does he just one day become a reverend?" Rebeckah asked.

"When Jimmy and John Doak graduate next month from Washington College, they will both be trained as ministers of the Presbyterian faith." Peggy shook her head, thinking about the shy and awkward boy she had tutored at Samuel and Esther Doak's school so long ago. Now he was going to be preaching the Gospel. She was proud of him.

"Looks like we're going to have two guests for supper tonight. Rebeckah, can you get things started? I have business to attend to with our new preacher."

"You always have business to tend." Rebeckah folded her arms in front of her.

"Be nice to me, and I'll take you to Philadelphia," Peggy whispered.

"Really! Do you mean it?"

"Do you mean what?" David asked.

"We'll talk more when there are six less ears listening." Peggy leaned toward Rebeckah.

Soon-to-be six-year-old James counted by twos the ears of his brothers. "They only have four ears—I just counted them."

"What about you?" The teacher in Peggy said to her little brother.

"Oh!" James put his hands over his own ears, and his face reddened.

His siblings had a good laugh at his expense.

Lulubelle came out from the dog run to greet them, her tail wagging. James and David wandered off toward the creek to play with the dog.

Adam, Jr. and Jimmy Witherspoon came out to help carry in the provisions.

"Adam, you and Samuel carry in and store the goods. Maybe the reverend would be kind enough to help me put up the team." Peggy smiled at Jimmy.

"I would be glad to, Miss Mitchell." Jimmy said.

Peggy curried one of the horses while he brushed the other.

"Two fine horses you have, Miss Peggy."

"Jimmy, you can call me Peg. We are no longer in school, and church is not in session."

"Reverend Doak says a minister must be respectful to his flock if he wants to earn their respect."

"Well, I'm not a sheep in someone's flock. So let's agree—when it's just you and me, we'll call each other Peg and Jimmy. Around others we can be more formal."

"That's fine with me, Miss Mit—Peg."

"See—you can do it, Jimmy."

He took the heavy load of tack from Peggy's arms, carefully hanging each piece on the wooden pegs protruding from the wall of the tack room. Peggy watched him with a new admiration. He seemed so sure of himself with her, unlike the Jimmy she knew in school.

"I want to show you something." Peg moved toward the loafing pen behind the barn.

Jimmy placed one foot on the lower rail and leaned his lanky arms on the top rail for a better view. "Wow! That's the best-looking horse I ever saw."

"Since when did you become an authority on horse-flesh?"

"Just because I don't have a fancy horse or a pretty woman doesn't mean I don't appreciate looking at them." He smiled at Peggy.

"Listen to you. Is this the bashful Jimmy I went to school with?"

The chestnut stallion let out a loud whinny, shaking its head and revealing a long, shiny mane. The horse, which had three white stocking feet and a white star on its forehead just between the eyes, pranced about as if recognizing he was being admired.

"I'm glad you like Star—for the last four years I've been training him to be your steed as you do God's work."

"I cannot accept such a gift from you, Peg."

"Then I'll let you earn him."

Jimmy turned his gaze from Star to Peg. "How? I would do anything for a horse like Star."

"I need you to accompany Rebeckah and me to Philadelphia."

"It would be an honor to escort two of the prettiest girls in Washington County to Philadelphia. When do you plan to leave?"

"I need a few weeks to prepare for the journey. When could you get away?"

"Well, that's what brings me to Knob Creek. I'll be graduating on the fifteenth of August, and I wanted to invite you and your family to attend the first graduation ceremony of Washington College. As you know, John Doak will be the other graduate. His mother and Reverend Doak are planning a big shindig on the grounds and are inviting everyone to attend."

Peggy put a hand on his arm. "I am so proud of you and honored by your invitation. I wouldn't miss your graduation for anything."

"Thank you."

"We'll need to leave at the crack of dawn the next day. Rebeckah and I must be back in time for the start of the school year. That will give us a month to travel and tend to business in the capital city. John and William will be making the trip as well." Peg counted out on her fingers the people she needed for the wagon train. "I'd like to have at least two more trustworthy men — we'll be transporting three wagons of furs. Would Willie and James be interested in going with us? I'll pay them well."

"I'll talk to them." He knew his brothers needed work.

Peggy looked toward the road at the sound of a lone rider. "I must greet Dr. Chester. We'll talk more about this later, Jimmy."

"I'm anxious to hear more. I've always wanted to see Philadelphia."

Dr. Chester dismounted, and Jimmy took the reins of his horse and tied it to the hitching post next to his mule.

Peggy said, "I see you found Knob Creek, Doctor. Reverend Witherspoon, have you met Dr. Chester? He recently set up his medical practice in Jonesborough."

"No, I haven't had the privilege." He extended his hand. "But I understand you've been appointed a trustee of Washington College, Dr. Chester."

"That's right, Witherspoon, and I'm sure we'll be seeing a lot of each other at the college when the fall semester starts." He pumped Jimmy's hand with his right hand and placed his left hand on Jimmy's shoulder.

"Yes, I plan to assist Reverend Doak and Sister Esther in teaching until I can obtain gainful employment elsewhere."

"From what Reverend Doak tells me, it won't take long for a church to employ your God-given talents," Dr. Chester said.

"Thank you, sir, for your words of encouragement."

"Come, Doctor and Reverend, let's go in the house. I want to introduce Dr. Chester to the rest of the family." Peg gestured toward the door.

The Mitchells were excited to have guests. When Rebeckah first told her father that Dr. Chester was coming for dinner, Adam went to his smokehouse and picked one of his best hams, one marked with the letter L, indicating that it had come from the pig's left hindquarter. Family legend had been passed down for generations that the ham from the left hindquarter was more succulent than from the other side as most pigs tended to scratch with their right leg.

Later, after they had eaten, Dr. Chester pushed his chair back from the table board. "One of the best meals I've had in sometime." He smiled and nodded at Rebeckah and Ibby, who had prepared and served the meal.

After dinner while there was still sufficient light, Adam showed the doctor Hebron Church and School that he and the men of Knob Creek had built with broadax-cut timber from the nearby forest. Adam explained that a log structure was all that the congregation could afford to build.

"The town commissioners recently decided that all new structures on Main Street would be built of either brick or finished planking. The Chester Inn will be the first building to be built on Main Street since that decision was made." Dr. Chester shrugged his shoulders.

"If you're considering brick for a three-story building, there are only two qualified brick masons in the county. It would take them many years to complete a project of this size, even if you could find that much kiln-dried brick in the area. Hauling brick from Baltimore or Philadelphia would be more work than the actual building of your inn." Adam shook his head as they walked back to the cabin.

Dr. Chester pulled the architect's plans from his case and spread them out on one end of the table board. "Once the inn is completed, I'll establish my medical office and apothecary shop on the first floor facing Main Street. The rooms to let will be on the second level and my living quarters on the top floor."

"For your situation, your only option is planking board."

Dr. Chester looked at Adam. "Where could I find the materials?"

"In these quantities, you'll need to get them out of Philadelphia. It would take the Little Limestone Mill a year just to finish your chestnut framing timbers."

"How could I get the materials shipped out of Philadelphia without it costing a fortune?" Dr. Chester asked with a frown.

"You need to ask my daughter Peggy about that."

"Ask me about what?" Peggy looked up from wiping the other end of the table board.

"I told the doctor you might have a way to get his materials for the inn from Philadelphia to Jonesborough."

Adam winked at her, and she grinned to show she understood.

"I might be able to help you. We can discuss it tomorrow when I come to town." Peg nodded toward her mother, who appeared to be asleep at the table.

Peggy motioned for Dr. Chester to move next to Elizabeth. Peggy sat down next to her and pulled Elizabeth's shawl up over her shoulders. The physician pulled out his pocket watch, found her pulse, and took a reading. Then he felt her face with his palm, shaking his head to indicate there was no fever. Reverend Witherspoon and the family watched as the doctor gave Elizabeth a once-over. He spent considerable time looking at the color of her skin and fingernails.

"Mrs. Mitchell, can you hear me?" The doctor spoke softly.

Her eyes slightly fluttered, and she nodded. She allowed him to look in her mouth, nose, and ears. Then, to everyone's amazement, she didn't resist when Dr. Chester raised her eyelids to examine her pupils.

"Let's put her in bed if we can, Peggy." The doctor on one side and Peg on the other gently raised Elizabeth from the bench.

Once the exam was complete, the doctor and Peggy returned to the table board where the family and Jimmy anxiously waited.

"She's resting well. I think the fact that she allowed me to examine her is an indication that she's aware something is wrong with her. Her heart sounds strong. Her color is pallid, most likely from not getting enough sunlight. Her nails and pupils, however, have good color, an indication that she has good blood flow. She is losing muscle mass, most likely from inactivity and natural maturation."

"What's causing this, Dr. Chester?" Adam asked. "She's a very healthy woman of fifty plus years. She's given birth to twelve perfectly healthy children, all of whom have survived to adulthood except one that was killed by lightning."

Peggy asked, "Why does she sleep so much?"

"My guess is she has nothing to do anymore, no reason to stay awake. I've watched this family closely tonight. You, Adam, and all your children show Elizabeth great respect, which she deserves. Your daughters have assumed all the duties from her of running the household. When I first saw Peggy come into town with your three boys, I assumed they were hers. Adam, I think Elizabeth needs her job back as the woman of this household."

The family sat in total silence for some time, slowly taking in what the doctor had said.

Peggy looked at Dr. Chester with her brow furrowed. "Mother needs something to do? That's all that's wrong with her?"

The doctor nodded. "That is my professional opinion. I don't wish to put her on any medications until the Mitchell family makes some adjustments. Let's see how she does."

"Please tell me what to do." Adam leaned toward the doctor.

"Tell her how much you miss her cooking. Ask her to fix breakfast just for you in the morning, and then tell her how good it was. Get her out of bed and this house and into the sunlight every day. Within a few weeks, I think you'll see some improvement."

After the guests left, Peggy gave her father his newspapers and mail while her sisters sat quietly talking with each other.

He looked at the mail and shook his head. "It will have to wait; my eyes are just too tired to read it now."

Peggy said, "I think you need to look at this letter." She pointed out the mysterious yellow envelope she had brought home from the courthouse.

Adam picked up the letter. "It's been more than three months since it was mailed—another day certainly won't make any difference."

"Father, it's from Martinsville. It could be news from your Uncle Adam's family."

"Will you read it to me?"

"Of course I will." Peggy opened the envelope without destroying the wax seal and quickly perused the letter. "It's from a John Hamilton. He starts by offering belated condolences on the loss of Grandmother Mitchell. Mentions her deathbed request that she sent to Reverend David Caldwell and his wife Rachel, how he cried when they read her letter to him."

I wonder what she said in that letter. Peggy didn't voice her thought to her father.

Adam sat waiting for Peggy to continue.

"Father, he writes that Lieutenant Armstrong who delivered Grandmother Mitchell's letter went with him to the farm, sat on the porch of the old house, visited the spring house, and drank from its spring." Peg clutched the letter to her bosom and thought of the day that the handsome soldier on his magnificent government-issued horse came to their corn field on the road to Jonesborough.

Adam made an impatient movement. "Peggy, please tell me what the letter is about."

"I'm sorry. I was just remembering that day when Lieutenant Armstrong came to see me—I mean us." Peggy skimmed more of the letter. "The lieutenant is now the assistant to Secretary of War Henry Knox, and he writes often inquiring about the 107 acres adjacent to the Guilford Courthouse. Lieutenant Armstrong is concerned that the Revolutionary War soldiers buried there not be disturbed. John Hamilton says he goes regularly to the corn field below the house and takes flowers which he lays on the large mounds of dirt of the mass graves." She paused and read silently for a few seconds.

"Go on," her father said.

Peggy read from the letter. "I frequently meet there a soldier's widow, a young person, a mother or father who comes to Martinsville just to see the ground that their loved one gave their life for. I have met survivors of the Battle for Guilford Courthouse, many with limbs missing or badly disfigured from their battle wounds. This morning, the fifteenth day of March 1796, was the fifteenth anniversary of that great battle. As I crested the hill above the battlefield, I looked down on a dozen or more wagons and at least twenty riders on horseback milling about the remains of your home.

These poor souls came all the way from Virginia, Delaware, and South Carolina to commemorate this date in history. It was as if they were on a religious pilgrimage to a holy shrine to remember their loved ones or patriot comrades that lay in those overgrown cornfields.

"On a previous occasion, there was an elderly man with a long white beard and moustache neatly attired sitting on the stone upping block in front of what used to be your home. I sat with him a good while as he told me about his only son that died in the battle. He asked me to pray with him for his son. I closed my eyes and said a prayer, not knowing which side he fought for. It did not matter.

"When I opened my eyes I was alone. The old man was gone—just vanished. I heard no horse or buggy leave and could find no sign of footprints in the soft soil. Others tell me of seeing a man of his description with an old woman late at night searching the fields of the battle, wailing and calling for their son.

"I often see your mother in my dreams admonishing me to never let the graves of the brave soldiers be disturbed. I cannot sleep worrying of the huge responsibility I inherited when I bought your property. I wish to get out from under the burden that this property has bestowed on me. When I purchased your mother's farm, I never once thought of the ramifications of being the caretaker of such sacred ground. I wish to deed back to you the 107 acres which I bought in 1784. I ask for nothing in return except that you take responsibility for your mother's wishes regarding said property.

"I hope to hear from you by return mail. Signed, sincerely, your friend John Hamilton."

No one said a word as Peggy folded the pages and handed them to her father.

After a long silence, Peg asked, "What are you going to do, Father?"

"I don't know, except for now I will say my prayers as always and go to sleep, for I am tired. In the morning, with your mother present, we can discuss it as a family." He rose from the table as if it hurt to get up and motioned to his daughters that it was time for them to retire to their cabin on the other side of the open dog trot.

"Do you think Mother and Father will allow me to go?" Rebeckah looked at her sisters as she sat on the bed combing the long strands of her raven hair.

"Go where?" Ibby asked as she pulled back the bedding.

"Peggy is going to take me to Philadelphia with her."

Ibby looked at Peg with a pained expression on her face. "What about me?"

"If it goes well with Becka, then next year I will take you. First Mother and Father must agree to allow your sister to make the journey." Peggy pulled the covers up to her shoulders.

"That's not fair," Ibby said. "I'm older. I should get to go first."

Peggy sighed. "Yes, you're older, and because you're older, you need to be the one to stay and help Mother. Besides, if we have any problems and don't get back in time, you can get school started."

"But—"

"Ibby," Peggy said in her schoolteacher voice. "Please snuff the candle and let's get some sleep."

Adam's daughters were awakened the next morning by the sound of the roosters crowing and their father's excited voice. "Trapper John is alive and well and living in New Garden with a Quaker woman."

The girls hurriedly scrambled out of bed and through the dog trot, almost tripping over Lulubelle on the way to the main cabin. They found their mother sitting at the table board, her hand over her mouth, crying with joy, as their father pranced around the room with Mr. Hamilton's letter in his hand. The girls had not seen their father so excited since the birth of Hezekiah.

After the girls had taken their places at the table, Adam smiled at them and said, "Thank you, God, for saving our Trapper John. Thank you; thank you!"

"How do you know Trapper John is alive?" Peg asked.

"John Hamilton's letter."

Peg looked at her father as if he had partaken of too much of the family recipe. "I read his letter and found no mention of Trapper John."

"You missed it, my dear daughter. Mr. Hamilton wrote the word *over* in the right hand lower corner of the last page of his letter and wrote a P.S. on the back."

Adam held the letter up for the girls to see the writing on the back of the page.

"Trapper John can't read or write, so he probably approached Hamilton after he heard that Hamilton was going to write me about the farm. The letter was already finished so Hamilton must have diluted whatever ink he had left with water in order to complete the task." He pointed to the letter. "The script is so faint it's difficult to see in daylight and impossible to see in the dark."

"That explains the blurred seal," Peggy exclaimed. "He had to reseal the letter!"

Elizabeth sniffed and said, "I'm so happy."

The girls and their younger brothers looked at their mother in disbelief to see her smiling and hear her utter the first words they had heard her say in some time.

"I fixed your father some breakfast. What can I fix for you children?"

Rebeckah started to say that she would fix breakfast. Peg put a firm hand on her arm and shook her head. Then she turned to Elizabeth. "We would love to have you cook breakfast for us, Mother."

Robert, John, and William had come in from their cabin and were getting brought up to date on the letter from Martinsville and the news that Trapper John was alive.

"Who is Trapper John?" asked eight-year-old David.

"He was a good friend to the Mitchells," Adam said. "He helped with the farm work after my first wife Jennett died. He was with me during the battle, then he had just disappeared in front of me when I was taken captive by the British."

"That's my name," Jennett said.

"That's right. Your mother chose to name you after Jennett to keep her name alive in this family." Adam held up the Mitchell family Bible for Jennett to see. He pointed out at the very top of the page *Adam & Jennett married April 5, 1766,* then the third entry—her death on February 20, 1767.

Rebeckah said "That's the year Robert was born." She put her hand over her mouth as if regretting her words.

"That's correct," Elizabeth said. "Robert was just three days old when his mother died. I never knew her, but God sent me to her red-headed little baby. Then all of you came along to be his brothers and sisters. So you, Jennett, I named in her honor. Whenever anyone asks you about your name, tell them proudly that you were named for your father's first wife."

The family continued to discuss the letter as Elizabeth cooked a big breakfast for her family.

"What do you plan to do about Mr. Hamilton's request?" Robert asked his father.

"I don't know. I must think about it and ask God for his guidance. When I make a decision, I'll let you know."

Robert nodded and looked around the table. Then a huge grin spread across his face. "I have an announcement to make. Elizabeth Allison and I are to be wed on October fourth."

William, John, and Adam let out a yell. The children screamed with delight. Everyone smiled and talked excitedly except Peggy. She began to worry about making it to Philadelphia and back before the wedding. The distance was almost six hundred miles, and according to those that had made the trip, it took three weeks if the weather was good and there were no major difficulties.

Robert noticed Peggy wasn't joining in the celebration of his announcement. "Peggy, aren't you excited for me?"

"Yes, I'm happy that you are marrying a wonderful woman like Elizabeth. But I am concerned about those of us that are going to Philadelphia being back in time for your wedding, that's all."

"Who is going with you other than William and John?" Robert asked.

"I hope to take Rebeckah. It would be an opportunity to broaden her horizons if Mother and Father approve."

Elizabeth looked at her daughters. "What about Ibby?"

"Ibby and I discussed her going but thought you might need her to help with the children."

"Jennett and I can manage just fine." Elizabeth put an arm around the thirteen-year-old, who nodded in agreement with her mother.

"That's good. Ibby, Becka, John, William, and I make five of the family going." Peg said. *It will be a small wedding without us if we don't get back in time.*

The family praised their mother for a wonderful breakfast and really meant it.

"You better like my cooking—it's just going to be Jennett and me here to cook for you while Peg, Ibby, and Rebeckah are away."

Peggy reminded John to get Deaderick's order loaded and meet her at the store. "If all goes well, we'll have a bunch of furs to load." She had a great deal to do to prepare for the trip and still needed to find at least two more riders.

She rode Star into town to have Daniel check the hooves and shoes. She didn't want any lame horses on the road to Philadelphia.

"I hear you're going to the big city." Daniel looked at Star's hooves.

"How do you know that?" Peg said.

"The Smith boys were in with Jimmy yesterday. They told me they all were going with you."

"That's good to hear as I hadn't heard for sure that they could."

Daniel reached for another hoof to check. "When you leaving?"

"Leaving the morning after Jimmy's graduation."

Daniel sighed. "I wish I could go with you."

"What's keeping you? You're not getting any younger."

"That's for sure."

"Business is going to slow down as soon as this celebration is over." Peg moved around to stand in front of Daniel.

He nodded. "That's true."

"I'll pay you well." Peggy cocked her head trying to determine if Daniel was serious about going.

"I know you would."

"Just think about it. I'll be back for Jimmy's horse after I take care of my business at Deaderick's."

"You gave Jimmy this beautiful stallion?"

"No, he is riding with me to Philadelphia for it."

"For a horse like this, I'd ride with you anywhere you said."

"I don't know if I could ever find another horse like Star, but I'll buy you any horse you want in Philadelphia if you'll go with us."

Daniel quit looking at the horse's hooves and looked at Peggy. "You're serious about me going with you, ain't you?"

"Yes, I am. With you along, I know if something happens to a wagon or one of the horses, you can take care of it. That's one less thing for me to worry about on the road."

"When did you say **we** leave?"

"The morning of the sixteenth of August, but for safety concerns I don't want it talked about." Peggy put a finger to her lips. "Talk to you more about it later—wagon master."

Daniel opened his mouth, but Peggy was already headed out the stable door on the way to Deaderick's. When she entered the store, a tiny bell jingled to announce her arrival.

"I'm here to grade your pelts, Mr. Deaderick."

"That's good, Peggy. They're out back in the shed." He led Peggy outside. "Don't allow those things in my store— that smell would run my customers off for sure."

"Whew, they do smell awful. Let's get that door open wide." Peg waved her handkerchief as if it would make the smell go away.

She set about sorting the pelts by type—a wooly buffalo; many deer hides; bear skins of several sizes; and beaver, otter, muskrat, and coon skins. In just a few minutes, she deftly graded the skins by size and quality. "I'll give you $200.00 for the lot."

"I can get twice that in York."

"You're not in York, Mr. Deaderick. Take it or leave it."

"Oh, all right." Mr. Deaderick raised his arms and shook his head as a sign of surrender. "You drive a hard bargain."

"You know I've given you a fair price—better than those brokers you've been dealing with." She counted the coin out as her brother John arrived with the wagon.

"John, get Mr. Deaderick's feathers and beeswax off the wagon, then load these pelts while I talk to Dr. Chester if he's in."

"I'm sure he is—saw him earlier," Mr. Deaderick said.

Peggy went upstairs and knocked on the door. "Dr. Chester, it's Peggy Mitchell."

"I've been expecting you. Do come in." Dr. Chester stood pouring liquid into small apothecary jars. "I sure enjoyed your family and the dinner your sisters fixed last night."

"My father enjoyed your company, and I appreciate your examining Mother."

Peggy opened her small clutch purse. "What do I owe you for your house call?"

"Not a thing." He motioned for her to put her purse away. "I want to hear how you can help me get my building materials from Philadelphia to Jonesborough." He filled the last bottle of medicine and wiped his hands on his apron.

"I'll be taking three wagons of furs and pelts to Philadelphia, leaving on the sixteenth of August. We'll be coming back empty except for a few supplies and purchases I make for the school and family. We could bring back to you whatever the wagons could carry."

"When will you return?"

"We must be back by no later than October fourth for Robert's wedding."

The doctor invited Peggy to sit to continue the conversation. At the end of the negotiations, Peg agreed to haul back three wagonloads of building materials from Philadelphia. Dr. Chester would pay her three hundred dollars, which would cover the cost of the riders, fifty dollars each.

In the next few days, Peggy purchased a wagon and rented another with a team of two Morgan horses from Daniel. That made the three wagons she needed.

Then she had a meeting to advise everyone what was expected of them on the long journey to Philadelphia.

"I ask that you not divulge to anyone except family the nature or details of the trip." In order to avoid frightening them, Peggy didn't stress the value of the cargo. "I want the men to bring your guns and ammunition. I will provide food and water, which will be on the wagons. We'll leave at daybreak on the morning of Tuesday the sixteenth. I ask that everyone stay here the night before to ensure an early start."

Chapter Nine

On the Banks of Sycamore Shoals

The weary travelers and their precious cargo had made it to Sycamore Shoals on the banks of the Watauga River where they would camp for the first night of the long journey to Philadelphia. Peggy wanted to ford the shallows of the river with the few hours of daylight that remained of the long summer day.

However, Daniel was concerned that a wagon could get stuck, a wheel might break, or something worse would happen crossing the river so late in the day. He feared that dark would overtake them, leaving a wagon stranded in the water until daybreak. He suggested to a protesting Peg that the men could better use the daylight to wade into the river to locate the best point to cross, making sure to remove any hazards lurking beneath the surface of the strong current. Respecting her wagon master's judgment, she agreed.

John and William foraged for game while the other men in the group cleared the path for tomorrow's crossing. The girls busied themselves with starting a campfire and preparing for the evening meal, confident that their brothers would have a successful hunt.

"Peg, if Jimmy and the Smith boys are brothers, why do they have different last names?" Rebeckah asked.

"Probably half brothers," Ibby said. She and her sisters watched the shirtless boys frolicking in the swift water of the riverbed, apparently finished with the day's work.

"There is no blood relationship between James Wither-spoon and Willie or James Smith." Peg stacked the kindling for the fire in a neat little pile.

Ibby wrinkled her sunburned nose. "Then how can they be brothers?"

"It's something that's not discussed, but I once overhead Reverend Doak say that after Mr. Witherspoon died, Jimmy's mother Anne married a widower named Smith who had three boys, William, James, and Thomas. One day Mr. Smith went off trapping in the woods and never came back. No one knows what happened to him. Their stepmother was the only family the boys had. She raised the Smith boys and her own son James with the help of Reverend Doak, Sister Esther, and the congregation of Salem Church." Peg added small twigs to the smoking kindling.

"Oh, those poor boys." Ibby looked toward the creek.

John and William clambered down a ridge through a thicket of mountain laurel and rhododendron. A large whitetail doe was strapped on the back of Jimmy's mule. When they reached the bottom, the brothers strained with both arms to pull the heavy carcass up on a limb of a sycamore tree, using a rope as a hoist.

"Looks like we're going to eat venison tonight." Daniel pointed to the boys struggling with the carcass. He shook his head. *Why don't they use the mule? Guess I best skin that deer myself; make sure it's done right.*

After dinner, James and Willie strummed their dulcimer boards, picking the tunes with their bone picks. Rebeckah and Ibby danced to the music of the ballads of the mountains around the flickering embers of the campfire.

"Looks like your sisters are enjoying themselves," Jimmy said.

"Music makes them happy. That's why I plan to buy a piano for the school while we are in Philadelphia—so they can learn to play."

"Do you play?"

"No, but I intend to learn once we have an instrument to practice on."

"Who will teach you?"

"I don't know a soul who can play. Guess I'll buy a book and teach myself." She put her arm in his. "Walk me down to the river's edge?"

"You know I play a few tunes, but Mother and Sister Esther both play quite well."

"I didn't know that." Peg looked across the rippling river to the other side.

"I'm sure either of them would be anxious to teach you and your sisters to play."

"That would be nice. I hope I will have time to shop for a piano in Philadelphia." Her mind wandered away from the discussion of music as she visualized the many obstacles that lay ahead, realizing the huge responsibility for the safety of everyone on the wagon train.

Jimmy turned to face her. "What's wrong?"

"We have so far to travel and so much to do once we reach Philadelphia, then return with Dr. Chester's materials, and get back home in time for Robert's wedding. I may have taken on more than I can handle." Peg bit her lip to keep from crying.

"God will not give you more than you can handle," Jimmy whispered. He put a hand on each of her shoulders and looked into her hazel eyes that reflected the moon's glow.

"That's what Grandmother Mitchell and my parents have always told me, but tonight I'm so unsure of myself." A tear ran down her sunburned cheek.

He put his arms around her waist and held her tightly. "I promise we will make it home safely and in time for Robert's wedding." He looked up to the heavens and said a silent prayer.

By dawn the next morning, Daniel had the men up rigging the extra tackle and safety ropes for the trip across the Watauga. The wagon master, who had laid out his planned crossing to the group the evening before, was reviewing it once more to make sure each member understood his duties during the dangerous undertaking.

The girls prepared a breakfast of eggs, venison, biscuits, and gravy. They wanted everyone to have a good meal as they planned not to stop until they reached Abingdon, Virginia, thirty miles to the east.

The day before, Daniel had James tie a large piece of cloth to a sycamore tree to mark where the team should come out on the other side. "We must keep our eyes on that tree and never allow the team and wagon to veer off course."

They planned to take only one wagon across at a time. John would drive the team of dapple gray Morgan horses from the seat of the wagon. The draft horses were trained for treacherous watering crossings and bred to pull heavy loads. Daniel would lead another team that was tied by a slack line on each end of the wagon's side, some forty feet upstream. Should the wagon drift into deep water and start to float, this second team would be used to hold the wagon. As an extra precaution, James would lead another horse upstream twenty feet in front of the Morgans at an angle, and Willie would do the same in the rear. With six horses, they should be able to hold the wagon against the current, but Daniel knew that if any of the horses spooked, the wagon would be doomed.

William and Jimmy would ride across in front of the draft horses, trying to stay directly in front of where the wagon wheels would roll, watching for large boulders the current might have shifted during the night. Never knowing what obstacles lay beneath the frothing waters, each carried a long-bladed knife that Daniel had sharpened to a razor's edge this morning. They were prepared to cut the ropes and harness to save the horses in the event the wagon went under.

The sisters packed the cooking vessels and bedding into what was to be the last wagon across. They each kept a watchful eye on the first wagon's progress as it moved slowly through the water. They didn't utter a word but each silently said a prayer.

Once the first wagon was on dry land, the men let out a holler, and the girls hugged each other in joy.

Peggy sighed. "We made it across once; we should be able to make it again."

The sun was high in the sky by the time all the wagons, horses, and travelers had safely crossed the river.

"No! Not there! Don't go in there!" Conversation stopped and the travelers looked up in surprise at the sound of Daniel's shouts.

A one-horse buggy was about to enter the river at a point just downstream from where they had crossed. Everyone saw what was about happen and began to yell. However, the lone traveler could not hear them over the roar of the fast-moving water.

"Damn. He's going into a deep eddy just off the bank," Daniel said.

Peggy said, "Stop him!"

Daniel called, "John and William, stay with your sisters. The others come with me."

As the rest of the men took off across the rocky shoals on horseback, the rig sank into the whirling pool of water. They could see someone swimming to shore. The horse and buggy went under. The horse fought desperately, lifting its head above the water twice during the horrific struggle to stay alive. The rescuers were too late to save the horse but found the man on the bank, gasping for air and coughing up water and bile.

The dripping man said, "Thank you," between gasps.

Daniel put a hand on his shoulder. "I'm sorry we couldn't save your horse and buggy."

"I seen you tried. Everything happened so fast. I thought I was in shallow water, but I guess I weren't cause the whole rig just went under." The man wheezed and panted.

The Smith brothers went to see if they could salvage the cart or any of its contents. They found only a small leather satchel of papers on the riverbank about 100 yards downstream. What was left of the two-wheeled cart washed up against a large boulder in the middle of the river.

"Who are you?" The drenched man lay on the riverbank, his wide eyes focused on the Negro and the gun and knife he carried.

"Everyone calls me Daniel. This here is Reverend Witherspoon. Who might you be?"

When he didn't receive an answer, Daniel again asked the man his name. The stranger acted as if he didn't know his own name.

Maybe he hit his head and lost his memory, Daniel thought.

James approached with a wet bag over his shoulder, water still dripping from it.

"Are you Robert Thigpen?" he asked.

"That's my satchel." The man grabbed the bag from James and clutched it to his chest with both hands.

"James Smith is my name. This is my brother Willie." The brothers both tipped their hats.

"Where were you headed, Mr. Thigpen?" Daniel asked.

"Be headed home. Where y'all going?"

"Philadelphia," Daniel answered.

"Seeing as I done lost my horse and buggy, could I ride with you to that town you just said?"

"That will be up to my boss. I'm just the wagon master."

The men put the still-dripping man on Daniel's horse and led him across the shallows to the wagons. When he got down from the horse, the stranger tried to straighten his clothes, which looked too small for him.

Daniel introduced Mr. Thigpen to Peg, and she introduced her siblings.

After the introductions, Thigpen turned to Daniel. "When can I meet your boss?"

"You just did." Daniel gestured toward Peggy and grinned.

Thigpen ducked his head. "I be sorry, Miz Mitchell. Didn't expect a woman to be the trail boss."

"That's all right, Mr. Thigpen. It happens all the time."

"I be much obliged if you let me ride on one of the wagons."

"Daylight's burning. Let's load up and try to make it to Abingdon before dark." She pointed their new guest toward her wagon.

"Would you want me to drive?" he asked.

"Not on your life, Mr. Thigpen. I've seen enough of your teamster abilities for one day."

The man didn't react to her comment. "What you want me to do?"

"Just sit next to me and look pretty." Peggy thought, *That will be a tall order.*

After the man was settled on the seat, Peg shook the reins once, and the wagon lunged forward. Her passenger gripped the buckboard hard with one hand but clung tightly to the wet satchel with his other hand.

Daniel and Jimmy scouted the road ahead, clearing it of fallen limbs and large rocks, always on the lookout for highwaymen who wanted to relieve them of the precious cargo hidden beneath the stalks of corn. Peggy was sure no one would suspect the wagon train was anything but a farm family taking their crops to market.

They made good time, and about noon, they passed the weekly westbound stage headed toward Jonesborough and on to Knoxville.

Daniel waited alone for the wagons under the shade of a large chestnut tree as Jimmy went on about half a mile in front of the first wagon.

When Peg's wagon reached the tree where Daniel waited, he rode up alongside her. "That stagecoach driver just told me the road's in pretty good shape up to Abingdon. There's a running creek a mile up the road. We can rest and water the horses there for a while, then drive them hard until dark."

The travelers were ready for the unscheduled break. The men led the dozen horses and the mule to a clear pool of spring water under a cluster of walnut trees. Peg opened the large Dutch oven that held the cooked meat, hand-pulled from the hindquarter of last night's venison. With the sourdough biscuits left over from breakfast, they ate a quick meal without building a fire.

Thigpen held the satchel over his arm while he ate as if he hadn't eaten in days.

"Which of them be your husband?" Thigpen pointed toward the men gathered around Daniel.

"I'm not married." Peg looked away from the man talking with his mouth full of venison.

"You be a widow?"

Her voice sharp, she said, "You sure ask a lot of questions for a man badly needing a ride." She was more aggravated at his grammar than his question.

He wiped his hand across his mouth. "I meant no harm."

"When I learn the truth about who you are and what you were doing so far from home, I will feel more comfortable telling you about myself."

She rose and motioned to the others that it was time to head out.

Once the Morgan draft horses fell into a comfortable gait, the teams that followed seemed to fall into the same graceful yet rapid pace. Daniel witnessed the beautiful sight from a hill above the wagon road. The cadence of the horses' hooves pounding the hard-packed dirt of the road, the jingle of the hardware on the leather tackle, and the sounds of loaded wagons creaking as they strained on each curve of the crooked road sounded like music to his ears.

Peggy lightly held the reins, and the team of horses did what they were bred to do. John drove the next wagon with Rebeckah seated beside him. William and Ibby followed. Jimmy scouted forward, and James and Willie guarded the rear. The wagon party had become a team, each doing their job without question or being told what to do.

Daniel had found peace with himself on the Great Wagon Road to Philadelphia. Like his draft horses, he was doing what he was meant to do. He enjoyed being Peggy's wagon master and was glad he accepted her offer. *Look at them go! Whoopee!* Daniel shook his head and grinned in admiration of his teamsters as he spurred his horse over the next hill to get in front of the wagons again.

They pulled into Abingdon with daylight to spare. Daniel slowed the train down gradually so the horses could cool down before arriving at the local livery stable.

From the stagecoach drivers coming through Jonesborough, he had heard good things about The Tavern, a stagecoach stop that could provide bed and bath for the women and good food for all. He rode ahead to make arrangements for the girls to share any available room. The men would sleep in the livery stable with the wagons and horses, protecting their cargo.

Mr. McDonald, owner of the inn, expressed excitement about having travelers from Jonesborough but asked Daniel, "Where will you be eating your meal this evening?"

"With my friends as always."

The innkeeper took a deep breath. "But I can't serve you in my dining room."

"Why is that?"

"You're a—a—a—Negro. What would my other guests think?"

"Mr. McDonald, I own the livery stable in Jonesborough where every wagon that comes through stops. I have a contract with the stage line and the U.S. Postal Department. I've heard nothing but good things about your inn, which I pass on to my customers. I don't think it would be good business to separate me from my friends."

"Uh—well—I guess—your group is quite large. I do suppose that I could close the dining room to the public this evening, if that would please you."

"If that pleases you," Daniel said.

"What's your name?"

"My friends call me Daniel. You can call me Mr. Daniel." He raised his head at the sound of approaching wagons.

Turning his back on the innkeeper, he walked into the road to greet his traveling companions.

Abingdon had been founded about the same time as Jonesborough but appeared much smaller. There was the inn, a log courthouse, and two log churches on Main Street. The area had originally been called Wolf Hills and was now the county seat of Washington County in the Commonwealth of Virginia.

William said, "Nicholas Fain told us the story. He said a pack of wolves came out of a cave and attacked Daniel Boone's dogs on a hunting trip so the frontiersman called it Wolf Hills. That's how it got its original name."

"That's right, and during the day you can still see the wolves' cave across the road." The barmaid, Molly McDonald, entered with a large tureen of steaming soup. Molly, the innkeeper's unmarried daughter, was about twenty years old, pleasantly plump with red hair, large freckles, and a rosy complexion that turned redder when a man complimented her.

"Grandfather McMachen came here for protection inside Black's Fort when Chief Bowles warned him of the pending Indian raid on the Quarters." Peg spread butter on her biscuit.

"That's where Grandfather McMachen met Nicholas Fain and our Uncle Fains met our Aunt McMachens." William laughed.

John joined in the laughter. "The three marriages that came about as a result of their fleeing to Fort Black certainly increased our family."

Peg's face took on a wistful expression. "I miss their stories. Grandfather and Mr. Fain used to laugh like you did when they were telling their stories."

"I miss them, too," Rebeckah said.

Ibby asked, "Can we go see the wolves' cave in the morning?"

Peg looked around the small dimly lit dining room. "Where is Pigpen?"

"Pigpen?" Jimmy asked.

"Well, he's so disheveled the nickname fits, don't you think?"

Thigpen had been in the room before Molly brought the soup but had just disappeared. Peg jumped up and hurried out the door toward the stable. Everyone in the dining room, including the innkeeper and Molly, followed her outside like ducklings in a row.

"Going somewhere?" Peg asked.

Thigpen was attempting to saddle one of their horses, but the leather satchel kept getting in his way. He ran toward the open stable door. John, who was near the door, stuck out a foot and tripped him. Thigpen fell face first into a fresh pile of horse dung. John yanked the man up, pushed him against the wagon, and grabbed the leather bag.

"Don't hurt me." Thigpen's voice came out in a squeak.

John threw the satchel to his brother. "There must be something in here more than a bunch of papers. Take a look at what he's been so watchful of."

William pulled out a bunch of papers bearing Thigpen's signature. At the bottom of the bag, he found a little hidden side pocket that was filled with currency. He tossed the bag and its contents to Peggy.

"Tell me what's in the bag besides money."

Thigpen trembled as he answered, "Just some papers."

"What are the papers about?" Peg stood with her hands on her hips.

"Bidness." He wiped at the green horse dung on his clothes, trying to whisk it away with the back of his hand.

Peg took a stub of lead pencil from the satchel and handed it and a small piece of paper to Thigpen. "Write your name for me."

Watching him struggle to hold the pencil, Peggy realized he couldn't write. The papers in the bag were signed Robert W. Thigpen in beautiful scrolled cursive penmanship. This illiterate person who couldn't even hold a pencil could not be Mr. Thigpen.

"Where is Mr. Thigpen?" she demanded.

"I don't know."

William took a step closer. "What did you do to him?"

"Nothing."

"Was the horse and buggy you drove into the river also his?" Daniel asked.

The whimpering man looked down at his feet. "I just found it."

"Was that what you were doing with my horse? Just finding it?" Peg watched him as he slid slowly to the ground. She turned to Mr. McDonald. "Who is the law here?"

"We just usually hang a horse thief when we catch him in the act. No need to bother the law."

"I am more worried that he killed poor Mr. Thigpen than his stealing a horse." Peggy glared at the innkeeper.

"Don't matter. We can only hang him once. Punishment's the same for horse stealing as it is murder in Virginia," Molly said.

"We could tar and feather him, except I'm just about out of tar. I got plenty of feathers, though," the innkeeper added.

Molly's hazel eyes shone with excitement. "Let the bears decide his fate."

"Let the bears decide?" Peg rolled her eyes.

"When the Indians discover a member of their tribe stealing, they strip him, tie his hands, hobble his feet, baste him in honey, and send him into the woods. The bears smell the honey and find the person. The bears either eat him on the spot or slowly lick the honey, depending on whether they're hungry for meat or honey." The barmaid blushed as she realized all eyes were on her.

Her father looked at Molly, his face filled with pride. "We got plenty of honey to spread all over him."

The horse thief sat on the ground staring at the dirt and shaking his head.

"We can't take the law into our own hands," Jimmy said, sounding like the preacher he was.

"Why not?" the innkeeper asked. "I think Sheriff Preston would appreciate us doing it for him."

"We can't be the judge, jury, and executioner," the minister insisted.

Mr. McDonald pulled a deputy sheriff's badge from his vest pocket and held it up. "We do it in Abingdon all the time. Sheriff Preston is my brother-in-law, and he can't always be here. That's why he deputized me."

"You've got a badge. Then let's hang him!" All the men but the preacher agreed.

Peg took charge. "Look, it's late. Our soup is cold, and I am tired. Just tie him up good, and in the morning we can decide the fate of whoever this idiot is." She turned and headed back to the inn with Ibby and Rebeckah following close behind.

The girls finished their cold soup and ate a little bread before retiring to their room.

Peg stood at the window that looked down on the stable, her hair blown back by the evening breeze that kept the small room comfortable on this muggy summer night. At times the wind carried in barnyard smells that were almost too much to endure. *I guess that's why the McDonalds gave us such a good bargain,* she thought.

Rebeckah sat on a three-legged stool in front of the large oval mirror that hung above the washstand, quietly combing her long black hair.

Ibby had already crawled under the covers of the bed. "Peg, how did you know?"

"Know what?"

"That the man we gave a ride to was dishonest. You didn't trust him from the moment we met him, did you?"

"I've been thinking about that too," Rebeckah said.

Peggy climbed into the rumpled feather bed.

Rebeckah crawled in with her older sisters. "When he disappeared from the dining room, you knew he was in the stable trying to steal our horse. How did you know?"

"I just knew."

"How?" her sisters asked.

"My distrust started when he had no remorse for his actions causing the death of his poor horse and the loss of his rig." Peg burrowed deeper into the feather mattress.

"I wondered about that." Rebeckah snuggled into the bed.

"He hung onto his bag, and he kept asking questions about us, but he wouldn't tell us anything about himself, including where he was going."

"You're right," Ibby said.

Rebeckah asked, "Will they hang him?"

"Most likely," Peg answered.

"Then we should pray for him."

"And for Mr. Thigpen, wherever he might be." Rebeckah motioned for Ibby to blow out the candle on the table next to the bed.

When the lights were out, the girls each said their silent prayers.

The men had tied the horse thief seated on the ground with his arms spread across one of the front wheels of wagon and tied at the wrists to the spokes. A cowbell had been tied around his neck to warn his captors when he moved. His legs were spread wide and his feet tied to pegs driven deep into the ground.

The next morning, a rooster's crowing awakened Daniel. The familiar sound and smell made him feel at home. From his bedroll spread out on the hay, he opened one eye then the other to see the man who until last night he had thought was Mr. Thigpen trying to shoo the big red rooster away from its perch directly over his head. The captive gently moved his tightly tethered wrists upward.

The rustle of the bedroll alerted the thief that Daniel was awake. "Please, please, shoo the rooster away from me. It's pooping on my head," he whined.

"That ole bird's got about as much respect for you as I do." Daniel chuckled as he shooed the fowl out of the barn.

As the men were washing up for breakfast at the water trough behind the stable, someone called, "Mr. Daniel."

Most likely not a friend, Daniel thought.

He turned to see a tall man with a red handlebar moustache and goatee walking toward him with a slight limp in his right leg. He extended his hand. "It is a pleasure to finally meet you in person, Mr. Daniel. I'm Robert Preston, the local sheriff. I understand you might have caught a fugitive I've been looking for."

"Tell me, Sheriff Preston. There are five other men standing around this horse trough. How did you know which one was me?"

"Been a lawman all my life. Let's just say you're the only man here that matches the description I was given of you."

Everyone had a good laugh.

Daniel took an immediate liking to the sheriff. "My friends call me Daniel, and I'd like you to call me Daniel," he said as he shook the sheriff's hand.

"Well, Daniel, breakfast is waiting for you and your friends, and I'm buying."

"You think Mr. McDonald will let me eat in his dining room this morning?" Daniel smiled at his new friend.

"Yes, I do." The lawman patted Daniel's shoulder and pointed him toward the inn.

At breakfast, Sheriff Preston questioned the men from Jonesborough about the horse thief they had pulled from the river. William told how last night the man had claimed he just found the buggy and the satchel with the money in it. The men knew little that could help the sheriff.

"You know, he never introduced himself as Mr. Thigpen," Willie said. "We just assumed he was because the satchel of papers had Thigpen's name on them."

"What's all the interest you have in this horse thief?" Daniel asked.

"He's just a small part of a much larger puzzle." The sheriff pushed back from the table.

Daniel asked, "What do you mean?"

"A gang of highwaymen have been preying on travelers along the Wagon Road for several months."

William laid down his fork. "Do you know who they are?"

"If I did, they would be in jail. The problem is no one has ever survived their attacks to give a description of the bandits." The sheriff leaned forward and talked in a low voice.

"That's why you're so interested in the horse thief." Daniel picked up a biscuit.

"Yes, and I am glad you didn't hang him or feed him to the bears last night. He may be the only person that can tell me about this gang."

"He's all yours, now. I hope he can answer your questions. Now, we need to be on the road." Daniel rose.

"You can't leave town," the lawman said.

"Why not?" Jimmy asked.

Peg looked up from the nearby table she was sharing with her sisters. "What do you mean we can't leave town? We should have left an hour ago."

"Sheriff Preston, this is my sister Peggy." John stepped over beside Peg and gave her a warning look.

"I'm honored to meet the lady trail boss and her sisters." Sheriff Preston bowed to the girls.

"It's an honor to meet you, Sheriff, but we must get on the road now."

The sheriff looked directly at Peg. "This could take months."

"Months!"

"Hear me out, Miss Mitchell, and please don't get excited." He motioned for everyone to sit back down. "What I have to say is only between us. I'm trying to help you and to fulfill my duties as sheriff."

The lawman explained that the only charge he could hold the highwayman on was his attempt to steal their horse. They would need to testify to ensure a conviction. He had no evidence any crime had been committed against Mr.

Thigpen, but he had eleven eyewitnesses to the attempted theft of their horse, which made for a strong case.

"A judge and prosecutor aren't scheduled to be in Abingdon until the November session," the sheriff said.

"November!" Peg said. "We have to be home way before then."

The sheriff said, "I have an idea. We could hold a quick mock trial and find the thief guilty and sentence him to hang. When the noose is put around his neck, I'll offer him a pardon if he tells all he knows about the highway bandits."

"Just how long will this quick mock trial take?" Peg asked.

"If you cooperate with me, I can have you on the road by noon."

John and William led the shackled prisoner over to the one-room log courthouse. After Willie and James scared off a family of raccoons that had taken over the county seat since the last proceedings were held there, court was hastily set up.

Peg testified that she saw the accused trying to saddle one of the horses, and the other ten witnesses swore the same. While the proceedings were taking place, Willie fashioned a hangman's noose, making sure the defendant observed his handiwork. The thief kept looking back at Willie neatly tying the knot, then at the witnesses. Large drops of sweat dropped off his face, and his shirt dampened under his arms.

The local undertaker, portraying the judge, pronounced the thief guilty and sentenced him to hang. They all hurried out to the gallows in front of the courthouse, prodding and pushing the convicted thief. A crowd gathered, not knowing it was a mock trial.

"Hang the scoundrel!" someone shouted.

The men guarding the prisoner pushed him up onto the gallows platform. When the hangman's noose was placed around his neck, the trembling man flushed a deep red as a wet spot appeared and widened on his trousers.

The sheriff leaned in close to him. "Tell me everything you know about the bandits, and I won't hang you. I'll protect you from this mob and from the bandits I'm sure are searching for you."

"I don't know much, but I'll tell you everything I know." He drew an audible sigh of relief when the noose was loosened and removed from his neck.

Chapter Ten

An Amazing Connection

The prisoner was taken back to the one-room log courthouse and seated at a small wooden table across from Sheriff Preston. The witnesses stood around the table, shielding the accused horse thief from the onlookers who thought there was going to be a real hanging, a popular diversion in Abingdon.

"First, I want to know your name, where you're from, and what your involvement is with these highway bandits."

"My name be Joshua Coffee. My folks was killed by Injuns when I was just a baby. My grandma raised me till I was about twelve, then she died. I pretty much fended for myself, learning how to herd hogs." His voice was shaky at first, but he began to relax and expound on the story.

He said he hired out to herd hogs for Mr. Thigpen, a pig farmer who lived near the Holstein River. He was to drive the hogs to a Mr. William Deery, who owned the Deery Inn and Tavern in Blountsville.

"Mr. Thigpen drove the buggy as he had bad legs, and I did the herding on foot. We got to Blountsville two nights ago and penned the hogs up for Mr. Deery in his stable. He offered us supper and a room, which we were much obliged. Driving hogs is mighty dirty work, and I was sure glad for a bath. The only clothes I had was the ones I wore to drive the hogs so Mr. Thigpen offered me a suit of clothes to wear."

"The clothes you are now wearing?" Sheriff Preston asked.

"Yeah, and they don't fit too good, Mr. Thigpen being a lot smaller than me."

Eager to be on the road, Peg said, "For heaven's sake, Mr. Coffee, please just tell the sheriff how you met the bandits!"

"I want to hear everything, Joshua." The sheriff looked up at Peg then back to the criminal. "Please continue and take your time."

"The next morning Miz Deery fixed us breakfast and Mr. Deery settled up with Mr. Thigpen. Cash on the barrelhead."

"How much cash?" the lawman asked.

"I don't rightly know."

"You were sitting at the table when Mr. Deery counted it out, and you don't know how much it was?"

"He's telling the truth," Peg said. "This man cannot read or write and doesn't know how to count."

"Whatever's in that bag is all of it. I never spent none of his money." Joshua raised his head and looked the sheriff in the eye.

Sheriff Preston asked, "What was the count in the satchel?"

"I counted three hundred twenty dollars," Willie answered.

Next the sheriff tried to determine how many hogs they delivered to the Deery Inn. Joshua shook his head up and down when the sheriff flashed ten fingers five times to indicate they drove fifty head.

"That would be about right. Six dollars a head," the sheriff said.

"I remember them both saying that."

"What?" Sheriff Preston asked.

"Six dollars a head. I remember them saying that."

"Now, Joshua." The sheriff looked into his eyes, searching for the truth. "Tell me how you met the bandits."

"Just outside of Blountville, I needed to be relieved after the big breakfast Miz Deery done fed me. I went back into the woods, and Mr. Thigpen stayed with the buggy. I heard riders coming. I could tell from the yelling and hollering they was doing, they didn't sound like friendly folks and was looking to make trouble. I was a-scared so I stayed where I was and watched from the woods." He closed his eyes and shuddered.

The sheriff waited a few seconds for him to continue. When Joshua remained silent, the sheriff said, "And then what?"

"I seen a rider with a feather in his hat shoot Mr. Thigpen in the head. The Indian took his gold watch and put it in his pocket. Then the others took what was left. They drug him back into the brush on the other side of the road from me. When they heard the wagon coming from the other way, they took off toward Blountville. They left Mr. Thigpen dead and his horse and buggy just a-standing in the road."

"How many?" Sheriff Preston asked.

Joshua showed five fingers on one hand and one on the other.

"Were they Indians? You said one wore a feather."

"One could have been. The one with the feather wore Indian britches. The others were mountain men."

"Mountain men?"

"You know—dressed like them men." Joshua pointed toward the six men sitting on the bench next to the Mitchell girls.

Sheriff Preston looked at the men from Jonesborough and then back to Joshua. "What about this other wagon?"

He raised his hand and spread his five fingers. "They was this many. They had tools in the wagon like they was a-going to work. I stepped out of the woods and waved to them. I climbed up on the buggy just like everything was all right. Then I tried to get as fur away as I could from them bandits."

Sheriff Preston wrinkled his forehead. "Why didn't you ask for help from the workers in the other wagon?"

"I was a-scared they wouldn't believe me. Nobody ever does."

"I believe you," the sheriff said.

Joshua tried to smile but his missing teeth distorted it.

"I wanted to take the buggy back to Miz Thigpen but got lost and that's when I seen the wagon train that looked like a family. I thought I be safe with them."

"Were you going to take the money back to Mrs. Thigpen?" the sheriff asked.

"I didn't know about no money or no satchel in the buggy until Willie found it on the riverbank and gave it to me. I guess Mr. Thigpen hid it somewheres in the buggy."

"Joshua did act surprised to see the satchel when I brought it to him," Willie said.

The sheriff looked at Joshua for a few seconds. "Would you recognize the bandits if you saw them again."

"Don't know. They was a fur piece from me."

The sheriff left and conversed with his brother-in-law, then returned to the table.

"Joshua, for your protection, I should lock you up. But Mr. McDonald has agreed to feed you and allow you to sleep in the inn's stable in exchange for your helping with some chores around the inn."

Joshua's voice quivered. "Thank you for not hanging me."

"There is still the matter of your trying to steal Miss Mitchell's horse," Sheriff Preston said.

"I wasn't stealing it. I was just going to borry it to get to Miz Thigpen to tell her what happened to her husband. She needed to know."

Sheriff Preston looked at Peggy.

"I won't file charges against Mr. Coffee if he agrees to stay here and work for Mr. McDonald until these bandits are apprehended."

"Thank you, Miss Mitchell. I'll stay here."

The lawman stood and looked down at Joshua. "Mr. McDonald is my deputy here in town. You best do what he says."

"Yes, sir."

Sheriff Preston turned to Daniel. "I would like to talk to you and Miss Mitchell alone."

Mr. McDonald motioned for Joshua to follow him, and the others moved to the wooden boardwalk in front of the courthouse.

When they were alone, the sheriff looked first at Daniel, then at Peggy. "Is there anything I can say or do to convince you not to continue on to Philadelphia?"

Daniel looked at Peggy, his eyebrows raised in a question.

She shrugged her shoulders and gave a deep sigh. "If we turn around and go back to Jonesborough, we may just as easily encounter bandits. It is behind us that Mr. Thigpen was killed, wasn't it?"

"According to Mr. Coffee, that is correct," Sheriff Preston answered.

"We could be attacked whichever way we go on the wagon road," Peggy said.

The sheriff said, "True."

She turned to her long-time friend for guidance. "What do you think?"

Daniel answered, "If we could get killed coming or going, I'd just as soon get killed going somewhere I never been, like Philadelphia."

"I need to talk to the others."

Daniel nodded and stepped outside where their traveling companions were enjoying the warm sunshine and telling stories. "We need you all in here."

Peg and Daniel described the situation to the group, giving them the options and weighing the dangers they faced. "If anyone wants to go back, we'll all go back together."

Everyone agreed they wanted to continue to Philadelphia.

The sheriff stood. "We best get going then."

"What do you mean—we?" Peg asked.

"I am riding with you, at least to Big Lick. If you get yourself killed, I don't want it happening in my county."

As Sheriff Preston had promised, they were on the road by noon. They would push the teams hard till dark to make up for the time lost due to the mock trial and interrogation. The sheriff tied his horse to the back of the lead wagon and rode with Peggy.

"I hope you don't mind me riding with you. This lame leg bothers me less on the buckboard than it does in the saddle."

"You'll certainly be better company than Pigpen," Peg answered.

"You mean Joshua?"

"Yes. Pigpen is the name I gave him in jest. It just stuck in my mind and every time I think of Joshua, the name Pigpen comes to mind." She spoke loudly to be heard over the noise of the wagons rolling along.

"A fitting name, I suppose, for a pig herder."

"Do you believe him?"

"Yes, I do." The sheriff held out his hands. "Let me take the reins a while."

"Why do you believe him?" She handed him the reins.

"He isn't smart enough to make up a story like he told."

Peggy thought the same thing but didn't want to let the sheriff know she agreed. She felt sympathy for anyone who couldn't read or write or do simple arithmetic.

They rode in silence for a good while, each deep in their own thoughts. Peggy worried more than ever about the group's safety. She wondered how her sick mother and the babies at home were doing without her. Tonight would be only the third night away from them, and she missed holding her brothers, Hezekiah, David, and Samuel, and sister Jennett.

One wheel of the wagon hit a large boulder that protruded slightly from the roadway; the Sheriff grimaced in obvious pain but never uttered a word.

Peg decided to bury her homesickness and anxiety in the recesses of her mind by engaging the handsome lawman in conversation. "How did you receive your injury that causes you such pain?"

"Fighting the damn British at the Battle of Guilford Courthouse."

"Really?"

"Yes, I was a Virginia Militiaman stabbed by a Hessian bayonet."

She looked intently at the sheriff. "Where?"

"Well, where I sit in the saddle, if you need to know." He squirmed in his seat.

"I mean, where on the battlefield were you injured?" She raised her voice to be heard.

"I'm not sure. Everything happened so fast during the battle. Why do you ask?"

"I was there, as were my brothers."

"You were there with John and William?"

"I'm afraid so. The battle ended in the cornfields on our farm that adjoined the Courthouse. My father was on the first line with the men of Guilford County and was captured by the British. My grandmother, mother, brothers, and sister and I hid in our spring house during the battle."

There was a long pause before the sheriff responded. "You would have been …"

"Nine years old. I remember it well, and I think often of what I saw and heard that day and the days following."

She and the sheriff sat in silence for a long time, listening to the clippity-clop of the horse's hooves and the constant creaking of the wagon. Both were thinking of that March day fifteen years ago that had changed their lives forever.

Putting the thoughts of war out of her head, Peg asked, "Do you have family?"

"I lost my wife a few years back during the birth of my son, Robert. My sister and her husband that you met are raising him."

"The McDonalds?"

He took a deep breath. "Yes. They can do a much better job than I can."

"Do you really think so?"

He looked over at Peg for a moment. "What kind of family could I make him? No wife to care for him while I am off chasing bandits across the county. He's best off with the McDonalds. His cousin Molly looks after him during the day, and they've become great friends." Looking straight ahead again, he asked, "What about you? What's a pretty lady like you doing not being married?"

"I have more than enough to keep me busy and have no time to marry."

"I've wanted to ask you about your business." His serious tone and his official stern lawman look didn't intimidate Peggy.

She pursed her lips. "I didn't say anything about business."

"Well, whatever your business, I've never seen such a load of pelts in my life. Where did you come by them?" The sheriff maneuvered the wagon slowly over a gully that had been created in the road by runoff from the last storm.

"I can assure you I came by all of them legally, Sheriff."

The sheriff glanced in her direction. "I didn't accuse you of anything—just asked where you got such a fine load of pelts as I've never seen before."

"While I was apprenticing in York, I met a furrier who admired the quality of the beaver pelts that I had brought from home to barter for books and supplies for the Hebron School. I started brokering furs and pelts for Mr. Astor, acquiring the high quality silver belly beaver pelts that he preferred and that are abundant around Knob Creek. It's become a business that provides well for my family and allows me to teach the children of the community."

Peg looked at movement on a hill above the road, then relaxed when she recognized Star. *Is Jimmy spying on me? If he is, that means he cares.*

"So many furs. Do you have any idea what these furs will bring in Philadelphia?"

"No. Why don't you tell me?" She frowned. "You obviously searched my possessions without my permission, and you apparently know everything we're carrying."

"As an officer of the law, I need to know what's coming and going through my county. As for the value of your load, I have no idea other than it is more than enough to get us all killed."

"That's why we put several layers of corn fodder on top, to conceal the furs and pelts from highwaymen, not the law."

"It didn't work."

She jerked her head in his direction. "How so?"

Before he could answer Jimmy came down the hill riding Star at full gallop hollering, "Riders coming!" He motioned for the rear guards to move up closer to the wagons as the wagon master had instructed them to do when approached by unknown riders.

The men instinctively checked their weapons as they had so many times before. The sheriff reached behind the buckboard under the dried corn stalks for his Brown Bess he'd carried since the Revolution. Needing both hands to retrieve the long weapon, he handed the reins to Peggy. He placed the gun, muzzle down for safety, next to his right knee.

Daniel had stopped three horsemen in the road about a quarter of a mile ahead, in sight of Peggy's wagon. After a short powwow with them, he signaled with his hand all was well.

Peg continued her conversation with the sheriff as if there had been no interruption. "Please continue telling me how you knew something was hidden in our wagons."

"You paid the inn for feed for your horses when you had what appeared to be three wagonloads full of feed."

"Oh."

"And besides, I noticed your wagon tracks were way too deep to be carrying just corn stalks."

Peg smiled at the sheriff. "I'm glad we have such a smart lawman escorting us to Big Lick."

"Where did you get that awful-tasting whisky you have in the big crock?" he asked.

"It's not whisky. That's our tanning solution to keep the dried pelts from becoming stiff and brittle; it also keeps them from smelling to high heaven. The whisky my family is known for is in the last wagon in little brown jugs. Once we make camp, I'll get you a bottle. It will help your pain and maybe improve your attitude." Peg smiled at the mental image of him taking a big gulp of her tanning solution. *It serves him right, but I sure hope it doesn't hurt him.*

"Who are you delivering the pelts to?" He grimaced again when the wagon ran over another deep wash in the road.

"Whoever will pay me the best price."

"You're hauling this load of furs all the way to Philadelphia and you don't have a buyer?" The sheriff raised his voice as the wagon lumbered over the next bump in the road.

"There will be plenty of buyers for my pelts." Peg waved at the official-looking party of three riders passing by. She wondered who they were, where they were going, and what they were up to.

"You seem pretty sure." He shifted his weight to the other hip.

"Supply and demand will ensure that I find a buyer and obtain a fair price."

"How's that?"

Peg explained how she intentionally held back last year's harvest of furs and bought up most of the pelts around Jonesborough this year in the hope of getting a much better price in Philadelphia than the smaller market of York. The Treaty of San Lorenzo had opened the Mississippi River to the port of New Orleans. Peggy figured the trappers to the west would float their pelts down river on flatboats, creating a shortage of fur pelts transported to the port cities on the east coast.

"It's just my observation and speculation of the fur market." She shrugged her shoulders as if it were not a major business decision.

The sheriff said nothing—just stared in awe at this mountain woman from Tennessee dressed in a simple light-weight linsey-woolsey dress.

"I find it hard to believe that you're a fur trader, a trail boss, and a schoolteacher."

"Well, I am. And I'm also a medical practitioner." She enjoyed watching the reaction of men after one of her dissertations on business. Like most men, Sheriff Preston seemed intimidated by her intelligence and business acumen.

Daniel rode up to report that he had located a good spot to make camp on the river, about four miles up the road.

"I know the spot you're talking about," the sheriff said. "It's a large meadow on this side of the South Fork of the Holstein River. That open area would make it difficult for night bandits to sneak up on us from the south, and the river will protect us on the north."

When they arrived at the campsite, they pulled the three wagons together to make a fort of sorts for protection. A fire built for cooking would also keep wild animals away. Two men would guard the camp as the others slept, dividing the duty into three watches.

Sheriff Preston and John took the first watch as the others turned in after a dinner of corn bread, pork, and beans.

"Want some more coffee?" the sheriff asked.

"Yes, thank you." John held out his pewter mug for the sheriff to fill.

"Is that an M embossed on your mug?" The sheriff examined the mug as if he thought it was his.

"Yes, it stands for McMachen, my grandfather's name." John wondered why the lawman showed so much interest in his pewter mug.

"Interesting vessel. I have only seen one other like it. I understand from your sister that you were on the field of battle at Guilford Courthouse."

"I was just shy of seven years old and holed up in a small limestone spring house with my mother, grandmother, and siblings." John shook his head. "Grapeshot was coming down on the roof and ricocheting off the rock walls, even splintering the wooden door, yet no one was injured."

"What do you remember the most about that day?" The sheriff added another log to the fire.

"How afraid I was, yet how calm Grandmother Mitchell was through it all. She even rebuffed a British officer who wanted her to allow him to search her trunk. She scolded him, and he just turned away and walked off."

"What was in the trunk?"

"Undergarments and a bunch of pewter. This is a piece of that pewter." He raised the metallic cup up toward the sheriff's face.

"How old was your Grandmother Mitchell then?"

"About seventy; she lived to be seventy-seven years old." A tear formed in his eye as he talked about his grandmother.

Sheriff Preston stared deep into the flames of the campfire. "I met her."

"How could you have?" John looked at the sheriff in disbelief.

"I was injured there. I lay in the stubble of a cornfield near a creek not too far from the Courthouse. "

"That had to have been our farm."

"Dark came, and it began to rain. I was in a great deal of pain, calling out for someone to help me. This elderly woman appeared and said I was on her farm. She helped me into a spring house for shelter from the rain. She stopped my bleeding with strips of cloth torn from undergarments from an old hair trunk. She gave me water and a little whisky in a pewter mug just like yours with an M on it."

John stared at the sheriff who was still looking down into fire.

"Then she lit a candle and went out into the rain to help others. She came back in the morning to check on me and brought a doctor. The angel who saved my life was your grandmother. I may have drunk from that mug you're holding."

John and Sheriff Preston stared at each other, neither saying a word as they contemplated the miracle of the wounded soldier meeting the grandchildren of the woman who had saved his life fifteen years earlier. Both wondered what God's plan was in putting them together on the Great Wagon Road to Philadelphia.

Finally, John stood and broke the silence. "I best go check on the horses."

Daniel was awake boiling more coffee as he and William prepared to take the next watch.

William put more logs on the fire and poured a cup of steaming coffee. He raised the pot and looked at Daniel and the sheriff. "More coffee?"

The men shook their heads.

John stepped out of the darkness of the night into the light of the campfire to say the horses were all tied securely. The men talked about the reward poster that the three stage line agents had given Daniel on the road yesterday. The stage line owners offered a five hundred dollar reward for information that led to the arrest of the six highwaymen that had been terrorizing stage passengers on the wagon road for months. They described the leader as a one-eyed Indian and the others as five mountain men. All were well armed, rode fast horses, and were ruthless, usually leaving no witnesses.

"Now we know Joshua told us the truth and at least one other person survived their attacks," the sheriff said.

"At least we know they're behind us," Daniel said.

The sheriff tossed the remains of his coffee grounds in the fire. "I want to lead us to Trollinger's outpost for supplies tomorrow."

William said, "I don't know that we need anything yet."

"I saw what you boys have in the way of ammunition. If we have to fight these bandits, I don't want to be short on firepower." The sheriff stretched out on his bedroll for the night.

The next day, they made it to the community of Trollinger's Station, as it was called by the few families that lived around the area. Henry Jacob Trollinger was a sixty-five-year-old German who had come to the New River Valley with his wife Barbara before the Revolutionary War. He acquired land that had a large cave underneath a limestone cliff on a hillside near their home. The cave had large deposits of potassium nitrate, called saltpeter, which was the main ingredient for making gunpowder. Trollinger supplied great quantities of gunpowder to the American Army during the Revolution, and received a lot of land from the struggling government as a reward.

"How are you, Sheriff Preston?" asked John Trollinger, the son of the founder.

"I'm good. How are your mother and father?" The sheriff lifted his aching buttocks off the saddle by stretching his long legs and standing upright in the stirrups.

As Sheriff Preston rose in his saddle, Peggy saw fresh blood stains on his right pants leg. His wound was bleeding; it must be worse than she realized.

"Not good. They been ailing," John said.

"Sorry to hear that. I'm escorting these folks as far as Big Lick, and we need a couple kegs of black powder." The sheriff introduced the entourage from Jonesborough to the boy, who looked to be about seventeen.

"Welcome to Trollinger's Station." The boy grinned. "That's a lot of powder. You plan on blowing them from here to there?" He laughed, then quickly turned serious. "Could you make do on one keg for now and pick the other up on your way back? I been so busy taking care of sick folks, got no time to mine saltpeter."

"One keg will have to do," the lawman answered. "Do you mind if we camp here tonight?"

"Glad to have some company and the protection of the law. Been a while since we had any visitors, especially pretty ones." John looked directly at the Mitchell girls.

There was little open space to make camp, as Trollinger's Station was nestled in the woods. Mining saltpeter left little time for clearing land and busting sod for planting. The family just traded the valuable powder to the farmers of the Little River Valley for the necessities of their table board.

Tonight the travelers would be the guests of the Trollingers, benefiting from the farm products their hosts had acquired. "Ma ain't up to fixing this pork shoulder and fresh vegetables. It's enough for all of us if you could fix it." John handed the basket full of food to a smiling Ibby.

"Thank you." Ibby made a short curtsy, then turned to show the fresh produce and pork shoulder to her sisters.

"Be here about dark-thirty for dinner and come hungry." Ibby smiled.

"Bring your parents if they're up to it," Peg chimed in.

"I doubt they will. Haven't been out of the house in months." He headed toward the log structure built into the hillside where ammo was stored and the family lived.

Sounds like my parents. Peg grabbed the other handle of the heavy basket from Ibby, and they carried it to where Daniel had started the campfire.

"Looks like we gonna eat good tonight." Daniel added wood to the fire.

Sheriff Preston had rolled out his bedroll under one of the wagons. Peg saw from a distance that he was in great distress; his color had faded away. He staggered and couldn't seem to get down under the shade of the wagon. She rushed to the lawman, and Daniel followed. They helped him onto his bedroll. He seemed to be delirious for a moment, then his eyes fluttered and he passed out.

"What's wrong with him?" Daniel asked.

"Help me get his pants off, and I'll show you." Peg started to unlace the lawman's britches.

Daniel gave her a strange look but did what she said. "Look at all the blood. What happened to him?"

"Stabbed by a bayonet," Peg answered.

The others had gathered around the wagon.

"When did that happen?" William asked.

"At the Battle of Guilford Courthouse. Please just get supper ready and let me tend to his wound." Peg motioned for everyone to go away. "Ibby, please boil me a pot of hot water. John, bring my medicine bag."

"That looks bad." Daniel pointed to the bleeding abscess and the scar on the sheriff's right hip.

Peggy cleaned and dressed the wound, keeping wet rags on the lawman's forehead in an attempt to reduce the fever and comfort him. She looked up to see Jimmy standing over her, his Bible in his hand.

"I've just about done all I can do for him, Jimmy. His recovery is in God's hands now. I hope your prayers can save him."

The preacher extended his hand to Peggy, helping her up from the ground. "I'll stay and pray for him, and I'll come for you if he awakens."

"Thank you." She gently touched Jimmy's bearded face with her hand. "He has a son named for him. Please pray for him also."

Tonight it was quiet around the campfire. Peggy had sent Ibby and her new admirer with supper for his parents.

During the night, Peg began applying hot poultices to the sheriff's wound trying to draw the infection out.

Her patient woke just as the sun began to appear above the dense forest. He drank a cup of broth and asked, "How long?"

"You've been out since a few hours before sundown yesterday."

He closed his eyes and was out again. At least he had some nourishment in his body. Peggy continued with the hot poultices. While cleaning the wound, she felt a sharp object barely under the skin that she hadn't noticed before.

"What have you found that is so interesting?" Her brother John stood above Peg observing her close examination of the sheriff's derrière.

"John, look at this."

"No, thank you."

"Seriously, take a look." Peg pinched the pale white flesh of the right buttock between her thumb and index finger.

"I see what you mean. What do you think it is?"

"I'm not sure, but it has to come out." Peg reached for her medicine bag and retrieved a scalpel and a small pair of forceps.

Others had gathered around the sheriff's pallet while she prepared to open the wound.

"William, you and John hold his feet tight. I can't have him kicking with this scalpel in my hand. Daniel, you and Jimmy hold his arms."

As soon as the men had the sheriff secure, Peg began to penetrate the skin with the sharp instrument.

The lawman shook and cried out in agony. The men held him tightly. Ibby and Rebeckah turned away, unable to watch.

"There it is." Peg held up the small piece of metal with the forceps for all to see.

"Is it a bullet? John asked.

"A piece of the grapeshot the British fired from their cannon at us that day."

"I remember the sound of that grapeshot hitting our spring house. One piece stuck in the door. It looked just like what you have in your hand." William eyed the small piece of metal.

"Looks like the sheriff received two wounds." Peg pointed to two separate scars very near to each other. "Either he was stabbed with a bayonet then hit with grapeshot in his right hip or shot first then the bayonet. Regardless of the order of the wounds, it's obvious that whoever treated the wounds thought both were from the bayonet and didn't look for anything embedded in the flesh."

"So he carried the metal fragment in his hip for fifteen years?" John asked. "That must have caused him much pain and suffering."

Peg began the tedious task of sewing the wound up with cat gut from her medicine bag. Sheriff Preston flinched with every stitch.

"How can you stand to do that?" Ibby asked.

"God's gift, I assume." Peg admired her own work and gave the sheriff's wounded behind a light pat.

Chapter Eleven
The Nation's Capital

Townspeople peeked out from behind draped windows. Neighborhood children excitedly ran into the street to get a closer look at the strange-looking travelers headed up Baltimore Road. The residents of Moyamensing Township just south of the city limits of the nation's capital stared at the Westerners as their thirteen horses and mule clip-clopped along the cobblestone roadway, young girls driving the teams and men riding in formation. The women were attired in simple housedresses made of blue linsey-woolsey in stark contrast to the city dwellers. The ladies on their way to church wore store-bought linen and silk dresses this first Sunday morning of September in the twentieth year of the nation's independence.

A reddish cur dog ran off a porch and nipped at the lead Morgans' heels, but, ignoring the dog, the well-disciplined horses strutted along the boulevard in a perfect gait as if they knew their long journey was about to end.

After the travelers crossed the river, ferrymen had told them to turn right at James Pemberton's Plantation to get to Mr. Cohen's livery stable.

Daniel waited for them at the end of the Baltimore Road where it intersected into South Street, which ran east and west between the Schuylkill and Delaware Rivers. Daniel had heard from freight haulers of his acquaintance that a Mr. Cohen maintained a stable near Front Street in the Dock Ward, not far from the Delaware River wharfs, a good place to barter and trade furs.

The sheriff rode up to Peggy's wagon. "We've made it to Philadelphia."

"Yes, we have," she said over the noise of the rumbling wagons."I'm sure glad to see you back on your horse instead of lying in the back of my wagon."

"Not half as glad as I am. If I'd stayed at Trollinger's Station, I might not have healed so well. And if you hadn't taken out that piece of metal, I wouldn't be here at all. Thanks for saving my life."

"You're welcome, Sheriff." She looked around at her surroundings and smiled as if she and her traveling companions had conquered the world.

Church bells began to ring, reverberating through the city streets and bouncing off the brick walls of the buildings. She had heard church bells before but had never experienced such a volume of sound. Neither had the horses, and they became more anxious with each ring of the bells.

"Out of the way; out of the way, I say." Two official-looking riders called out the warning as they escorted an exquisite white-and-gold-trimmed coach pulled by two beautiful white horses and driven by a well-dressed coachman and his assistant. Peggy stared as they passed to the left of the caravan.

When the Tennesseans reached the intersection of South Street and Fourth Street, they could see a throng of people and horses surrounding the stately carriage that had just passed. The crowd cheered as the passengers unloaded in front of a large church two blocks down at Pine Street.

They found Mr. Cohen's stable attended by a Negro boy named Ezekiel. He was about ten years old but seemed much wiser than his years.

He flashed a proud smile. "You can call me Zeke." His eyes widened when he saw Daniel giving the white men instructions. He leaned over and asked, "Are you the wagon master of this outfit?"

"Yes, I am. Why do you ask?"

"You're a Negro!" The boy whispered in his ear so the others couldn't hear.

"You don't say." Daniel smiled at the young boy and put an arm on his shoulder. "Where can the ladies find room and board with a warm bath?"

"Mrs. Cohen might have a room for them. I'll go see if you want."

"Please do that while we feed and curry the horses." Daniel patted Zeke's shoulder.

Zeke returned with the stable owner and his wife. It was apparent that the Cohens wanted to have a look at their prospective boarders before inviting them to stay in their residence. The couple spoke with a slight German accent, and Mr. Cohen wore a crocheted yarmulke on the back of his balding head. After the usual questions of "Where you are from?" and "How long you will be staying?," the travelers and the Cohens agreed on a price for the girls to stay in a room and the men to bunk in the tack room of the stable. This would allow them to keep a close watch on the rigs and cargo, even though Mr. Cohen assured them everything was secure at his stable. He would have been concerned if he had known the value of their cargo, Peg thought.

Zeke put the ladies' things in a wheelbarrow and led a procession of the girls and Cohens on the short walk to the Cohen home. They passed the Pine Street Presbyterian Church with the impressive coach in front, its coachmen in waiting.

Peg looked at Mr. Cohen. "Who owns that beautiful coach?"

"John Adams, our next president." Mr. Cohen motioned for the sisters, who stopped to marvel at the magnificent conveyance, to move on. "Hurry before those blasted bells start to toll again."

"This way." Mrs. Cohen turned down a short alley beside the church.

When the bells began to ring, the girls covered their ears. Peg shouted, "How do you stand it?"

"You get used to it," Mrs. Cohen screamed back as she waddled along the cobblestone as fast as her short legs would carry her.

Once inside the spacious home with the ornate front door shut, they could carry on a conversation again. Zeke carried the belongings up the back way as his mother, Mattie, showed the guests to their room. The Cohens invited the Mitchell sisters to make themselves at home, then excused themselves to retire to their room to rest after the brisk walk in the muggy heat.

Ibby and Rebeckah peered out the window and pointed out features in the surrounding neighborhood that caught their eyes. On their tiptoes, they could see the Delaware River a few blocks east. Peg put their things away in a beautiful oak armoire. The beveled mirror on the door revealed the dust of her long journey.

"Look! They are so beautiful," Rebeckah said.

Peg turned to look out the window with her sisters.

"Who is that couple?" Ibby asked.

"Most likely Vice President John Adams and Mrs. Adams," Peggy answered.

Rebeckah's eyes widened and her voice rose in excitement. "Really? I've heard of him. That man is the Vice President of the whole United States you've told us about in our civics lessons?"

"Thank you for bringing us." Ibby threw her arms around her big sister, and Rebeckah joined the hug.

Mattie spoke from the hallway. "I'll have tea for you at three in the sitting room downstairs and dinner at five in the dining room. Zeke will be bringing up hot water shortly, and I'll prepare your bath."

"Thank you. A warm bath sounds wonderful," Peg said through the door.

Rebeckah said, "I want a warm bath, too. Please don't stay too long or the water will get cold before it's my turn."

Each sister took a relaxing bath in the long, narrow copper bathtub. They washed with the scented soap and dried with the luxurious, thick, linen towels Mattie brought them. They each examined several small bottles of perfume in a velvet-lined box on the washbasin before choosing a fragrance. Perfume was a rarity back home.

The girls became giddy thinking of their elegant surroundings and the new sights and activities they would see and experience in Philadelphia.

"Are you ready for tea, my ladies?" Peg playfully stepped out from behind a hand-painted screen that cordoned off the dressing area, holding a pearl-handled fan over her face like a mask.

"What is this tea thing?" Ibby wrinkled her nose as she always did when she didn't understand something.

Peg fluttered the fan, then used it to motion her sisters toward the door. "It's fashionable to have tea in the afternoon; it's a British custom that has apparently remained in favor here in Philadelphia. We don't drink tea back home because tea is difficult to come by and very expensive."

Peg opened the door, and the three young ladies stepped into the hallway and started down the narrow stairs.

Rebeckah asked, "What do we do at a tea?"

"Don't worry," Peg told her sisters. "Just sit like a lady as I've taught you and follow my lead."

Mrs. Cohen, who had changed into a silk skirt and matching blouse, poured steaming hot tea from a sterling silver teapot into small china cups. She offered the girls fresh cream and a choice of coarse-ground brown or white sugar. On the tea table, a large silver serving tray held fresh-baked scones and tea biscuits filled with assorted flavors of fruits.

"Please help yourselves. I know you must be starved after such a long journey. Zeke will be taking an early supper to your men," their hostess said.

"Thank you." Peg reached for a tea biscuit, motioning to her sisters to partake of the treats.

"What brings you all the way from Tennessee to Philadelphia?" Mrs. Cohen asked. She appeared to be about the same age as their mother.

Here goes the interrogation, Peg thought. She knew she should tell her hostess everything, but not just yet. "My sisters and I are on a shopping trip. And tomorrow being my birthday, I want to buy something special for myself."

"That sounds like fun. What do you intend to buy?"

"A new wardrobe for each of us, a suit of clothes for Reverend Witherspoon, and a piano if we can find one I can afford."

"Such a large order you have! No wonder you have brought three wagons. Let me tell you I have a cousin that has a dry goods store around the corner and my brother-in-law Charles Albrecht manufactures pianos just blocks from here. I would be glad to take you to their places of business tomorrow if you wish."

"Yes, that would be most kind of you. However, I must post an advertisement in the Gazette and Daily Advertiser first thing in the morning. May I use your address for responders?"

"Certainly, my dear. The newspaper office opens at nine. We can take care of your post, and then go to my cousin's for pretty things for you darling girls." Mrs. Cohen sighed. "I just love to shop. And it's your birthday! How old will you be?"

"Twenty-four."

"Oh, to be so young."

The next morning at the newspaper office, Peg placed her advertisement and ordered broadsides of the advertisement that would run on Wednesday and Friday of the twice-weekly paper. She also ordered engraved calling cards for Jimmy and herself; they would be ready with the broadsides by day's end if the ink was dry.

After the girls picked out their first ready-made clothes, the seamstress marked them for alterations. They headed home for afternoon tea and to meet Jimmy, whom Peg had asked to join them.

Mrs. Cohen said, "I've never met anyone who traveled with their own man of God and a lawman."

Peggy just smiled.

As Jimmy chit-chatted with the ladies, Mr. Charles C. Watson, a well-known Philadelphia tailor, appeared at the front door at half past three.

"I'm here to fit Reverend Witherspoon for a suit of clothes," the tailor announced to Mattie.

The minister heard Mr. Watson at the door. "I didn't send for a tailor."

"But I did, Reverend," Peggy said. "If you're going to take me to church on Sunday, I want you dressed like the preacher you are." She extended her hand to the tailor and introduced the clergyman.

"But—I can't," he stammered. "I—"

"I want you looking pretty to perform the ceremony for Robert's wedding next month." She sighed. "I wanted to have suits made for William and John, but they said if the groom didn't have a tailored suit from Philadelphia they wouldn't have one either."

"Well, uh, if your brothers—"

"Regardless of what my brothers wear, the preacher will be properly dressed for this wedding."

"Mattie, show the reverend, Peggy, and Mr. Watson to the parlor upstairs. If Mr. Cohen is in there, run him out."

"Yes, Mrs. Cohen." Mattie led the group upstairs.

"Tell me what you have in mind," the tailor said.

Jimmy didn't respond; he just stared at the tailor. Mr. Watson figured out who would be paying for the suit and turned to Peggy.

"Tell me who you have made suits for, Mr. Watson."

"James Madison, John Adams, and the late Dr. Franklin, to name but a few."

"What about preachers? Presbyterian preachers?" she asked.

"I did do a suit for a Methodist minister once. I made him a traditional dark grey suit with a collar trimmed in black silk and matching stripes down the seam of the trousers. Quite impressive it was." Mr. Watson looked up at Peggy, then quickly looked down to the floor.

"Can you have it finished by Saturday afternoon?" she asked.

"I could if the reverend would be available for fittings each day."

"That can be arranged," Peg said. "When can you start?"

"Tonight with a deposit of a quarter eagle for the material."

"When it is finished?" she asked.

"A double eagle."

She did the math in her head. "So the total cost is three-fourths of an ounce of gold."

"If you wish to use currency, a twenty dollar note will do."

She reached into her clutch purse for a quarter eagle and handed it to the tailor. "Coin is good." She knew three quarter eagles were less than a twenty dollar note.

The tailor turned to the minister. "Reverend Witherspoon, I will have dinner with my family, then meet you at my shop at a quarter past six. That will give us two hours before the sun sets to work on your new suit." He handed the preacher his card as Peggy escorted him to the front door.

"Peggy, that is a lot of money for a suit," Jimmy said once they were alone in the foyer.

She patted his shoulder. "You must look like a preacher when you are interviewed for your own church."

"Thank you. I know every preacher needs a good suit."

Zeke arrived with the broadside advertising posters and the two sets of calling cards. Peg's calling cards read

Margaret Mitchell, Broker of Fine Quality Furs.

The other set of cards read

Reverend James Witherspoon, Minister, Hebron
Presbyterian Church.

She handed Jimmy his calling cards. "These social cards are for you."

He looked at the cards for some time. "It says Minister of Hebron Church by my name." Jimmy looked at Peg for an explanation.

"That's right, Reverend Witherspoon. You are the minister at Hebron Presbyterian Church until some wealthy congregation hires you away from us." She gave him a radiant smile.

"You mean the congregation has called me to preach at Hebron?"

"Yes, and you will deliver your first sermon there the Sunday after we return. Reverend Balch will still visit occasionally, but we look forward to having a preacher every Sunday."

"Thank you."

"You know we can't pay you, but my father and I thought it would be easier for you to find a clergy position if you already have a church." They also knew preaching for free at Hebron would give him practice and confidence.

"I don't know what to say. How can I thank you?" He put both arms around Peg and pulled her close to him.

"You can thank me by taking Zeke and putting up these broadsides around the wharf and Front Street before it gets dark. Remember not to divulge to anyone where the furs are. I'll have pelts to show the quality of our furs at the Cohens starting at nine in the morning." She handed him the cards. "Take some of my cards and give them to anyone that shows a genuine interest in purchasing my lot of furs and pelts. Take your cards; you might have the opportunity to save a soul. Remember to be at the tailor's at a quarter after six." She hurried toward the door, motioning Jimmy and Zeke out. "You can eat later."

Mattie announced dinner was being served. When Peg entered the impressive dining room, her sisters and Mr. Cohen were already sitting at a long oak table with room to seat twelve. Mrs. Cohen entered the room followed by Mattie, both carrying food from the kitchen. Once everyone was seated, Mr. Cohen blessed the food and the dinner conversation began.

"Do you know the minister of the Presbyterian Church around the corner?" Peggy asked Mr. Cohen.

"Yes, I do. Reverend Robert Annan boards his horses at my stable, so I see him frequently. He and his wife live in the small cottage behind the church."

"Would you be so kind as to introduce Reverend Witherspoon to him? He might be able to give Jimmy—I mean Reverend Witherspoon—some direction in his theological pursuits."

Mr. Cohen looked to his wife; she looked down at her plate, which Peg interpreted to mean she didn't want to get involved.

Mr. Cohen took a deep breath and waited a few seconds before speaking. "You understand that we are not Christians?" He looked over his glasses directly into Peggy's eyes.

"With the mezuzah on your door post and the yarmulke on your head, I assumed you are of the Jewish faith."

Ibby squinched her nose and turned to Rebeckah, who looked from Ibby to Peg to the Cohens and back to Ibby.

"You have no problem with us not believing in your Jesus?"

Ibby and Rebeckah gazed at the Cohens with wide eyes; they had never known anyone who didn't believe in Jesus.

"I was taught that your faith and mine share the same God, and I am aware that you do not accept Jesus as the Messiah."

"Please understand that we believe that Jesus lived and died on the cross. Jews just don't accept him as the Messiah. That bothers many Christians like Reverend Annan, and for that reason my introducing you to him might not have the effect that you wish. I would be honored to make the introduction, but it may be best if you introduce yourself, as I know that he is not as tolerant as you concerning our faith."

"Thank you, Mr. Cohen, for your concern. I understand. I am aware that many well-intentioned Christians sometimes let the zeal for our religion impugn the beliefs of others."

"Miss Mitchell—"

"Please call me Peg."

"Peg, you appear to be the tzur of your group."

"What's tzur?" Rebeckah asked.

Mr. Cohen looked at Rebeckah. "A tzur is a strong rock— like flint rock. Peggy seems to be the strong foundation of the family." He turned back to face Peggy. "As a man many years your elder, I can see and appreciate your care and concern for those you love. I know you girls are sisters, that John and William are your brothers. Are the others you're traveling with family also?"

"We come from a very small community, Mr. Cohen, where if you aren't kin, you're a friend. Jimmy—I mean Reverend Witherspoon—went to school with my brothers and me. James and Willie Smith are his stepbrothers. Daniel, our wagon master, has been a member of our family since his birth." Peg took a sip of claret from a hand-cut crystal goblet.

"You don't say." Mrs. Cohen looked at Mattie, who was paying close attention to the conversation.

"My grandfather inherited Samuel and Bessie, Daniel's parents, along with a plantation," Peg said.

"So they were slaves?" Mr. Cohen nodded and looked at his wife for her reaction.

"Yes, they were, but they were very dear to my grand-parents. Bessie nursed and comforted Grandmother until her death. Grandfather McMachen sold the plantation and moved west. He gave Bessie, Samuel, and their children Daniel and Samantha their freedom. The McMachens were the only family they knew, and they begged to go west with Grandfather and his family. Daniel became like a son to Grandfather, who taught him about horses as well as the basics of reading and writing. Daniel is family." Peg's voice cracked with emotion.

"Daniel owns the livery stable in Jonesborough?" Mr. Cohen asked.

Peg took a deep breath. "Yes, he does."

"Is Sheriff Preston a member of your family?"

"He is no relation. He only wanted to get us safely out of his county, as a gang of highwaymen were attacking travelers on the wagon road. Along the road, a war injury became infected, and it became necessary that I remove a piece of metal that was causing him great pain. He was unable to ride horseback so we brought him with us in the wagon to Philadelphia."

"You removed the metal from his body?" Mr. Cohen asked.

"From his backside!" As soon as Rebeckah blurted out the words, her face turned red.

"From his tuchus?" Mr. Cohen asked, gesturing with a knife as if it were a scalpel.

Mrs. Cohen and Mattie looked at the shiny knife in Mr. Cohen's hand and then at Peggy.

Mr. Cohen asked, "Are you trained in medicine?"

"I didn't go to a school of medicine, if that is what you mean. I learned by doctoring my family's illnesses and injuries as they occurred, reading *Beecham's Family Physician*, and studying human anatomy in any book I could find on the subject." Peg's voice was filled with pride.

The conversation stopped while the Cohens and Mattie, who was now seated in a wingback chair near the buffet table, gathered their thoughts.

Mrs. Cohen shook her head. "You're such an interesting person."

"I told you she was a tzur."

"We must introduce Peggy and her sisters to our friends," Mrs. Cohen said.

"Would you be our guests for Sabbath dinner this Friday evening?" Mr. Cohen asked. "My brother, Rabbi Cohen, and his wife will be joining us."

Rebeckah leaned over to Ibby and whispered, "What is he talking about? Sabbath is on Sunday."

Mr. Cohen overheard the whispered conversation. "Yes, Christians celebrate the Sabbath on Sunday, but we celebrate our Sabbath from sundown on Friday until sundown on Saturday. "

"We would really like to have you and the girls and Reverend Witherspoon with us this Sabbath," Mrs. Cohen said. "It is our turn to host the family. I know they would love to meet you and hear your wonderful stories of the west."

"We would be honored to attend your celebration." Peg knew that being invited was a great honor and that turning down the invitation would be an insult. She thought it would be a learning experience that Ibby and Rebeckah would never forget and an opportunity for Jimmy to discuss religion with a rabbi. Not many Presbyterian ministers had done that.

After dinner, they sat in the parlor and visited. Later, Zeke and Jimmy came in from distributing the posters.

Peggy asked, "Did you see the tailor?"

"Yes, I stood there forever while he measured me all over."

Mattie said, "Come in the kitchen, and I'll fix you both something to eat."

After the reverend and Zeke had finished Mattie's leftovers, Jimmy joined Peggy in the sitting room. "Your posters have drawn a lot of attention."

"How do you know that?"

"As soon as we put a poster up, men would come over to read it and write down the address."

"That's a good sign!"

Peg heard Mattie at the front door.

"No callers after dark!" Mattie said.

"I am pulling up anchor at first light," a man said in a booming Irish brogue.

Peggy and Jimmy went to the door to see who was calling so late. Peg stepped in front of Mattie and walked out on the steps. "May I help you?"

"You can if you're Margaret Mitchell, the **fur broker**." He emphasized the words **fur broker**. "If you're one of the usual women that advertise on a broadside, I'm not interested."

Peg was determined to know who he was before she listened to anything he said. "I am Margaret Mitchell. Who may I ask is calling?"

"I want to buy the furs and pelts you have offered for sale. That is if you really have furs for sale. The only thing I've seen women advertise on a broadside is themselves."

Peggy said, "I'm not listening to a word you say until you tell me who you are."

"I'm a prospective buyer for your furs. May I see them?"

"As my broadside said, they will be available for viewing after nine in the morning."

"That will not do, Madam. My ship is sailing at daybreak."

"I identified myself to you, sir. Would you be so kind to do the same for me?"

"Excuse me, Miss Margaret Mitchell, Fur Broker, from someplace called Jonesborough that I have never heard of." The white-bearded man removed his seaman's cap and bowed.

Peggy smiled, intrigued by his brusque style and the horizontal-black-and-white-striped shirt he wore.

"My name is Patrick McDuffy. I'm the captain of the Lady Ann, which should have sailed three days ago with a load of furs for Amsterdam. Your Highness, do you want to sell your damn furs or stand on the porch and chitchat about it?"

"I am quite enjoying our conversation, but I am concerned about your haste to do business so late in the evening," Peg answered.

"You have furs and pelts. I need furs and pelts. What difference does the time of day have to do with anything? Do you want to do business or not?" the captain demanded.

"The banks are closed. How would you pay?

"As I always pay—in gold coin."

"Are you aware of the size of my lot, sir, and the monetary value of it?" Peg asked.

"Yes, I am. I have your inventory." He pulled a folded broadside from his pocket.

"You tore down my poster!"

"If you and I make a deal for the lot of furs, it won't matter about your blasted sign, now will it?"

"If you will meet me here at first daylight, we can do business in an hour and you can sail away to Amsterdam. An hour shouldn't make that much difference on such a long journey."

He turned and walked away shaking his head, muttering about doing business with women, and thrusting his short arms up in the air as if to say *you win.* "I will see you in the morning."

"Interesting fellow, that Captain McDuffy," Peg said to Jimmy as she entered the house.

The next morning, Peggy awoke to the sounds of the neighbor's roosters crowing and the traffic of horses on the cobblestone street in front of the house.

Mattie knocked on the door. "Miss Peggy, you got callers out front waiting for you."

When she reached the front door, Mr. Cohen met her with a frown. "Do you see what your advertisement has brought to my home?"

He opened the door to a yard full of men with all kinds of conveyances, none of which was large enough to haul off the entire lot of furs.

She looked at the motley crew that had responded to her advertisement. "I will take care of this, Mr. Cohen. I never suspected anything like this."

Someone in the crowd yelled an obscenity.

The men howled and hooted at the vulgar remark until Captain McDuffy took a swing at the person that made the comment. Then a full scale brawl was on in the Cohens' front yard. After several minutes, the constable arrived to restore order and to run off the ruffians who were making sport of Peggy's business. He allowed only those he identified as prospective buyers to remain.

Captain McDuffy flashed a big Irish grin. "You should have dealt with me last night."

"If you want to see the inventory, follow me."

She led Captain McDuffy and the other two sincere-seeming prospective buyers to the stable. The entourage included Mr. Cohen and the constable. Sheriff Preston and the men from Jonesborough were caught off guard, as they weren't expecting potential buyers for at least another hour.

"Daniel, please remove the oilcloth from the wagons for inspection of the furs," Peg said.

When the cloth was off the wagons, the buyers began picking through the stacks of furs.

"If your inventory is accurate, Miss Mitchell, I will give you fifteen hundred dollars in gold coin for the lot, and I'll be on my way," the captain whispered to her. "The others are bickering about not wanting the buffalo hide or the deer skins."

Peggy climbed up onto a wagon and raised her voice. "Gentlemen, Captain McDuffy has offered me fifteen hundred dollars in gold coin for the lot you're picking over. If either of you would like to counter his offer, you may do so now. Otherwise, the lot is going to Captain McDuffy."

Each of the men made an offer, which Captain McDuffy countered.

When the bidding ended, Peggy said, "Sold to Captain McDuffy for eighteen hundred dollars."

"Can your men leave the pelts on the wagons and haul them to the dock for boarding? I will give each of them a quarter eagle for their help," the captain said.

Peggy asked Daniel to harness the teams for transport, and the group headed to the Lady Ann. John and William went with Peggy to the captain's quarters for the money exchange. Captain McDuffy removed a worn-looking oilcloth sack from the ship's safe. From the coins inside, he made eighteen stacks of ten-dollar gold coins, with ten coins per stack. The sack still appeared to be almost full of gold when he placed it back in the safe. The Mitchell siblings had never seen so much gold.

"You count it, Miss Mitchell?"

"I counted it as you stacked it."

He shook her hand. "It was a pleasure dealing with such a lovely lady. If you wish to sell your furs next year, the Lady Ann will be here again at the same time."

"Would you have something I could carry the coin in?" Peg asked.

He handed her an empty bag from the safe and smiled. "Next year bring your own money bag."

"I'll be sure to do that, Captain McDuffy."

"Once the pelts are aboard my ship, give each of your men a double eagle for their efforts." The captain handed Peggy the double eagles.

"Now what?" John asked.

"First to the bank and then to make amends to the Cohens," Peggy said.

"Amends for what?" William asked.

"Apparently our actions have led some to believe that we have opened a brothel in their home."

Her brothers stared at Peg, with their mouths agape.

They stopped at the bank and deposited all but thirty of the gold coins, removing a few broadsides along the way.

When they arrived at the Cohens, riffraff that included working girls from the city's bordellos thronged in front of the house. The men made catcalls and the women hollered obscenities about Peggy moving in on their territory.

"What is going on?" John said.

"Oh, no!" Peg groaned. "The advertisement in the Gazette came out this morning. The whole city of Philadelphia thinks we're prostitutes!" She covered her face to hide the tears.

As the constables on horseback and on foot ran the rowdies off, more of the derelicts appeared. A female bordello owner came at Peggy with a folded parasol but was diverted by a constable.

Peggy's brothers got her inside where they found Rebeckah, Ibby, and Mattie hiding in a closet. The Cohens were cowering in their room upstairs.

"What's going on?" Ibby asked. "Why are these men being so mean?"

"They think we're prostitutes. Oh, what have I done?" Peggy moaned.

Rebeckah put her hands on her hips. "We're not prostitutes! We're Presbyterians!"

From the yard came a loud voice. "Listen up. I said listen up!" Then came a loud boom that sounded like a cannon shot. "Now that I have your attention—I am the sheriff of Abingdon, Virginia. As your local constabulary has failed to maintain order, I am declaring martial law. I have deputized the men you see in front of me as well as the local constables. I ask that you leave the premises of these fine folks immediately. Anyone that doesn't will be arrested and hauled away."

The eleven deputized men started moving in a single line, slowly pushing the crowd back toward the street and away from the Cohens' home. When the yard was clear, they would take turns guarding the perimeter, not allowing any loitering.

Peg watched the chaos in the yard turning into order. "There is something to be said for bringing your own sheriff to town."

Chapter Twelve
New Friends

"Easy does it, John. If we put a scratch on this instrument, Peggy will be selling our hides like a silver belly beaver," William joked to his brother as they loaded the pianoforte on the wagon. Jimmy and Daniel held the bridles of the restless Morgan horses, which had become wary of the strange block and tackle being used to load the heavy wooden crate.

Mrs. Cohen's brother-in-law, Charles Albrecht, had been commissioned by a prominent German-born businessman to make a small rectangular pianoforte at his shop at Third and Green Streets. Before the instrument could be delivered, the businessman's family succumbed to the cholera epidemic that ravaged Philadelphia in 1793. The shiny, reddish-brown mahogany instrument sat in a corner of Mr. Albrecht's shop for years, a sad reminder of the victims lost that year. Because it had been custom made for his client, Mr. Albrecht had been reluctant to offer it for sale.

However, once Peggy saw the beautiful ornate case with its inlaid stripes and heard the piano master play a minuet, she had to have it for the Hebron School and Church. The case was only five feet long perpendicular to the keyboard by two feet wide and one foot deep, not much larger than her teacher's desk. Its removable legs could easily be set up and dismantled.

"I'm happy that this special pianoforte now has a home where it can at last bring smiles to the faces of those that hear the sweet sounds made by her mellow strings." Mr.

Albrecht smiled and patted the tarpaulin-wrapped shipping crate after it was securely tied down in the wagon.

"Please know that the children of Hebron School who play this instrument will know the story of the craftsman that built it." Peggy smiled back at the piano maker.

Mr. Albrecht's chest seemed to expand a little and he winked. "Should they ever forget, the maker's name is painted in the oval on the name board, and his mark and the date under the music rack."

"We shall never forget you." Peggy placed her hand on his shoulder for a second then climbed into the buckboard and sat beside Jimmy.

"I happen to have four tickets to the *Archers of Switzer-land* tomorrow night at the Chestnut Street Theatre. It is obvious that you love music. I would like you to have the tickets as appreciation for your purchase."

"Thank you. We would love to go to the opera. Wouldn't we, girls?" Peggy looked over her shoulder at her excited sisters seated on the crate that housed the pianoforte.

"I will bring the tickets tonight to Shabbat dinner," the piano maker said.

"You will be joining us tonight?" Peg asked.

"It is tradition; our family breaks bread together every Sabbath in one of our homes."

"I look forward to sharing Shabbat with you and Mrs. Albrecht this evening."

Jimmy moved the team gently forward as Ibby and Rebeckah waved goodbye. Daniel, John, and William tipped the brims of their dusty hats as they rode past the craftsman.

"Shalom." Mr. Albrecht waved as they drove away.

As the wagon moved south down Third Street, Ibby and Rebeckah talked excitedly about going to the theater that Mrs. Cohen had pointed out to them while shopping. Built on the plans of the Theatre Royal in Bath, England, it could seat 2000 people in the three tiers of boxes in a horseshoe-shaped gallery around the orchestra pit. All the seats looked down on the stage, giving every patron a good view of the performance.

Peggy smiled back at her sisters, then turned toward Jimmy. "It's been four days since Sheriff Preston left for home. How far do you think he has got?"

"Traveling alone by horseback, Robert ought to be in Big Lick by now and should be home by Sunday." Jimmy gave the team a shake of the leather reins.

"That's good. I know he is anxious to see his son again." Her voice carried surprise when she asked, "You call Sheriff Preston Robert now?"

"Yes, he asked that I call him by his given name, and we have become good friends. His close call with death, all of us praying for his recovery, discovering that it was your grandmother who saved his life in the spring house on the battlefield so long ago, and then you—her granddaughter with the same name—removing the piece of metal from his backside ..." Jimmy took a deep breath. "I suppose all that made him realize that God has a plan for him. I baptized him before he left."

"You did! Where?"

"In the water trough at the stable. He'd never been baptized before so I immersed him completely for good measure."

"I would have liked to have witnessed that. Why didn't you invite me?"

"He wanted it to be just between him and God—and, of course, his minister."

"Then his is the first soul you have saved as the new minister of the Hebron Church." Peg beamed at Jimmy, then looked up at the dark clouds beginning to roll in from the nearby Delaware River.

As they approached the entrance of the livery stable, they saw that a large Conestoga freight wagon pulled by six huge draft horses had the right of way blocked.

"Daniel, you and John best help the wagoner with his team before it starts to rain on us." Peggy grabbed her bonnet with her left hand as the wind lifted it off her head.

Daniel quickly removed the leather collar and harness from the wheel horse's head and the back straps and britchens from its back as Zeke and the Smith boys helped the driver remove assorted tackle from the lead and middle team.

Jimmy raised his voice to be heard above the wind. "Peg, you and the girls should get under the roof of the barn. It looks like it's going to be a gully washer."

James ran up to the wagon and held up his hand to help Ibby and Rebeckah. A bolt of lightning struck with a loud crack. The horses whinnied and shook their manes vigorously to demonstrate their displeasure. Fortunately, they didn't move the wagon as Peggy and her sisters were stepping off at that instant.

Daniel called from the barn, "Good horse, Nick. Good horse, John. Good horse."

At the sound of their master's voice, the animals quickly settled down.

The girls and James reached the barn just in time to keep from getting drenched. Under the cover of the roof of the open barn, they watched the sky unleash its vengeance. The strong wind blew the rain almost sideways, and white pebbles of hail the size of mustang grapes fell from the heavens, followed by almost-solid sheets of water.

"Oh, the pianoforte will get wet." Peg looked at Jimmy, her brow furrowed and her hands clasped as if in prayer.

"Mr. Albrecht sealed the crate with tree sap and then John and I wrapped it in a tarpaulin. It'll be fine."

As soon as he finished his sentence, Jimmy headed into the blowing rain to move the nervous horses and wagon out of the storm. The other men pushed the large freight wagon over enough for Jimmy to maneuver the small wagon in beside the large Conestoga so they could remove the harness from the horses.

Once all were under the high-gabled roof, Daniel walked over to the young, red-headed teamster. "Good-looking team of horses you have."

"Thank you for the compliment and for all your help. They are fine animals, indeed. I am going to miss them."

The teamster reached out to shake Daniel's hand. "My name is Jake Thompson."

Daniel introduced himself and the others. The group hollered and strained to hear over the sound of the thunder and the rain pounding on the roof.

The storm subsided as fast as it had appeared, leaving a rainbow hanging over the Delaware River and a great deal of water in the streets. The Mitchell girls took advantage of the break in the weather to walk to the Cohens. They took off their new high-top shoes, tied the strings, and hung them around their necks to protect the shoes from the water as they walked barefoot on the cobblestone street. They chattered excitedly about the new clothes they would wear for the Shabbat tonight.

"Why did you say you were going to miss that fine team of horses, Mr. Thompson?" Daniel asked.

"My teamster days are over, I'm afraid." He sighed. "I promised my wife this would be my last haul. I'm going to sell my rig and get a job where I'll be home every night with her and the boys." He looked over at his horses. "I'll miss sleeping under the stars, watching the teamwork of these horses I spent years training for freight hauling. Only a teamster like you would understand what I mean."

"This is my first long haul, but I know what you're talking about," Daniel replied.

"Really? This is your first haul? You unharnessed my team like an experienced teamster, and your Morgans are so well disciplined, I assumed—"

"I own the livery stable in Jonesborough. Harnessed many a team in my day and been training horses all my life." Daniel wiped rain droplets from his face with a red bandanna.

"You got the call of the road, I can tell."

Both men admired the draft horses in the loafing pen as if they were treasured works of art.

"That I do. Got it the second day on the road watching Nick and John pulling that wagon around the curves of the road, hooves pounding the road in cadence like they was dancing to the sweet music of the bells jingling on their leather harnesses." Daniel shook his head then grinned at the broad-shouldered teamster.

"It sure sounds like the road is calling you. Tell me where you came up with the names for your horses. Nick and John just happen to be my two boys' names."

"Named my best horses for two of the most dependable and honest men I ever knew. John McMachen gave me my freedom and taught me to read and write. Nicolas Fain set me up with the livery stable. They made me who I am today. You've given your sons honorable names."

Thompson acknowledged Daniel's comment then changed the subject. "Sounds like you want to own a big rig like mine. If you're interested, I'll make you a good deal on my six-horse team, all the rigging, the wagon, and pending bills of lading. You could have two four-horse teams for normal loads and an eight-horse team for heavy loads. There would be no limit to what you could haul."

"What do you mean—bills of lading? I've heard the word before but don't know what it means."

"My book of business. I have six months of shipping backed up right now. A bill of lading is an order from a shipper to deliver freight to a receiver. Sometimes I have two or three bills of lading to deliver at one stop. That's like gravy on a biscuit; that's where the money is made."

"How did you find all this business?" Daniel asked.

"With a rig like mine, the big shippers find you." The teamster motioned toward the wagon. "This Conestoga is twenty feet long and can carry six tons. Not many like it."

"Six tons?" Daniel admired the light blue Conestoga wagon.

"Yes—12,000 pounds of freight. Those Germans over in Lancaster sure know what they're doing."

"What kind of work will you do if you sell?"

"My wife says it doesn't matter as long as the work is honest and I'm home every night."

Daniel looked the tall teamster in the eye. "You must have some idea what you want to do."

"The City Tavern at Second and Walnut has an opening for a bartender that I'm going to inquire about."

"I know it's none of my business, but if you have family problems now, you're really going to have them if you become a bartender in a tavern. Think about it. You'll be working late at night cause that's when a bar does its business and the devil does his best work. That's no job for a family man," Daniel said emphatically.

"You sound like you have some experience in the work of the devil," Jake said.

"Running a livery stable for twenty-five years, I've seen the devil do his work. Good young men like you with families at home come to town, leave their rig with me, and get their nose into a jug—then don't have money left to pay me the stable fees. I seen them coming and going." Daniel looked to see if the young teamster was listening.

Jake Thompson gazed around the wet barn and horse pens, closed his eyes, and took in a deep breath. He held it for a second or two then slowly let it out. "I love that sweet barnyard smell of fresh horse dung. I think I'd like to have a livery stable like Mr. Cohen."

Daniel smiled and nodded. "How much do you want for that rig of yours?"

"It ought to be worth at least a thousand dollars."

"That sounds like a fair price for a going business. That's about what I think my livery stable business is worth," Daniel said. "If your family has the same appreciation of barnyard smells, your wife and children can be with you day and night, living in the livery stable and blacksmith shop that goes with it."

"It has a blacksmith shop and a place to live! That sounds like a wonderful opportunity, and I could still work with horses. If I understand, Daniel, you're proposing a swap of my rig for your livery stable and blacksmith shop. Is that right?" Jake's voice rose, and he couldn't stand still.

"That's what I said."

"I must discuss this with my wife. We live just a few blocks away."

"You do that, but please get back to me soon cause we're gonna be leaving," Daniel called after the excited young man as he hurried away.

"Sounds like you have a trade in the works. I'm happy for you if that is what you want." Jimmy sat down across from Daniel.

"It depends on what his wife says, but I sure like that rig."

"If it is meant to be, it will be. Jonesborough wouldn't be the same without your smiling face. Won't you miss us?" Jimmy asked.

"I'll be coming through Jonesborough regularly on my way from Philadelphia to Nashville."

William, who had been listening to the conversation from his position a few feet away, said, "Let's all go down to City Tavern and have a drink and celebrate."

"Your being with me could cause problems. Remember this isn't Jonesborough where everyone knows us. Besides, I have a jug of some of the finest whisky your father ever made right here." Daniel pulled the bottle of Adam Mitchell's best out from under some straw where he had hidden it. "Anyway, I expect Mr. Thompson will be back to talk business soon, and I want to be here if he comes. Opportunities like this don't come around often."

Daniel took a draw and passed the crock jug to William who took his turn, passing it to Jimmy.

"No, thanks," Jimmy said. "I have a Shabbat dinner to attend this evening and best start getting ready."

William looked at John, who shrugged his shoulders. Then he turned to Daniel. "What's a Shabbat?"

"Don't know." Daniel shrugged. "But your sisters been talking about it all week, how they was going to dress up for it and all."

Zeke had been listening from his perch on top of the gate to the loafing pen, a place where he could see and hear everything that went on in the livery stable. He climbed down and joined the men's conversation. "It's just like Sunday dinner after church, except the Jews do it on Friday night."

"You don't say? You mean a Shabbat isn't some critter that you eat?" Daniel teased.

William wrinkled his forehead. "You mean Shabbat is the Jewish word for dinner?"

"It is the word for the Sabbath, and the Shabbat dinner is a very special dinner." Zeke started toward the barn door. "I best get home to help my momma get things ready for it."

"Goodbye." Daniel smiled at the young boy.

"You have become fond of Zeke, haven't you?" William asked.

"Yes, I have and of his momma Mattie, too." Daniel grinned and reached for the brown jug of whisky.

"Sounds like Daniel got some interest in Mattie." John made a funny face at his brother William, trying to tease Daniel.

"How come you never married?" William asked.

"You wouldn't understand," Daniel said, looking at the young men he had known since their birth.

"Tell us."

"You boys and your cousins can have any woman you want in Washington County. Your family has land, and any father would be honored for his daughters to marry into your clan." Daniel took another swig.

John and William had never heard their friend talk about his personal life.

"What's that got to do with you not marrying?" John asked.

"Who would I ask in Washington County? Far as I know, I'm the only free Negro for miles. If I find a slave girl I like, you think her master going to give her up? Only if I sell myself to him, then I'd be his slave. If I asked a white girl, I'd be promptly hung from the nearest tree."

It got very quiet in the livery stable. The jug was passed again among the three friends.

"I never thought about that," John said.

"Me neither!" William chimed in.

"Mattie is the only Negro woman I've met that could be my wife."

The Mitchell brothers looked down. John scratched the dirt floor of the stable with his boot toe.

After a few seconds, William looked up and said, "John, I'm hungry. Let's go to the tavern."

John stood and looked at Daniel. "Come join us."

"No, thank you. Mattie said she'd bring me some chicken soup after a bit."

"See you later," the brothers called as they left.

"Be careful as the devil will be there looking for you." Daniel grinned and waved.

***

The Cohens' house smelled of fresh baked challah, the bread that Mrs. Cohen had taught Mattie to twist and braid. In a large pot on the stove, the cholent, the stew that would be the Sabbath meal, had been cooking slowly all day. Mr. Cohen had bought fish for the Gefilte from a fishmonger on the wharf.

Watching Mattie grind the fish, Rebeckah squinched her nose. "Phew. Why do you grind your fish?"

"Don't know. The Cohens say it's an old family recipe, and I fix it the way they ask." Mattie added shredded carrots, onion, and Matzah meal to the ground fish.

At the sound of a knock at the door, Rebeckah asked, "You want me to see who it is?"

"Please, child. My hands are a mess."

Before Rebeckah could get to the door, Peggy had already opened it to a well-dressed woman about her mother's age. Locks of curly white hair protruded from under her shiny silk bonnet. The matron seemed to be confused and distressed.

"May I help you?" Peggy asked.

"I am Mrs. Annan, the wife of Reverend Annan from the Pine Street Church around the corner. I hate to bother Mrs. Cohen on her Sabbath, but I understand from Mattie that there is a young woman staying here who has some medical experience."

"That's me. I'm Peggy Mitchell." She gestured to the girls who had joined her at the door. "These are my sisters, Ibby and Rebeckah. I'm not a doctor, but I do take care of my community's medical needs back home."

"My poor Robert is running a very high fever and has lost his voice. I sent word to Dr. Rush but was told he is away tending a sick infant. Could you take a look at him? He must get his voice back for his Sunday sermon."

"Let me get my medicine bag."

"Thank you so much." Mrs. Annan wrung her hands and stood first on one foot then the other as Peggy hurried upstairs.

"Whatever is wrong with your husband, my sister Peggy will make him well," Ibby said.

Rebeckah nodded in agreement.

Mrs. Annan made a half-hearted attempt at a smile. "Ibby is such an unusual name. How did you come by it?"

"I was named Elizabeth after my mother, but everyone just calls me Ibby."

"How old are you, Ibby?" Mrs. Annan's voice didn't sound like she really cared but was simply trying to make conversation.

"I'll be sixteen in December."

Peggy came rushing down the stairs and directed Mrs. Annan out the door.

"Ibby, tell Mrs. Cohen where I've gone. I'll be back shortly," Peg called over her shoulder.

The Annans lived in the manse behind the church. Mrs. Annan invited Peggy in and took her to the bedroom. Though the house was small, it was comfortable and elegantly furnished.

Peggy pulled a small straight-back wooden chair next to the bed. The reverend's face felt hot to her touch. She looked into his throat and saw the swollen glands that made his throat sore.

"When did he last eat?" Peggy asked.

"He ate a good meal after Bible study Wednesday evening," Mrs. Annan said.

Peg turned sideways in the chair and looked at the minister's wife. "Will you bring me a pitcher of water and a small spoon? Then return to Mrs. Cohen's and bring a cup of her chicken soup. If Reverend Witherspoon is there, bring him with you."

Mrs. Annan stopped pacing and looked at Peggy in confusion. "Reverend John Witherspoon died two years ago. I attended his funeral."

"This is Reverend James Witherspoon from Washington County, Tennessee." Peg's voice took on an edge as she thought about all she had to do before sundown.

The woman moved toward the door as fast as her aging body allowed, muttering "Oh, my poor Robert." She returned promptly with the pitcher of water and a spoon.

"Thank you, Mrs. Annan. Now please go on to the Cohens' for that chicken soup."

Peggy began to give the sickly minister water, just a few drops at a time from the spoon, and gently wiped his brow with a cool wet rag.

A few minutes later, Mrs. Annan returned, followed by Jimmy, who entered the room carrying a ceramic bowl filled with hot soup. "What can I do?" He placed the bowl on the bedside table.

Peggy smiled at Jimmy, seeing him for the first time in his new suit of clothes. Then she returned her attention to her patient, who pointed at Jimmy and tried to say something.

"Who are you?" Reverend Annan managed to choke out.

"I am Reverend James Witherspoon, minister at the Hebron Presbyterian Church in Tennessee."

Reverend Annan struggled to ask. "Can you preach?"

"Certainly. That is my calling," Jimmy answered.

"This Sunday." Reverend Annan pointed toward his church.

"You want me to preach to your congregation?" Jimmy asked.

Reverend Annan nodded.

"It would be my honor, Reverend Annan."

The minister, relieved, lay back and fell asleep.

"Mrs. Annan, when he wakes, spoonfeed him all the water and chicken soup he'll take. He needs lots of fluids. Reverend Witherspoon and I must get back to the Cohens for dinner. I'll be back later to check on him."

"Thank you so much," Mrs. Annan said.

The Cohens' family members had walked from the synagogue, as was their Sabbath custom. Mr. and Mrs. Cohen introduced Reverend Witherspoon, Peggy, Ibby, and Rebeckah as their *Christian friends from Tennessee.*

Then Mr. Cohen introduced his family members, including his brother, Rabbi Jacob Cohen, the rabbi's wife Rebekah, and their son Abraham. Peggy was intrigued that Rabbi Cohen had lived in so many countries and spoke three languages. Rebekah and Rebeckah talked about the different spelling of their names, and Abraham entertained Ibby and Rebeckah by explaining the customs and rituals of the Jewish Sabbath.

The Philadelphians were excited to meet the Westerners and the lady fur broker who had created such a sensation in the Cohens' front yard two days ago. Some were a little disappointed the strangers weren't dressed in buckskin as they had envisioned.

The Sabbath table was set with two candles, a glass of wine, and two whole loaves of challah bread covered with a cloth.

"The two candles represent God's dual commandments to remember and observe the Sabbath," Abraham whispered.

As sundown approached, Mrs. Cohen said, "Come. It is time to light the candles."

As the woman of the house, she lit the candles, waving her hands reverently over them. Covering her eyes with her hands, she recited in Hebrew the blessing over the candles, then she stepped back from the table to make way for her brother-in-law, Rabbi Cohen.

The rabbi picked up the cup of wine and recited the Kiddush, a prayer to sanctify the wine.

Rebeckah whispered, "What are we supposed to do?"

"Follow me and do as I do," Abraham told the girls and Jimmy.

Mattie had set out a warm cup of water and a small towel for each guest to wash their hands. Before wiping their hands on the towel, each said an individual blessing. Mr. Cohen stood at the end of the table. He removed the covers from both challah loaves and blessed the bread. Then he indicated that the meal could begin.

After the meal, the conversation quickly turned to questions from the Easterners about the advancement of the West and the sixteenth state, called Tennessee.

Once the last Shabbat guests left the Cohens' home, Peggy and Jimmy walked back to the manse. They found Reverend Annan more alert but still very weak. His wife was exhausted; Peggy put her to bed. Jimmy fed the patient more chicken soup, which the Cohens claimed was a miraculous medicine.

Peggy sat in a straight-back wooden chair next to Jimmy and took the spoon and bowl of soup from his hands. "You do the praying, and I'll do the feeding."

"I'll be praying in the study." He stood and stretched.

The study adjoining the bedroom was finished in dark mahogany wainscoting and matching shelves filled with leather-bound books, the most volumes that Jimmy had ever seen, even more than in Reverend Doak's collection.

He sat at the shiny desk and felt the fine finish with the palms of his hands. He bowed his head and started praying. His head began to drop lower and lower. He jerked up and shook his head and continued praying. His head drooped again. He jerked awake and started to pray again but soon his head dropped to the smooth finish of the polished wood.

As tired as he was, he fell asleep as soon as his head touched the surface of the desk.

The sounds of labored coughing woke Jimmy, refreshed from his short nap. He heard Peggy encouraging the preacher to spit it up. Jimmy entered the bedroom and saw Reverend Annan sitting up in bed. His color was much improved. Peggy stood behind his back, firmly but gently beating on it with her palms cupped to release the mucus built up in his lungs. She had learned this from *Beecham's Physician Manual*, and the method had worked many times in the past.

Reverend Annan looked up at Jimmy, waved, and fell back to sleep.

"I don't have a sermon. I've never spoken to such a large congregation," Jimmy said.

"You best get cracking. You have all the books you need at your disposal." Peg nodded toward the library.

"Yes, I do." He returned to the study, rejuvenated and excited about his first sermon.

Peg smiled. *That's my Jimmy.*

The young preacher admired Reverend Annan's library of theology books and fought the urge to touch the leather-bound works that provided the thoughts and ideas of sermons for this well-known and respected minister. Then he realized he didn't have to resist—he could handle those beautiful volumes. He perused the shelves to find the books he would use to prepare his sermon.

Someday, I'll have an office and a library like this. He remembered his impoverished childhood, reflecting on how Reverend Doak and Sister Ester had taken him in and prepared him for the ministry. He vowed to make them proud of him as he started planning Sunday's sermon.

Mrs. Annan walked into the bedroom and smiled to see her husband looking so much better. Peggy taught her the cupped-hand lung therapy, emphasizing how important it was to eliminate the mucus in his chest that could block his airways. She added the last of the eucalyptus leaves from her medicine bag to the kettle on the brick hearth of the bedroom fireplace.

"Be sure the water in the eucalyptus pot doesn't evaporate while I take a nap."

Mrs. Annan nodded, and Peg lay down on the short day bed across the room.

She awoke to find Reverend Annan sitting up and Mrs. Annan sitting on the bed feeding him hot porridge.

"Good morning, Reverend."

Peg acknowledged his weak wave and smiled when she saw a twinkle in his eye that was not there earlier.

Mrs. Annan laid her palm on her husband's forehead. "His fever is gone."

Peg walked over to the bed. "Your color looks good. How do you feel?"

He nodded and pointed at his throat to indicate that he couldn't talk yet.

Peg pulled a pint-size crock of the family recipe out of her medicine bag. "You have any honey, Mrs. Annan?"

"Certainly do—fresh from Mr. Pemberton's apiary."

"Please bring the honey. I'll make the reverend a hot toddy that will help that cough and make him rest better."

Peggy mixed the honey, whisky, and hot water, showing Mrs. Annan how to make the toddy. She handed the minister's wife the crock. "Prepare this for your husband whenever he wants it. Reverend Witherspoon will stay with you while he finishes tomorrow's sermon. I must take care of some business. I'll be back to check on your husband tomorrow. Tonight we're going to the opera."

"Robert and I love to go to the opera." Mrs. Annan said.

"He'll be able to take you soon."

"Thank you for all you have done." Mrs. Annan sounded like she was about to cry.

"You're welcome." Peggy walked out of the bedroom and stuck her head into the study. "The girls and I will be ready at seven, Reverend. Don't be late. You'd better take a nap so you'll be wide awake for the opera."

Chapter Thirteen

The Archers of Switzerland

Peggy struggled to stretch the white kidskin opera gloves up her arms to just above her elbows. Unaccustomed to wearing long sleeve gloves, she found them annoying to pull on but considered them elegant and fashionable accessories for evening wear.

Ibby and Rebeckah wore round gowns of embroidered muslin trimmed around the neck in lace. The girls' dresses were of similar design but different colors—silver for Ibby and light blue for Rebeckah. Mrs. Cohen and Mattie took great pleasure in transforming the mountain maidens into mavens of the opera. They adorned Peggy with a string of pearls that set off her multi-hued dress, which reflected the colors of a peacock. Mrs. Cohen found Ibby a ruby pendant and Rebeckah an heirloom brooch in her jewelry box.

Mr. Cohen paced the downstairs parlor as he waited for the excited women. He had a surprise for them.

As soon as they came down, he opened the front door wide for all to see. "Ladies, your chariot has arrived."

The shiny town coach that awaited them accommodated up to four passengers sitting face to face in pairs. Daniel and Zeke smiled and waved from atop the coachman's box in front of the enclosed coach. John and William jumped from the rear groomsman's platform to open the door for Jimmy. The usually shy reverend stepped down to the applause of the entourage gathered on the porch. He removed his silk-trimmed beaver top hat and took a bow, which impressed Peggy immensely.

He offered Peggy his arm and escorted her, while John and William escorted their sisters to the waiting coach.

The multitude of ruffled petticoats consumed most of the space inside the coach. The long-legged minister placed his top hat on his knees and scrunched up in the corner seat across from Peggy next to Ibby.

"You look very debonair in your new clothes," Peggy said.

His face turned faint red. "Thank you." He looked first at Peggy and then at Ibby and Rebeckah. "You ladies look very charming this evening. It is a great honor to have you all in my company."

"Well, thank you, Reverend Witherspoon."

Peggy nodded and smiled. The girls had responded just as she had taught them.

Rebeckah fidgeted in her seat and reached to roll down the leather curtain, which was tied in a neat roll that hung above her window.

Peggy placed a gloved hand on Rebeckah's arm. "That's to be pulled down only during bad weather." She shook her head in disapproval as only a school teacher can do.

Embarrassed at being disciplined in front of the reverend, Rebeckah made a face and turned her head to the outside of the coach.

Peggy looked at Ibby and Rebeckah in their new clothes, realizing how attractive her younger sisters had become. Ibby sat so proper and ladylike next to Jimmy. *They would make an attractive couple*, Peg thought. *She's closer to his age than I am.*

Peggy asked, "Are you going to tell me where you acquired this stately coach?" The noise of sixteen hooves striking the cobblestone street would have drowned out her voice if she hadn't raised it.

"Reverend and Mrs. Annan offered it to us as they won't need it until he is better," Jimmy said.

"Why are the horses' manes braided with blue-and straw-colored ribbons?" Ibby asked.

"Zeke did that all by himself—took most of the day to intertwine the narrow little ribbons in the horses' manes," Jimmy answered.

Rebeckah pointed out the window. "Look, those horses have the same color of ribbons in their manes."

"That whole carriage is covered in blue-and-straw-colored ribbons." Ibby looked out her window as their coach turned onto the busy street.

Jimmy said, "The carriages are decorated in blue and straw color in honor of George Washington's service to the nation. Reverend Annan and the congregation of his church came up with the idea last Sunday to show respect for our retiring president, and word has spread throughout Philadelphia."

"It is a wonderful tribute. But why the colors blue and straw?" Peggy asked.

Jimmy answered, "Those were the colors of George Washington's uniform during the American Revolution."

"That makes blue and straw ribbons very suitable. I so dread to see our first president retire." Peggy sighed.

"Reverend Annan says President Washington is anxious to return to Mount Vernon and a farmer's life," Jimmy said.

"Speaking of Reverend Annan, how is he doing?" Peg asked.

Jimmy turned his attention from the passing carriages to the ladies. "Dr. Rush came by shortly after you left. Reverend Annan rebuffed him for wanting to bleed him. He told the doctor you were taking good care of him, and your medicine was better than his."

"He told the renowned Dr. Benjamin Rush that? He must be feeling better."

"The reverend has finished the elixir that you left for him and wants more," Jimmy said.

Peggy frowned. She had left Reverend Annan enough whisky for a week.

"We're here," Rebeckah announced.

Daniel reined in the four horses from a canter to a complete halt at the steps of the Chestnut Street Theatre. His expert horsemanship brought envious stares from opera goers milling about the entrance. Opening night for *The Archers of Switzerland* was sold out. Throngs of opera devotees were in line trying to buy tickets, but none were to be had.

Peggy watched many patrons of the opera turned away at the ticket booth. "I'm glad we have tickets."

"Look at the juggler. Isn't he good?" Ibby pointed to a man with three balls in the air, then four. Mimes and musicians performed on the sidewalk in front of the theater for any gratuity thrown their way.

Street vendors peddled all sorts of wares. Peggy bought a pearl-handled folding fan for each of them. The hand-held fans, similar to the one she had used at the Cohens', would deflect the smoke of the oil lamps as well as provide a cooling breeze in the crowded venue.

The orchestra was warming up as the foursome inched their way up the crowded steps toward the entrance.

Ibby tugged on Peggy's sleeve for attention. "It's that mean man."

Someone bumped into Ibby, and she dropped her fan. By the time she picked it up, she had to hurry to catch up with the rest of the group, who were already at their seats in the middle of the second tier of boxes just above the orchestra pit.

Jimmy looked around and smiled. "The best seats in the house."

"Yes, they are." Peggy sat down, then opened her new fan.

The oil lamps on stage flickered and then lowered. The orchestra began to play, and the curtains opened. The Tennesseans were spellbound from the opening curtain until the last note of the opera was sung.

As the curtains closed, the audience gave the production a standing ovation that resulted in two curtain calls and adulation that seemed to go on forever.

Peggy had wished to show her siblings, who were also her students, some Eastern culture as part of their education, and she was pleased at how it had come about.

With such a large crowd exiting at once, the carriage couldn't have gotten within blocks of the theater so they were glad they had told Daniel they would walk home. Besides, Daniel and Mattie needed the time to be together.

"There he is again, Peg." Ibby poked her sister on the arm.

"What are you talking about?"

"One of the mean men that said vulgar things about us in the Cohens' front yard is following us." Ibby tried to point him out, but he disappeared into the crowd.

"What did he look like?" Peggy asked.

"He's missing one eye and has a large scar on his face. He looked like an Indian to me," Ibby said.

"Why do you think he was an Indian?" Jimmy asked.

"He looked like an Indian and wore a feather in his hat." Ibby shrugged.

"A one-eyed Indian." Peg looked at Jimmy with fear in her eyes.

Jimmy turned to Ibby. "You said again. When did you first see him?"

"On the way up the steps to the theater. I told Peggy."

"I guess I didn't hear you. I'm sorry. If you see him again, get my attention."

Jimmy looked at the girls with a reassuring smile. "Nothing to worry about. I'm sure it's just a coincidence that Ibby saw this Indian twice tonight."

Peggy whispered, "I hope you're right."

After sitting for almost three hours during the opera, the group enjoyed the walk in the pleasant weather. Once home, Ibby and Rebeckah went upstairs to their room. Peggy and Jimmy lingered for a while on the porch discussing tomorrow's sermon and the long trip back to Jonesborough starting Monday morning.

"I'll see you at church in the morning." Jimmy rose from his chair and held out his hand to help Peggy up.

She took his outstretched hand, then touched his arm. "Thank you, Jimmy."

"For what?"

"Just being my friend."

He smiled and led her into the Cohens' house. After she was inside and the door secured, Jimmy headed over to the manse to check on Reverend and Mrs. Annan.

***

Church members entered the sanctuary and saw the young stranger occupying Reverend Annan's seat. Alarmed whispers and speculation spread through the congregation. The voices grew louder and the crowd more restless by the minute as the fear of what might have happened to their beloved spiritual leader increased.

A few minutes early, Elder Cunningham sensed the concern of the congregation and introduced Reverend Witherspoon as a visiting preacher. Reverend Witherspoon started his sermon by giving the worried congregation an update on their minister's condition. He assured them Reverend Annan would be back in the pulpit next Sunday.

Jimmy's sermon, his first since his graduation from Washington College, was based on the story of David and Goliath and about life's many challenges. The young minister knew challenges well, and this sermon was one of those challenges. He was apprehensive about speaking to a congregation that was larger than the whole town of Jonesborough, but Peggy's assurances gave him the confidence that he needed.

After the service was over, he received many compliments from the members, especially the women of the church who adored him and his Western accent. Elder Cunningham asked him to preach again should he be in the area in the future and discreetly placed a stipend in Jimmy's watch pocket.

Once the last member had shaken Reverend Witherspoon's hand and exited the church, he and Peggy scurried to the manse to check on Reverend Annan.

"Good day, Mrs. Annan. How are you and our patient this afternoon?" Peggy asked as she entered the house.

"I had a good night's rest, thank you. The reverend is sitting up in bed waiting for you and Reverend Witherspoon."

"Come in here, you two angels of mercy," Reverend Annan called out from his bed.

"You sure sound much better," Peggy said.

Jimmy walked over to the patient's bed. "You certainly do."

"Do you mind if I give you one last examination?" Peggy asked. "We'll be heading to Tennessee in the morning.

"As long as you brought me some of your tonic." Reverend Annan strained his voice to be heard.

"Yes, I brought you another bottle, but you should only take it in moderate amounts, Reverend."

Jimmy stepped back to give her room.

She felt his pulse, checked for a sign of fever, then placed an ear to his back to listen to his breathing. She moved away from the bed and looked at her patient's wife. "Mrs. Annan, are you still giving Reverend the cupped hand treatments I taught you?"

"Yes, I do it just before I feed him, and it wears me out."

"Continue the treatments at sunrise and sunset for two more days. Get him up to walk as much as he can stand; that will also help to eliminate the congestion. Make sure he drinks lots of water, and do not let anyone bleed him."

Jimmy returned to the side of the bed. "Reverend Annan, your congregation misses you and is praying for a speedy recovery. I told them you would be back in the pulpit next Sunday."

Reverend Annan nodded his appreciation and whispered a faint "Thank you."

As they left the manse, Jimmy put three quarter eagles in Peggy's hand.

She looked at him in surprise. "What's this for?"

"Paying you back from my first stipend for the suit of clothes you bought me." Jimmy smiled.

"I bought your suit as a gift."

"You've done enough for me already, and I appreciate it."

She put the coins in her pocket and gave Jimmy an approving smile.

***

Mattie and Mrs. Cohen prepared a traditional Sunday dinner for the Westerners. Daniel had received a special invitation to make sure he understood that he was expected to be there. The dinner would also be an opportunity for everyone to say their goodbyes, knowing that the chance of seeing one another again was a slim possibility.

James and Willie brought their dulcimer boards, instruments that the Cohens had heard of but had never seen played. After dinner they played their instruments in the parlor as the Cohens tapped their feet to the unique sounds of Celtic music. Zeke was intrigued by the strange-looking instrument and liked the unique sounds that the small strings made when plucked with a hand-carved bone the size of a thumbnail.

Daniel and Mattie slipped outside. He held her hand tightly as they walked through the neatly manicured cemetery behind the Presbyterian Church. He sat her down on an old stone bench that had turned a shade of pale green from years of growth of air-borne algae created by the heavy humidity from the Delaware River.

Mattie, an attractive woman of about twenty-five years, had long, wavy black hair, dark eyes, and a deep bronze complexion. She had been born on a small island in the Caribbean that Daniel couldn't pronounce. The Cohens had brought her to Philadelphia from the islands when she was fifteen years old. Mattie was as attached to the Cohen family as Daniel was to the Mitchells.

She looked deeply into Daniel's eyes, her eyes glistening.

"Mattie, I'll be leaving tomorrow, and I don't know how to say this except that I want you and Zeke to come to Jonesborough with me. I'll build a nice log cabin big enough for the three of us. Jonesborough is a nice little town where everyone knows everybody. I could teach Zeke the trade of a farrier—it's a respectable trade to learn."

"What about me?"

"You would be my wife and never have to change any bed linens that your family hadn't slept on."

Mattie's mouth opened into a surprised O. "Are you saying you want to marry me?"

"That's what I'm saying. I want to marry you and take you and Zeke home with me to Tennessee."

"I have to talk to the Cohens. I don't know what they are going to say."

"They're happy for you." Daniel looked at her intently.

"You asked their permission and they said yes?" Mattie looked up at him with wide eyes.

"They're sad to see you go, but they want you and Zeke to be happy. That's what's important to them."

"We leave in the morning?" Mattie clasped her hands together in joy.

"As soon as Dr. Chester's materials are loaded."

"Then we must get married tonight. How can we do that?"

Daniel grinned. "That's no problem because the preacher is waiting for us at the house."

She let out a happy scream. "That's right. I forgot you have a minister with you." She grabbed Daniel and hugged him.

They kissed under an old hickory tree.

"Yes." She raised her voice into a cry of joy. "I'm so happy."

"Careful, woman, you might wake the folks that are buried here." Daniel kissed her again.

The proposal was no surprise to anyone except Mattie. Reverend Witherspoon performed his first marriage ceremony in the parlor of the Cohen house with the couple's closest friends and family as witnesses. It was a joyous occasion for all.

The Cohens cried, knowing they would miss Mattie and Zeke who were like the children they never had, but they were happy for them. The elderly couple had been concerned about Mattie and Zeke for some time, worried about the future of the mother and son if anything happened to the Cohens. This marriage ended their worry—they knew Daniel would take good care of Mattie and Zeke.

***

Eager to get to Jonesborough, Jake Thompson and his family were waiting at the lumber mill in Kingsessing Township just west of Philadelphia and the Schuylkill River when the Swedish proprietor and his help arrived. The mill workers easily hoisted the heavy timber trusses on the Conestoga using a forty-foot gin pole with a boom and large block and tackle. The last truss was being loaded as Daniel and the other three wagons arrived. The Mitchell entourage was amazed to see the pine timber truss weighing a half ton or more lifted so easily. Then it was swung out toward the wagon and laid gently on the wagon bed. *Like a water fowl setting down in the still waters of Knob Creek*, Peggy thought.

"How are we ever going to get those heavy trusses off your wagon once we get to Jonesborough?" Daniel asked Jake.

"Same way we loaded them."

"We don't have an apparatus like that to unload," John said.

"Yes, we do." Jake smiled at his traveling companions and pointed toward the heavy rigging attached to the side of the Conestoga wagon. "When we're ready to unload, all you and William have to do is cut down a tall pine tree to make another gin pole and boom."

Daniel grinned and shook his head at Jake. "You're as handy as a pocket on a shirt. Come over here and meet everybody." He patted the teamster on the back.

"Let me get my wife and boys."

Daniel stepped over to the wagon carrying Peggy.

She said, "Good thing you made the deal for Jake's wagon, Daniel. I don't think we could have loaded it all with just the three wagons we have."

Daniel leaned over and whispered. "The deal won't be final until Mrs. Thompson approves of the swap. That's why she's coming along—to see my stable. Then if she likes what she sees of it and Jonesborough, we got a deal. Even if we don't make a trade, we got free use of that big wagon of theirs."

"Makes sense that she would want to see what her new home is like." Peggy hoped Mrs. Thompson liked the barnyard smell, remembering the nauseous moments she had encountered attending to business at the livery stable.

Jake Thompson and his family walked over to Peggy's wagon. Daniel introduced Jake; his wife Sara, a petite girl of no more than eighteen years; Nick, a toddler; and John, an infant, to their new traveling companions. Daniel's chest seemed to expand and a big grin covered his face as he introduced his new family to the Thompsons.

As soon as the other wagons were loaded with the smaller framing lumber and hardware, Daniel said, "We best get rolling—daylight's a-burning. Mrs. Thompson, you and the boys can ride with Peggy, Mattie with Ibby, and Zeke with Rebeckah."

The Conestoga led with Jake riding the left wheel horse of the sextet team. Peggy came next, followed by Ibby, then Rebeckah. The wagon train consisted of fifteen people, four wagons, eighteen horses, and a mule. The canvas top of the Conestoga was taken down and stored to make room for the large wooden trusses neatly stacked one on top of the other in the bed of the mammoth wagon. The load, securely fastened by stout ropes braided from hemp, extended four feet over the sideboards and five feet out the back of the wagon.

Everyone was warned to stay a good distance from the Conestoga wagon out of fear the heavy trusses could break loose during a load shift. That meant Jake could not sit on the lazy board attached to the left side of the freight hauler. He would have to ride on the wheel horse or walk alongside the Conestoga holding the reins a good distance from the load—not convenient but safe.

"Sure glad the mill was on the west side of the Schuylkill River. It would have been scary crossing that floating bridge at Grays Ferry with this load," Peggy said to Sara.

"A load like that is scary on dry land." Sara eyed the precarious load that obstructed the view of her husband on the wheel horse.

"I see why you want Jake off the road," Peggy said.

"Being a teamster is dangerous work. I worry the whole time he is away. I don't know what the boys and I would do if something happened to him. He's all the family we have." Sara wiped a tear from the corner of her eye with the cuff of her long sleeve.

"You have no family?" Peggy asked.

"All my family but me died in the cholera epidemic a few years ago," Sara said. "Jake found me in the City Tavern prostituting myself for something to eat. I just turned fifteen; we been together ever since."

They rode on not saying a word, each lost in her own thoughts. Peggy thought of how lucky she was to have a large loving family. Sara contemplated what lay ahead on her first journey away from Philadelphia. Baby John began to cry, as Nick slept on a pallet, protected from the sun in a small space between the piano and the sideboard of the wagon.

"Must be feeding time." Sara picked up the infant and unbuttoned the top of her one-piece dress to nurse him.

The caravan made camp about halfway between Philadelphia and Baltimore on a small creek where a flock of turkeys roosted. Two of the birds became dinner for the hungry travelers, thanks to John's expertise with a slingshot. Mattie made cornbread and beans, and Peggy picked some edible greens along the creek bank near a flowing spring.

Zeke strummed the translucent strings of the dulcimer boards and tried to make the sounds the Smith boys did. James warned Zeke about breaking the strings, explaining the difficulty of making new ones. Zeke didn't believe the strings were made from dried and stretched gut, the larger strings from a cow and the smaller ones from a lamb or goat.

"You can help the next time we slaughter an animal," Willie said.

James gave Zeke a hard stare. "Harvesting intestines is not a fun job. Are you sure you want to help?"

Zeke smiled and nodded.

"We have enough strings to make a dulcimer for you, but we need a good piece of dried cedar to carve the instrument's sound board." Willie showed Zeke the carved shape of the dulcimer he had been playing. "We can start the search tomorrow in good daylight."

The boy went to sleep for the first time under the stars on the road to his new home in Tennessee. Excited about the dulcimer that his new friends were going to help him make, Zeke lay in his bedroll with a smile on his face for several minutes before drifting off to sleep.

After supper Peggy and Jimmy took a walk along the creek, listening to the babbling water flowing toward the river and tree frogs adding to the melody of the night.

Walking beside Jimmy and looking straight ahead, Peggy asked, "Will we make it home?"

"Of course, we will. Why would you doubt it?"

"I meant will we make it home in time for Robert and Elizabeth's wedding."

"If we can continue to move as we have today we should. My calendar says it's the twelfth day of September; that gives us twenty-two days to make it back. We made it up the same road in eighteen days. Barring any unforeseen events, I see no reason why we shouldn't be home for the wedding," Jimmy answered.

"Thank you for your assurance." Peggy put her hand on his shoulder for a moment, then snatched it away.

"What's wrong?" Jimmy placed a hand on each elbow and looked into her face. Moonlight reflected on her forehead.

She put her finger over her mouth in a sign for silence. "Someone is there." She pointed toward a large tree behind Jimmy.

She watched the tree for a second and saw her brother John making his rounds of the first watch. Peggy let out the breath she had been holding. "Oh, it's you."

"What are you doing out here in the dark?" John leaned his rifle against a large cypress tree that had long, tentacle-like roots running down into the water of the creek. John sat on an exposed root large enough and at the right height to be a comfortable resting place.

"We're enjoying this beautiful evening God has given us," Jimmy said.

John smiled at his friend. "You sure are starting to sound like a preacher."

"Thank you. After years of preparing for the ministry, I would hope that I sound like a preacher."

"It's just that we spent so much time together growing up that it's hard for me to realize you're now our reverend."

"Nothing has changed between us, John. I'm the same person. I still pull my pants on one leg at a time."

"I know that." John shook his head. "It just doesn't seem the same between you and me as it does with Reverend Doak or Reverend Balch."

Jimmy stepped forward. "It's about time I relieve you for the next watch."

"Good. I'm ready to get some sleep." John stood and stretched his long arms, then picked up his weapon and headed to his bedroll by the campfire.

"Don't worry. We'll be home in time." Jimmy put an arm around Peggy's shoulder and walked her to the circled wagons.

Peggy stopped beside her sisters, already asleep, curled up in their bedrolls under the wagon. "Thank you for coming with us."

"My pleasure." He squeezed her hand, picked up his gun, and walked into the darkness to begin his watch.

On the fifth day, the party made it to the Roanoke River near Big Lick where they camped. Peggy bought three barrels of salt from the trading post the next morning and would have bought more had there been room in the wagons.

"What are you going to do with all this salt?" Sara Thompson touched one of the wooden casks. The staves were stained black and the metal bands rusted from the caustic substance inside.

"Salt is hard to come by over those blue-looking mountains you can see in the far distance." Peggy pointed to the southwest of their position, then turned back to pay the salt purveyor.

"We better get going."

"I know—daylight is a-burning." For the first time, Sara laughed at the Tennessee expression.

The salt man loaded the last cask on the wagon. "You best be careful on your journey as bandits have been working the Wagon Road between here and Abingdon."

"What's he talking about, Peggy?" Sara, looking more worried than usual, picked up the restless Nick.

"There are always highwaymen on the wagon road looking for some poor soul to rob or horse to steal. Don't worry, Sara. Thieves are cowards looking for an easy mark. They'll be afraid to take on a large party like ours." Peggy thought about the one-eyed Indian that Ibby had seen at the theater last Saturday night. *He could be ahead of us if he left on Sunday.*

"What's Jonesborough like?" Sara gazed at the western horizon.

"A lot smaller than Philadelphia, but much bigger than Big Lick." Peg flicked the reins to encourage her team to tighten up the distance between wagons.

"What about the people?

"Just like people everywhere. They came from all over, looking to make a better life for their family or to get away from something." Peggy told Sara about Mr. Deaderick, Dr. Chester, her family (including all the children's names and ages), and her beloved dog, Lulubelle.

"I look forward to meeting them. I know the boys will love Lulubelle." Sara looked at the mountains ahead.

"You'll get to meet all my cousins, nieces, and nephews at Robert's wedding." Peggy said.

"I'm glad to hear that."

The wagon train camped that night on the north side of the New River crossing near the narrows which Jake said offered easy access to the other side.

While gathering fire wood Zeke found the wood for his dulcimer board. "Here it is, James."

"Where did you find this? It's just the right length and width with the grain running in the proper direction and seasoned just right for whittling." James removed the bark, revealing a unique pattern found only in the grain of mountain cedar.

"I found it on that hill over there." Zeke pointed a short distance away. "The tree it came from looked like it had been hit by lightning years ago. Is that what we need?"

"I don't think you could have ever found a more perfect piece of cedar to make a dulcimer board." James caressed the exposed wood, admiring the slightly curved strips of white running alongside the red strips. The grain looked as if it had been designed by an artist rather than created by nature.

Zeke turned to Daniel. "Can I borrow your jackknife?"

"I can do better than that; I have a spokeshave in the tool box of Ibby's wagon," Daniel answered.

"You brought a spokeshave." Zeke's eyes shone with excitement. "That will be a lot faster than a knife."

Handing his new son the jackknife, Daniel said, "When you get that cedar whittled down to where it ought to be with the knife, I'll show you how to shape a piece of wood using a spokeshave."

Zeke had been walking beside the wagons during the days to fend off boredom. Now that he had the wood to whittle, he chose to ride in the back of a wagon so he could work on the dulcimer board.

"You be careful with that knife, Zeke," Mattie warned.

"Yes, Mother."

Two days later the wagons were camped on the north side of the seven-mile ford in view of a high mountain to the south.

"I wonder how Mr. Pigpen is doing." Peggy leaned back against Jimmy to watch the golden rays of sunset bouncing off what Sheriff Preston had told them was the highest mountain peak in the whole state of Virginia.

"We'll know soon how Mr. Pigpen is," Jimmy answered.

Zeke climbed the knoll that the couple had chosen to watch the sunset. "What you doing?"

"Watching the end of a beautiful day," Jimmy said.

Peggy motioned Zeke to sit down and show her his dulcimer board. "That looks good."

"It's hard to whittle with the wagon bouncing up and down. I get my best work done just before bedtime." The sun went behind the mountains, and Zeke folded the jackknife and placed it in his pocket. "That's all for today."

"Tomorrow will be another day." Jimmy patted Zeke on the shoulder as the trio watched the sun fade into darkness at the end of the Wagon Road.

"Where is that sun setting now?" Zeke asked.

"At your new home in Jonesborough," Peggy said.

"When will we get there?"

Jimmy smiled at the boy's eagerness. "Six to eight days time."

The next morning, Daniel said, "We should make Abingdon before dark."

Peg smiled. "I sure hope the McDonalds have a room available. A warm bath sure would feel good."

"It sure would," Ibby agreed. "I don't like going so long without a bath, but it's too cold to bathe in a creek now."

They broke camp early. Daniel scouted the road ahead while Jimmy stayed about a hundred feet in front of the load of trusses in Jake's Conestoga. The other wagons followed in the same order as they had been traveling. John and William rode close to the wagons, one on each side. James and Willie covered their flank.

So far, the trip home had been without incident, not even a broken spoke.

Chapter Fourteen

Homeward Bound

The Conestoga stopped in front of Peg's wagon.

Jimmy rode up hard. "Hold up. A rider and his horse are down in the middle of the road up ahead."

All the men rode off with Jimmy to see if they could help.

"What happened here?" Daniel asked the man on his knees stroking his horse's neck. His face rested on the horse's head as if he were comforting the injured horse.

"My horse took a bad fall—I think she broke her leg." The horseman continued to hold his head against the young filly as she kicked as if trying to get up.

"Were you on her when she went down?" Daniel asked. He thought, *I don't see any signs of such a large animal falling, and the horse and rider have no scrapes.*

Jake came running to help. "Let's try to get her up."

Daniel knelt with much difficulty, stretching out his bad leg in an effort get down to the horse's level. Jake knelt to examine the back legs, trying not to get kicked, while Daniel inspected the front legs.

"I don't see any injury," Daniel said.

William looked at the downed horse. "Here, let me help get her up."

"You get a hold of her bridle," John said.

"That won't be necessary." The kneeling horseman put a pistol to Daniel's head.

Jimmy didn't see the drawn weapon. "Can I help?"

He received the same answer the gunman had given John.

Damn! One man and a horse got the drop on all of us. The wagon master blamed himself for falling prey to this well-planned trick.

The men jerked their heads back as they heard screams from the wagons.

"Don't worry. It's just my men taking your pretty women." The sadistic smile on the face of the man with one eye made the long scar down his left cheek from his eye to just above his lip even more hideous.

At the sound of his young sons' crying, Jake jumped up. Another bandit appeared out of nowhere and knocked him unconscious with the butt of a rifle.

On the Indian's command, the downed horse got up on all fours. Nothing appeared to be wrong with her. Had the circumstances been different Daniel would have been impressed. Training a horse to lie down and get up on command was one of the most difficult tasks to teach, something that Daniel had never been able to accomplish.

Zeke had been asleep in the back of Rebeckah's wagon when the commotion began. She whispered to him to stay hidden, then she disappeared from his sight. Through a crack in the sideboard, the terrified young boy could see the highwaymen with their guns drawn. He heard the women's screams but didn't know what to do. He had to find Daniel and the other men. Why hadn't they come to help? They must have been captured as well.

Zeke slipped carefully over the sideboard of the wagon on the opposite side from which the bandits took the women. He stayed low, going under the belly of the wagons, watching where the bandits were taking the women, seeing only their legs. When Zeke reached the Conestoga, he saw that six highwaymen had their guns drawn on all of his traveling companions. The large freight wagon stood in the middle of the road on a steep downhill curve. Everyone was on the lower side from where Zeke hid behind the large rear wheel.

He couldn't see the leader, but he could hear him.

"Shoot the men—all of them."

"First, let's have them tell us what these things are they're hauling," another said.

Peeking under the Conestoga, Zeke could see three sets of feet moving toward the wagon. Then he heard what sounded like at least two men climb up the sideboards.

"What in the world could we do with those timbers? They're worthless to us," one of the bandits said.

The voice of another sounded a little louder. "Let's check out the next wagon."

Just above his head, Zeke saw the neatly tied slipknot of the hemp rope that held the trusses in place. He remembered Jake telling Daniel that one pull on the end of this rope would untie everything. Just as the bandits started to climb down, Zeke gave the slipknot one hard pull. The bandits had been holding on to the top truss; their weight and the angle of the wagon's position all worked congruently so the top two trusses tumbled off at the same time. Zeke, realizing that the six Conestoga horses would be startled, moved quickly to the lead horse and grabbed the harness. If the horses bolted, Zeke knew he couldn't hold them.

"Good horse; good horse." Zeke soothed the scared horses with a calm assertive voice as he had been taught.

The large trusses cascading down on three of the bandits distracted the other three. The mountain men easily disarmed them.

Daniel looked at the pile of timber, the dust still settling, then at Zeke holding the large lead horse as if it were a small pony. "Did you do that?"

Zeke looked down at the ground. "I'm sorry."

"Sorry! You saved our lives!" Daniel continued to hold his gun on the three bandits that weren't crushed by the timbers. "I would come and hug you if I didn't have these bandits to deal with."

It took a moment for the others to realize what had happened, then Mattie and Peggy followed by Ibby and Rebeckah ran to Zeke and took turns hugging him. Pride beamed from Zeke's face.

Daniel said, "Let's get these bandits tied."

John grabbed some leather straps from the wagon. "What about the ones under the timbers?"

"They aren't going anywhere." Willie held out his hand for some of the straps.

Sara swayed. "Jake's bleeding. Somebody do something."

Jake raised his head a little as he slowly came around from the horrific blow. "Where are my sons?" He rubbed the protruding knot on the back of his head.

"Oh, my babies, my poor babies. Where are my boys? They were left all alone in the wagon when Peggy and I were captured."

"They're just fine." Peggy hurried down the dusty road, lugging one of the boys on each hip and her medicine bag in one hand. When she reached the group, she handed the boys to their terrified mother. "Let's take a look at Jake's head wound."

"Is he—is he going to be all right?" Sara's voice trembled as she looked down at her injured husband.

"There's a laceration about an inch long I need to doctor, but he's going to be fine."

While the women hovered over Jake, the men kept their attention on the bandits and the fallen load.

James and Willie tied the three bandits to a wheel of the freight wagon. "If you outlaws make a commotion and spook those big Conestoga horses, you're going to be in for one hell of a ride." James laughed and made a rotating motion with his finger, as if the large wheel was turning.

John pointed to the wood on the ground. "Jake said we'll have to cut a tall tree for a gin pole to load those trusses."

"Best get started." William groped around in the back of Peggy's wagon for the broadax.

"I'll fetch the mule—time that jenny earned her oats," John said.

It was nearly dark by the time the badly mangled bodies of the three bandits were buried in a mass grave beside the road. Jimmy said a few words but was certain the bandits were headed straight to hell.

The stagecoach from Baltimore to Abingdon came through as they were burying the bandits. The driver, who knew both Daniel and Jake, promised to tell Sheriff Preston that the wagon train from Jonesborough would be in tomorrow with three prisoners, including the so-called one-eyed Indian.

The trusses were reloaded and Peggy had Jake's wound cleaned up and stitched. The men hobbled the bandits and forced them to stumble along the road as the wagon train moved a few miles down to make camp.

After dinner Daniel checked on the prisoners and relieved John, who had been guarding them.

"Did you get enough to eat?" Daniel asked.

John nodded. "Yep."

"What about our guests?"

Two of the bandits, who were hobbled but had one hand untied to eat, nodded. The leader just hissed at his comrades.

"That's good because they mostly likely will hang you before you eat again," Daniel said. "Folks in Abingdon look forward to a good hanging."

"We shall see."

The leader showed no fear though the other two looked at one another with wide eyes.

"You dress like an Indian. Are you an Indian?" Daniel looked directly into the prisoner's only eye.

He stared coldly at Daniel. "My mother was a half-breed prostitute; I have no idea who my father was. So I dress like an Indian and am known as One Feather."

"One Feather, how did you lose that eye?" Daniel struggled to tie the bandit's free hand back to one of the spokes. He motioned to John to do the same for the other two.

"In a barroom fight, the last fight I fought by rules. Now anyone threatens me I shoot them before they get close enough to hurt me." One Feather spat toward Daniel but missed.

"A man tied up spread-eagle like you are shouldn't do that, as I have this sudden urge to kick you in your crotch. That urge might go away if you were to answer a couple of questions. Did you kill a pig farmer just outside Blountville a little over a month ago? Robert Thigpen drove a little one-horse buggy and was shot in the head for only his pocket watch." Daniel positioned himself for a swift kick to the groin.

One Feather sneered. "Why do you care?"

"An acquaintance is suspected of killing him. I'd like to know that he is innocent."

"In my pocket is a gold watch. If it's the pig farmer's watch, then yes, I killed him." One Feather glanced at his vest pocket and smiled as if inviting Daniel to dare reach for it.

Daniel carefully reached into One Feather's pocket. The bandit attempted to bite Daniel's arm. The strong blacksmith slammed the bandit's head back hard against the wagon wheel with only his elbow.

Another sinister hiss came from One Feather.

Each of the prisoner's legs was tied to a wooden stake driven deep into the ground, holding him in a sitting position with his legs spread-eagled. Daniel stepped into the center of One Feather's spread legs and lifted his large right foot, showing him how easy it would be to crush his unprotected manhood.

"I have two more questions." Daniel ignored One Feather's frown and hiss. "We have nothing in the wagons but building materials for an inn, timbers too big for a house or even a barn. Our cargo would be worthless to you as it would be difficult to sell." Daniel turned his head sideways to look at the grotesque little man tied to the wagon's front wheel. "Why bother ambushing us?"

"You have the most valuable cargo of all, more precious than gold. The five attractive women you travel with would fetch a good price—more than all your horses and wagons."

"That's what I thought." Daniel nodded his head. "Next question: I want to know how you taught your horse to lay down and get up on command."

"I didn't teach him. I stole him from a one-legged man who couldn't get up on a horse." One Feather let out a sadistic laugh. "I asked him to show me how he got the horse down and then up. After he showed me three times, I was sure I could get the horse to respond to my commands. I shot the cripple between the eyes." One Feather seemed to enjoy describing killing people.

Daniel stepped back from his intimidating position, opened the pocket watch, and saw the initials R.W.T engraved inside. He remembered the papers in the attaché case were signed Robert W. Thigpen and the case fished from the river bore the same initials. Daniel felt sick realizing how close they had come to hanging the innocent pig herder for a crime this murderer committed.

***

"Riders coming! Everyone up and at your post. Get your guns." James woke the travelers.

The men took their positions around the inside of the circle of wagons, guns placed on the sideboards ready to fire. The women huddled together under the big wagon, shielding the children with their bodies.

"Can you make out how many?" Daniel asked.

James squinted. "I can only see two."

"Well let's find out who they are before they get any closer." Daniel fired a round that whizzed over the riders' heads.

The approaching horsemen responded as expected, pulling back on their horses' reins and stopping them almost in their tracks. The defenders of the wagon train could hear the horses whinny in response to being stopped so abruptly during a hard run.

John looked around at the other men. "What do we do now?"

"Just wait. If they're friendly and want to talk, they'll ride in slowly with their hands up," Daniel said. "If they don't, get prepared to fight."

The early-morning riders rode slowly toward them.

"It's Sheriff Preston and Deputy McDonald," John said.

Daniel put his gun down, and the men from the wagon train grinned at each other and waited for the visitors to reach the wagons.

"Good to see you." Jimmy gave the sheriff a preacher's bear hug as soon as he was off his horse.

"Thanks for the warning shot." The lawman looked at the men who were putting away their guns.

James shrugged. "You could have been some of One Feather's tribe coming to spring him for all we knew."

"No harm done. Good to see you, Reverend, and you, Daniel." The sheriff acknowledged the others with a smile and a nod. When he saw Zeke and his mother, he shook his head and looked again. "What are you doing here?" When Daniel put his arm around Mattie and Zeke, Sheriff Preston realized the answer and said, "Congratulations."

Daniel introduced the bandaged Jake and his family, and the sheriff introduced his brother-in-law. Peggy hugged Sheriff Preston, and Ibby and Rebeckah curtsied.

Daniel gave Mattie one last look and shoulder pat, then turned back to the horsemen. "We sent word that we were coming in today. What brings you out so early in the morning?"

"I got your message from the stage driver, but as I now have a family to support and need to get reelected, I'd like the townspeople to see me and my deputy somehow involved in this capture."

Peggy asked, "Did you say family?"

"Yes, I'm going to give McDonald here the opportunity to be my father-in-law as well as my brother-in-law by marrying his daughter Molly." Sheriff Preston placed a hand on the shoulder of a beaming Mr. McDonald.

Peggy smiled at the two men. "Is your son excited about your remarrying?"

"He knows his cousin Molly well—she's been taking care of him for a long time. I think she will make him a good mother." Sheriff Preston smiled. "It was you that made me realize I need to make a home for him, and I thank you for that."

"I wish your new family happiness," Peggy said.

The lawman looked at Daniel. "Where are those bandits that have caused so much fear on the wagon road?"

"They're tied to the Conestoga wagon over here." Daniel pointed. "Careful—One Feather will try to spit on you or bite you if he gets half a chance."

"That's quite a wagon." The sheriff gave the Conestoga a quick glance then looked at the outlaws bound to its large wheels with leather straps. "That scrawny little Indian is the leader of the highwaymen that killed Robert Thigpen? He's one of the men I ran off from the Cohens' front yard, isn't he?"

Daniel nodded. "Now that you mention it, I remember him being in the mob at the Cohens. He was also watching the carriage at the theater when I drove away after dropping the girls and Jimmy off."

"Ibby told us a one-eyed person dressed like an Indian had been following us," Jimmy said.

"I told you I'd been following your women." One Feather sneered at the men.

"He's not much taller than Zeke. I didn't consider him a threat when I first saw him in the crowd in Philadelphia," Sheriff Preston said.

"I've killed more men than all of you put together."

"It don't take much of a man to kill a fellow with a gun or a knife when no warning is issued and your victim is trying to help you out." Jake looked like he wanted to squash One Feather like a bug with his boot.

"He got the drop on us using his horse as a Judas goat. Had it on the ground like it had broken a leg. We all fell for his trick." Daniel placed his arm around Zeke as the young boy joined the circle of men.

"Only a few have ever survived an attack by this gang of bandits. How did you manage to escape them?" The lawman bent down for a better look, and One Feather hissed at him. "You do that to me again, and it'll be your last time."

"Zeke saved us." Daniel pulled the boy closer and received a hug in return.

Everyone started talking at once, trying to tell the sheriff about Zeke's heroic actions.

"You don't say." Sheriff Preston smiled and nodded at Zeke and then looked at Daniel.

"Breakfast is ready," Mattie called.

"We can talk about it over some of Mattie's biscuits and gravy," Daniel said.

"I look forward to eating Mattie's cooking again and hearing how you and your party apprehended the bandits." Sheriff Preston followed Daniel and Zeke to the campfire inside the circle of wagons.

"Mattie, whatever you have in that Dutch oven sure smells good." Daniel gave his new bride a wink as he reached for the pot of coffee.

"You should have seen those big timbers crashing down on those bandits," James said.

The men relished telling the story of Zeke unloading the pine trusses on top of the thieves and the ensuing capture of the three survivors of the gang. Zeke's face turned somber when they talked about the deaths that resulted from his actions.

Mattie noticed. "That's enough talk of that incident. I would appreciate you not discussing it around Zeke."

"But Zeke's our hero," James protested.

Daniel gave James and the others *the look*, rolling his eyes, which meant to those that knew him there would be no more talk of this matter. Peggy and Jimmy nodded in agreement, and the subject was dropped.

Peggy looked at Sheriff Preston enjoying his breakfast and a second cup of strong, black coffee. "When is the wedding?" she asked.

"As soon as I can get you all and the prisoners back to Abingdon." He turned to Jimmy. "I need my minister to perform the ceremony if he's willing."

"I would be honored to marry you and Molly."

"I want every one of you to attend and enjoy the feast afterwards at the tavern," the soon-to-be-groom said.

"Sure a lot of people getting married." John looked at his brother William.

"Your time is coming. I told you I'd sign your marriage bond to marry Mary Ann Barnes."

John nodded. William knew his brother appreciated the offer to post a large marriage bond of fifteen hundred dollars—the largest ever posted in the county. The customary bond was only one hundred fifty dollars posted to the governor. No funds would change hands unless the groom backed out of the marriage.

Peggy had suggested ten times the usual bond to get the attention and admiration of Mary Ann Barnes and her father as other suitors were seriously courting the pretty maiden. Peggy wanted to post the marriage bond for John, but women were not allowed to post surety bonds.

"You best do it as soon as we get to Jonesborough." Peggy looked at her brothers with that schoolmarm look that meant don't you forget.

John lowered his eyes and nodded.

***

Deputy McDonald rode ahead to tell the townspeople that their sheriff would be bringing in the murdering bandits shortly. A crowd curious to see the notorious One Feather and his gang had gathered in front of McDonald's Tavern for their arrival.

Out of sight of the townspeople, Sheriff Preston stopped the wagon train and unloaded the shackled prisoners for the walk through the dusty main street. It was an impressive sight—the sheriff riding his large black stallion and the three prisoners hobbling along, tethered one after the other single file behind him. Following them at some distance as the sheriff requested came the wagons and riders, now with six more horses in the pack.

The crowd cheered and called out bravos for Sheriff Preston. One Feather crouched low and hissed at the crowd like a rattlesnake, which made the sheriff's grand entrance even more dramatic.

"Wouldn't the crowd be surprised to know that the actions of an unarmed young boy caused their apprehension?" Peggy looked at Mattie and smiled.

Mattie nodded. "Remember we promised not to discuss that. Let's just let the sheriff have his glory and keep my Zeke's name out of it."

Peggy pulled back on the reins to stop her team in front of the Tavern Inn as Joshua came running up to her wagon. "Good to see you again, Miss Mitchell." He removed his hat and bowed to Peggy. "Let me take care of your wagon and team for you."

Someone has been working on his social skills, Peggy thought. "Thank you." She fought the urge to call him Pigpen. *I owe Joshua an apology when the time is right.*

The prisoners were put on public display in front of the courthouse in wooden stocks built for the occasion. Each prisoner had his own stock that held his head in the large center hole with a hole on each side for an arm. A heavy timber crossbar locked in place by a large padlock secured their head and arms. Word spread quickly of the capture of One Feather, and people came from miles around to see what was left of this band of thieves. The sheriff and deputy took turns guarding the prisoners in the stocks, which provided a great opportunity to invite all who viewed the prisoners to the wedding ceremony and festivities that were to commence shortly.

"Remember your sheriff on election day," the lawmen told everyone who passed the courthouse.

"It looks as if you will have an easy reelection, Sheriff Preston." Peggy looked at the prisoners and spoke low so no one overheard her.

The sheriff glanced around. "I appreciate you and your party going along with me on this."

"I have concerns about your capturing the moment for your own gain, but for the sake of Zeke and his mother, I think it's best to divert the attention away from him."

"When I arrived back from Philadelphia after an absence of two weeks, a political rival had started a rumor that I was off courting three young maidens from Tennessee and neglecting my sworn duties to the county. My deputy and I insisted I was in pursuit of the highwaymen that killed Mr. Thigpen. Your allowing me to bring in One Feather saved my political career, and I will be forever grateful."

"Were you in Philadelphia courting young maidens?" Peggy flashed a teasing smile.

"I wanted to court one young maiden, but I also knew that three young girls on a wagon road were prey for highwaymen like them." He gestured toward the men in stocks.

"You failed to show much interest in the young maiden." Peggy looked into the eyes of the handsome lawman.

"I soon saw that her heart was taken by another."

"How would you know that?"

The sheriff smiled. "I'm a good lawman, and I know these things."

Joshua walked up and spoke to Sheriff Preston. "Everyone is ready to start the wedding out back under the big tree behind the inn."

"I have to go, Peggy. Thank you for all you've done for me."

Joshua said, "Miss Mitchell, can I talk to you?

"Yes, let's walk over to the ceremony." Peggy took his arm.

"You sure you wanna walk with me?" Joshua looked down at his feet.

"Yes, I want to tell you something."

"Well, I gotta tell you something first. I know you thunk I was stealing your horse, but I was just gonna borry him. I got to thinking bout poor Miz Thigpen. She needed to know what happened to her husband, and she needed that money for her young uns. I was just gonna borry your horse to ride all night to try to find her. I was gonna get your horse back to you, somehow, someway."

Joshua stumbled as he tried to stay in step with Peggy's slow steps.

"I was wrong about you, and I'm sorry," Peggy said. "Will you forgive me for thinking you killed Mr. Thigpen?"

"There ain't nothing to forgive you for. You helped me find a good job with the McDonalds. They teaching me a trade and to read and write. I can even spell my first name and print it on paper. I don't have to herd pigs no more on account of you, and I thank you for bringing me here."

Joshua escorted Peggy to the front of the large crowd gathered to witness the marriage ceremony.

"Thank you," Peggy said.

Joshua's face lit up as he stood next to her during the short ceremony. She looked with pride at Jimmy Witherspoon in his new tailored preacher's suit. She looked at Ibby and Rebeckah in their new clothes, her brothers, her new friends the Thompsons, and Daniel's new family. *I'm so thankful for all my family and friends, and I'm ready to be home with the rest of the family.*

***

They arrived in Knob Creek on Saturday afternoon on the twenty-fourth day of September of 1796. Hezekiah, the baby, had grown at least an inch. He jumped into Peggy's arms, then came James, David, Samuel, and Jennett scrambling for the attention of their sisters.

"Where's Lulubelle?"

Peggy, Ibby, and Rebeckah looked around the barn.

"She went off after eating one morning last week and didn't return as she usually did in the afternoon," Adam said. "I found her dead down by the creek. I buried her where she breathed her last breath. Old age finally caught up with her. It looked like she died peacefully."

Rebeckah and Ibby looked like they were about to cry, and Peggy wore an expression of pain.

Adam knew the girls would miss their dog, but he didn't want their homecoming to be filled with sorrow. "I'm glad to have my daughters home."

He opened his arms for a hug, and they all embraced him at once.

"Where is Mother?" Ibby asked.

"She's coming as soon as she gets her fire started for dinner."

"How's she doing?" Peggy asked.

"I think Dr. Chester was right. She needed to have something to do. While you girls were away, she and Jennett spent a lot of time together. Your mother taught Jennett to knit and spin wool like she did you girls when you were Jennett's age." Adam looked at his daughters and smiled. "She's now the same woman I married twenty-five years ago next month."

"Where do you want the piano?" William said.

"You brought a piano from Philadelphia?" Adam's face lit up with excitement, and he hugged Peggy "Your mother will be so happy. She has missed the music of a piano."

"What's this about a piano?" Elizabeth rushed toward her oldest daughters, her arms stretched out for a welcome-home hug.

Rebeckah pulled away from her mother. "Peggy bought a custom-made pianoforte in Philadelphia."

"I can't wait to hear it played," Elizabeth said.

"Jimmy, can you preach tomorrow?" Adam asked. "The deacons planned a special tribute to honor George Washington for his service to our nation. I will read his farewell address that was published in the Philadelphia Gazette. If we had someone to play the piano, that would be wonderful— maybe some patriotic tunes as well as music for worship."

"Don't worry. I can preach, and I will bring Mother, who can play any instrument and knows most of the Presbyterian hymns by ear."

"Thank you, Reverend."

"You are the first elder of Hebron Church to call me Reverend." Jimmy beamed with pride.

Peggy smiled. She was at home with the family she loved.

Other Books in The Westward Sagas

The Westward Sagas began with **Book 1: Spring House,**
available at www.westwardsagas.com and Amazon.com or
at bookstores by special order.

> The Mitchells just wanted to be left alone to farm their
> land, practice their faith, and raise their family. But
> their response to the extraordinary circumstances of
> frontier life, politics, and war made heroes of these
> ordinary citizens.
>
> Adam fought the British, while his mother, wife, and
> children endured deprivation and danger on the
> family farm in the midst of the battle.
>
> The story of Adam's two loves – his first wife Jennett
> who died bearing their son and his second wife
> Elizabeth who bore him twelve more children –
> creates the human backdrop to the historical events
> of Revolutionary War times.

The story will continue in *Book 3: Rebeckah.* In 1805,
Rebeckah married Thomas W. Smith, who followed
Andrew Jackson as a Tennessee Volunteer in the War of
1812. The family moved to Texas in the early days of the
Republic. Like generations of Mitchell women before her,
Rebeckah endured the hardships of the frontier. After her
husband and brother-in-law were scalped by Indians and
her nine-year-old nephew taken captive, Rebeckah and her
widowed sister-in-law began a three-year crusade to find
and rescue the boy.

Fact or Fiction: A Note from the Author

As stated in the Preface, everything in *Adam's Daughters* is compatible with known history. However, because there are gaps in recorded history, I have imagined what might have happened and included these imagined events in the story.

For example, there is no record that Andrew Jackson courted Peggy Mitchell. However, it is possible—perhaps likely. We know Andrew was in Jonesborough in 1788. He and Peggy were both young and unmarried, and there were not many marriageable men and women in the area at the time. Judge McNairy was a close friend of both the Mitchell family and Andrew Jackson, so it is probable that he would have introduced his friends to each other. Andrew Jackson recorded Margaret Mitchell's will in Nashville, so he obviously had some contact with the Mitchell family. Did Andrew Jackson court Peggy Mitchell? No one knows. Is it possible? Absolutely.

A few people thought I invented the State of Franklin, but everything in the book about the State of Franklin is true. I spent months researching this strange and fascinating bit of history to ensure that what I wrote was accurate.

Some may wonder if there really were German Jews in Philadelphia shortly after the Revolution. Not only were there German Jews, but the piano maker Charles Albrecht was a real person, a craftsman who received the first patent issued for a piano.

I have included details, such as specific locations, to identify real places and incidents. Vague descriptions indicate that the place is a product of my imagination or there isn't enough historical information available to be more specific.

If you want to learn more about history and genealogy, the resources on the next page have been invaluable to me in my research.

RESOURCES

Arthur, John Preston. *Western North Carolina: A History from 1730 to1913*. Overmountain Press, 1996. ISBN 978-1570720628.

Brands, H.W. *Andrew Jackson: His Life and Times*. Anchor, 2006. ISBN 978-1400030729.

Calvin M. McClung Collection. East Tennessee History Center, Knox County Public Library, Knoxville, TN.

Cox, Joyce and Cox, W. Eugene, compilers and editors. *History of Washington County Tennessee, Washington County Historical Association*. Overmountain Press, 2001. ISBN 978-1570722028.

Cox, Joyce and Cox, W. Eugene. *Jonesborough's Historic Churches*. Heritage Alliance of Northeast Tennessee and Southwest Virginia.

Fink, Paul M. *Jonesborough: The First Century of Tennessee's First Town*. Overmountain Press, 2002. ISBN 978-0932807380.

Gibson, Jo Chapman. *Salem Presbyterian Church*. Overmountain Press, 1993.

Guilford County Genealogical Society, Attn: Publications, PO Box 49104, Greensboro, NC 27419-1104. Publication list available upon request.

James, Marquis. *The Life of Andrew Jackson*. Bobbs Merrill, 1938.

Meyer, Annie Galbreath. *History of Our Mitchell Ancestors from 1743 to 1959*. Dorite Press, 1960.

Miller, John. *The First Frontier: Life in Colonial America*. Doubleday, 1996. ISBN 978-0999107324.

University of Tennessee, Knoxville, Special Collection Library, Knoxville, TN.

Washington County Tennessee Inventories of Estates Volume 00 1779-1821. Mountain Press.

Williams, Samuel Cole. *History of the Lost State of Franklin*. The Watauga Press, 1924. (Revised edition: Clearfield, 2006).

About the Author

David Bowles, a native of Austin, Texas, lives in San Antonio with his best friend and constant companion Lulubelle, a yellow Lab. He grew up listening to stories of his ancestors told by family members in the generation before him. The stories fascinated David so much that he grew up to become a tale-spinner, spinning tales through the written word in The Westward Sagas and through the spoken word speaking to groups of both adults and children.

David started writing stories of his family to ensure that his children and grandchildren had accurate records of the family history. However, while the original versions, written in narrative textbook style, did maintain the records, they didn't maintain the interest of the readers. So he used his imagination and creativity to fill in the gaps of what might have happened when the details weren't available. He created dialogue and scenes to add true life drama to the story of the Mitchell Family from colonial days to the settlement of the West. He hopes these stories fascinate his readers as much as the stories of his ancestors have always fascinated him.